THE FRIEND REQUEST

BY

CHARLES SOTO

Copyright © Charles Soto 2014

Copyright © Charles Soto 2015

All rights reserved.

Copyright© Cover Design

Najla Qamber Designs

All rights reserved. No part of this book may be reproduced, scanned, or distributed in any printed or electronic form without permission.

This is a work of fiction. Names, characters, places, and incidents either are the product of the author's imagination or are used factiously, and any resemblance to actual persons, living or dead, business establishments, events or locales is entirely coincidental.

The author does not have any control over and does not assume any responsibility for third-party Web sites or their content.

The scanning, uploading, and distribution of this book via the Internet, or any other means without the permission of the author is illegal and punishable by law. Please do not participate in or encourage piracy of copyrighted materials in violation of the author's rights. Purchase only authorized copies.

THIS BOOK IS DEDICATED TO EVERYONE WHO BELIEVES IN A SECOND CHANCE

ACKNOWLEDGMENTS

Once again I would not be the man I am today without the love and support of my family. To my beautiful wife Patty, you have blessed us with two wonderful daughters and for twenty-seven years you have stood by my side asking only to love me and that I love you. You are my harshest critic, my biggest fan and true to all, you are my best friend. I love you…and I thank you for all the second chances you have ever given me. A special thank you to Publicist, Sara Benedict for her help during the publication process. You are simply wonderful and I owe you a huge hug! Also, thank you to Penny Sansevieri for believing in my work and her entire staff at AME for their patience and care. You have all been fantastic! To my legal advisor and friend, Attorney Tim Dodd, I thank you for your kind advice, which has led me here. I would also like to give congratulations to Phyllis Frias for the new Charlie Frias Park in, Las Vegas, NV. where the Butterflies still flourish. You are forever in our hearts Uncle Charlie. Most of all, as always, my most heartfelt gratitude goes out to *you*, my readers. With no one to read, words serve no purpose.

CHAPTER ONE

It was a city that served Chase Bishop's purpose, giving him the financial freedom that secured him through his life. He had been here through the boom and turned his small construction management company into a multi-million dollar firm overlooking some of the largest construction phases throughout the United States.

It was the end of September and the usual hot, arid, scolding air that baked through the summer months was now replaced with a temperate desert climate that would make up much of the winter. It's the perfect time to be in Phoenix, as far as the weather went. This city was dry and desolate, with majestic, cratered mountains that served as an outline to Arizona's Sonoran Desert, making up an imposing, spectacular view that stretched across the Western horizon.

The Salt River breaks free from the Gila River, sharing the city's outer borders as Fortune five hundred companies make up its metropolis. A vast, thriving industry composed of a medical district, factories and retail centers, divided the city into sections stimulating the economy into functioning at full capacity. That was all before the housing crash. Banks and businesses folded, property seizures and foreclosures reached into the thousands. Everybody was feeling the aftermath and no one more than the construction industry.

Sure, he had his success. But, the lengths he took to achieve them never went unnoticed to those who worked for him and his brother Sid. He had no kids, had never married, but that was about to change. If Chase had any weakness at all, it was his consumption of women. Lucky in life, unlucky in love became his signature and tonight came with no exception.

Chase lived large. His massive estate bordered the Salt River, private and secluded, taking up five acres of shoreline in an area built on prestige. There was a guarded gate to the entrance of the Costa de Oro Estates, a premier village that made up one of the most affluent suburbs of Phoenix. Each home was articulately developed in a wealthy atmosphere that read power and indulgence and Chase Bishop's home fit the scale in abundance.

Three levels of Spanish style stucco built the exterior, giving way to a series of lavishly perched decks. Each deck housed the roof of the bedroom below it, creating a valley of peaks that towered to ceramic tiled roofs. The elaborate sandstone cobbled driveway, which guided visitors in from the main gate, stretched in a chain of curves five-hundred feet long, ending in a loop at the steps to the massive double cherry wood doors.

Tonight the enormous home hosted a grand gala; a celebration for a huge contract his company was awarded for the country's stimulus money program. As always, the guest list included the most vital people in the community. Bankers and attorneys, politicians, his entire office staff and his brother/partner Sydney were all in attendance.

In the eyes of those that gathered tonight, what met their reluctance was a reminder of what Chase had been missing. He was a man of one weakness and the entire room knew who that weakness was. With ground breaking only a month away, the impromptu announcement of Chase's engagement took everyone by surprise, especially his brother.

What should have brought on elation instead drew concern. As Sydney stood there with his wife Kelly elbow-to-elbow in the ballroom, the expression on his face was a picture of a thousand regrets.

"Did you know anything about this?" Kelly leaned into Sydney, her glass toasting with everyone else as they all tipped their drinks to the now engaged couple. Though, seeing the expression in her husband's eyes, it was obvious Sidney was just as taken aback as she was.

"Hell no." He nodded as puzzlement and shock betrayed his deepest fears. His brows squished tightly together and his entire body stood despondent, unwilling to toast and unable to think. Still holding his glass down at his side he turned to his wife and said, "What the hell's he thinking?"

"Sid!" Kelly snapped, widening her eyes. "People are gonna hear you."

"So what! I'm sure they're all thinking the same thing."

Kelly dipped her head as if to agree, matching his concerns in a thought that was just too overwhelming to comprehend. *Why her? Why now?*

"I know." Her hand faltered in a gesture of uncertainty. "She's not exactly…" She lost her focus, trying to find the words to soothe over a bad situation.

"Yeah," he sneered. "That says it all." His sarcasm outweighed any source of a compromise.

***

Across the room, Chase watched Sidney from the moment he made his announcement. The shock and dismay on his brother's face reflected every one of Chase's own. The news that Heather shared blindsided him for over a week. The thought of actually raising a family of his own was the one thing he had been missing from his life.

Could it be true? Was it even possible? His thoughts battled with his conscience for so long that it consumed every bit of his reasoning. Truth or fabrication, trust or deceit, whichever he weighed against, whichever he took for granted, only time would tell what lay ahead.

His fiancée Heather took his arm as he maneuvered through the guests. Congratulations and courteous nods mixed with forced smiles. Her pretentious demeanor highlighted her extravagance; harnessing the power of a woman built to seduce and control.

It was a black tie affair and everyone dressed accordingly except for Heather and a few of her friends. Her flamboyance, of course funded by Chase, flaunted her taste for the most lavish designers. She was a woman built by fabrication, she lived in the moment, and for a woman of humble means it was a perpetual struggle fitting into Chase's lifestyle. Her short cut skirt and gaudy jewelry tempered by a revealing blouse that exposed her cleavage was both bold and incredibly out of place. She was ten years younger than Chase, but he was definitely in her league. He was a man that took good care of himself. Athletic and devastatingly handsome, Chase hit his prime at the age of thirty-four.

"What's wrong, bro?" Chase teased a smile at Sydney. Feigning interest, Heather stood beside her future husband. "You look like a kid who just got turned down for the prom."

"You mean more like a hunter with no bullets, standing in front of a charging Rhino."

"Ahhh," Sydney's wife Kelly gasped. "*Why*, Sid," she chuckled. "You should congratulate Chase and Heather."

"Why?" Sydney shot a weary look at his brother. The wrinkles on his forehead confirmed his distress. Never one to conceal his thoughts he remained hush about his disdain for the pending nuptials.

"Because," Chase glared. "It's the polite thing to do."

"I should say so," Heather interrupted as she caught an opening just to taunt him. "After all, we're going to be family." She gestured with her hand, quickly patting Sidney's chest. "I'm sure it's just a formality," her chin turned upward. "But, shall I refer to you as, *brother* from now on?"

Sidney cringed at the sheer thought, finishing off his drink in one long gulp as he just stared at the two of them.

"Well, *I'll* certainly congratulate you, Chase," Kelly looked to him and said graciously.

"And me?" Kelly remained sternly in Heather's focus. Regardless of what Sid or Kelly thought, she had manipulated her way into this family and there was nothing they could do about it.

"You're included in that, dear," Kelly added. "You're going to be a Bishop now. You don't have to fight for attention. Or...does that come naturally for you?"

Heather scowled, refusing to incite a battle at what was now her engagement party. She planned it to perfection and refused to let anyone spoil it. She was the one at the center of attention and if the two people she most despised didn't like it then she knew she had succeeded regardless of her moderate background. She was a woman at the top of her game and despite how *they* felt; she would soon have Chase all to herself.

Her eyes gave a taunting, sarcastic roll as she comfortably turned to Chase. Her beautifully layered and highlighted auburn brown hair rested softly against his chest. The delicate, supple touch of her lips met his as she pulled his attention to her. Seductive and alluring, the pure control of her beauty entrapped him in her web. It was clearly an open and deliberate show of affection used to tease her future in-laws, revealing the power she now wielded even before taking the 'Bishop' name. Like a mantra, she repeated it. *Heather Jessica Bishop*.

"I need another *goddamn* drink." Sid's look said it all, disgust and hate teetering along a border he swore he would never cross. He was a man who never interfered in his younger brother's affairs, but this time it was different. Somehow, someway he would have to get Chase out of this. Make him see Heather for what she truly was; a woman who could never give him the kind of love he deserved. Sydney had already devised a plan that would remind his brother of the man he used to be and he knew it would bring the past into focus, when Chase was different, happier and aware of what was truly important. "Care to join me?" He stared at Chase, a demand more than suggestion.

Knowing what was coming, Chase raised a halfhearted grin. His objections were obvious and so was the argument that was sure to follow. Regardless of how Sid felt, he had made his decision. If Sid didn't like it then he had better get used to it, because Chase never had, nor would he ever need to explain himself to anybody, including his older brother.

Chase turned to Heather. "Will you excuse us, Hun? I think that's Sid's subtle way of saying he wants to talk to me." His smile was a meager attempt to dispel Heathers worry.

"Of course, darling. I don't have to be tied to your side every moment, like some women I know," she paused briefly. "Besides, I wanted a chance to talk with the ladies." Heather nodded toward her friends standing nearby. "I'm sure they're all dying to know the details." Turning to Kelly, she held up her hand in a small, parting gesture as if to save Kelly from any embarrassment. "Not that you're not one of them, Kelly, but we never did have much to talk about did we? Must be on account of our age difference."

Kelly finished her drink, ignoring Heathers biting sarcasm. The sooner she got away from her the better. Regardless of what Heather thought, whatever fantasy world she clung to, she would never be accepted into this family, not like a true Bishop. As Kelly stood there and stared, there was one thing that became apparent; Sid wasn't the only one who needed another drink.

"Well," Kelly paused. "You seem to presume a lot. It's obvious that's the one thing in life you still have to learn. Now," She glanced away. "If you'll all excuse me, I think I need another drink."

They all watched her leave, each in their own thoughts, As Chase and Sidney listened to Heather excuse herself as well, the showdown to follow brought tension between them both.

"Still want to get that drink big brother?" Chase raised a smile, his eyes comforting his thoughts to exactly what Sid had wanted. After all it was expected since he gave no warning. The announcement of his engagement had come as a complete surprise, even to him, but before Sid could say something he might regret, Chase realized he would have to explain his reasoning just to never have to discuss it again.

"What the hell are you thinking, Chase?" Sid's eyes focus sharply. Even though he was five years older and a bit shorter than his younger brother, both men shared the same features. It was obvious they were brothers, with light blue eyes and all the same expressions. Short dark hair trimmed their handsome, masculine faces. Not a hint of gray had touched either of them. Even living in the desert all these years hadn't dimmed their looks. Their complexions were a bit darker now, but still smooth and unlined. As Sidney stood there and stared, he realized the only thing that made them different were Chase's lifestyle and the poor choices he'd made with women and tonight only proved his theory.

"Now, don't start, Sid." Chase grabbed a couple of drinks from off a waiter's tray, making his rounds through his guests.

"I'm going to need something a bit stronger than champagne, if you don't mind?" Sid's impatience mounted, as he looked to Chase with all the misgivings and uncertainties that waited for an explanation.

"Well," Chase reluctantly answered. "I can see this is going to be a fun night."

"What the hell do you expect? I mean really," he said as he shook his head. *"Heather?* Are *you* serious?" Sid's voice was strong, shocking and incredible doubt emphasized each word. "I need to know—"

"Relax, would you?" Chase interrupted. "Come on, I have some private stock in my office."

The two set down their glasses as Sid followed Chase out of the ballroom, through a long corridor off the main entrance to the home.

With each step they took their thoughts collected the rejections that were sure to follow.

With every minute that passed, Chase could feel Sidney's eyes blanketing him with disappointment.

Silence remained a burden as they stepped inside Chase's spacious, yet secluded office. It was a room much different from the rest of the home with a private collection of memories he kept throughout the years.

"I'll tell ya bro," Sydney breaks the tension. "I can never get tired of coming into this room. All this memorabilia from your baseball days at Arizona State, these Little League and high school baseball trophy's crowding every spot on the shelves, sure bring back a lot of good memories. Huh Chase?" Sydney planted the seed of reminiscence. The first of many he would have to initiate for Chase to realize his mistakes.

"I guess." Chase dimmed his brows finding his comment random, especially for a man who makes a point with every word he says. "*Now* what are you getting at Sid?"

"Nothin' man." Sid shrugs it off. "I'm proud of everything you've accomplished in your life so far and you should be too, Chase.

"Who says I'm not?"

"I'm just saying you let it get away from you sometimes, that's all." Sydney swayed his eyes up to the framed pictures that hung on the walls, the ones from Chase's high school and college graduation days; taking particular notice the one picture Chase had always kept just as fresh in his mind since the day it was taken. The one Chase had to look at whenever he was in this room, Chase's senior prom picture and the girl that stood beside him. One way or another, Sid knew he would have to come clean, confide in his brother and trust that Chase would revert to the man Sydney once knew and try to bring him the happiness he'd been missing. He needed to remind his younger brother what life was all about, back before they built their business, before the influence of money had found him; when his dreams were much simpler and his heart was more tamed.

Chase took out a bottle of Patron Tequila from his liquor cabinet and poured each of them a shot. Trusting his patience he began to figure out how to fill Sid in on the details about everything that had brought him here in the first place and how he would handle it.

The moment Chase quit pouring; Sid downed his shot and then held it back up in one swift motion. Whatever Chase was going to tell him, he knew there would be objections.

"I think I'm going to need two shots for this one, bro."

"Yep." Chase poured again. "You're probably right."

"Why, Chase?" Sid's tone came in a plea. "Why didn't you tell me? Why the surprise?"

"Because," Chase sighed, releasing the anxieties that crowded his every thought. "It came as a surprise to me too." He finished his own shot, waiting for Sid to lower his as he topped them off. "I didn't know I was getting married until tonight."

"What the hell you mean, you didn't know?"

"She gave me an ultimatum." Chase's eyes dimmed in embarrassment, no longer sharing the indifference he had showed when he was with Heather. Whatever this was about, Sid knew there had to be more to it than that.

"What kind of ultimatum? She threaten to leave you or something?

Hell," he toasted his glass. "That's the best news I heard all night. Tell her good riddance."

"Yeah, well only you would think that," Chase said as he finished his drink. "On Monday she told me she was pregnant, Sid." Chase watched his brother's eyes widen in shock. "Yeah," he nodded in agreement. "I've been chewing on it all week, so tonight before the party I thought I would do what's right, that's why I asked her to marry me."

"*What?*" Sid's doubts overrode his caution. "You and I both know that ain't possible."

"You don't know that, Sid?" His voice firmer, determined and rational. "Hell, *I don't even know that.*"

"What are you talking about? You told me what happened…what the doctor said."

"That was a long time ago." Chase tried to find some fragment of a truth to keep it in perspective. He was a man who always held his composure when deciding his own outcome and if after tonight Sid couldn't get past this, see it and accept it as Chase had, then the differences that stood between them would never go away.

"Come on, Chase," Sidney's words stirred concern. "I thought the doctor said you couldn't—"

"He said probable, Sid." Chase cut him short, not wanting to hear the words he refused to consider. Unable to accept what he'd always known, as if not hearing him somehow kept his manhood, Chase would lay deaf forever.

"Oh, come on, Chase." Encouraged, Sidney continued, "then why was this the first time it's ever happened? Never heard of anyone not having an oops in their life, especially with all the tail you've chased over the years." He remained resolute and refused to let Chase off the hook. "Either she's full of shit or she tricked you and quit taking birth control. Whichever the case, she can't be trusted. Hell, how do you even know it's your baby?"

"Now, you just wait a minute, big brother." Chase turned abruptly; his eyes livid with the sheer thought of what Sidney had suggested. His usual low-keyed, calm voice had come out strong and assertive. "Let's not go there, alright. Whatever the future holds, it's my decision. Regardless of what you think of Heather, out of concern for me, you ought to start treating her with respect. Life isn't about waiting for the storm to pass, Sid, it's about learning how to dance in the rain."

"Shit," Sydney said disappointed. "Don't throw around that old cliché of yours like it means something. Not here. Not now. What the hell happened to you, bro?"

"What are you getting at, Sid?" Chase read through his brother's stare, knowing he always had a point.

Sidney shook his head, finding the inevitable truth. "You're a hard man, Chase. But what people see as short tempered and greedy, I see as calculating and respectful. I mean…your revered, bro." He waved his hand. "You've changed the way builders do business. You're the 'closer'. You succeed where others fail."

"Your point?" Chase drew his brows, taking none of it as a compliment.

"Why is it you can handle some of the biggest projects anyone's ever heard of, take on some of the largest banks without ever being taken advantage of, but when it comes to women, you fold like a cheap suit?"

"That's not fair, Sid." His eyes held the reflections that countered every part of his soul. What he'd been missing. "I'm not getting any younger." His pace began again, a slow, calming pace that researched every thought that compromised him. "I envy you and Kelly…what you have. You don't think I want that, kids, a beautiful wife to spend my life with? Hell man, I don't care about heather's background. So she wasn't born with a silver spoon in her mouth Sid. So what, neither were we. I couldn't care less if she worked in a department store. You don't think I'm tired of chasing tail? I—I know Heather isn't exactly what you call, the 'refined type'. But, she's a good girl, Sid. Exciting in the sack and will turn a head wherever she goes."

"Well, congratulations, Chase." Sydney cocked his head. "You just described a 'call girl' because if that's the only thing that matters to you, then you're in for a world of hurt."

"I didn't mean it like that." His hand waved him off. "And I don't like your comparison. I just think it's time, that's all. You're the one with a family. It's my turn to have the same."

"If it is your kid. You at least owe it to yourself to get tested." Sidney paused, pouring them each another shot.

"And how do you know I haven't already, huh?" Chase shrugged and grew more frustrated.

"Yeah, right. Then what did the doctor say?"

Chase looked to him with blatant disregard.

"He said my body's too small for my dick, Sid," Chase's sarcasm shouted through his eyes. "It's none of your damn business if I get tested or not."

"Fine," Sid shrugged. "You can make jokes if you want. But trust me little brother, you shouldn't marry someone when you have doubts and uncertainty. And for God's sake," he handed Chase his tequila. "Tell me you got a prenup?"

"Back off, Sid," Chase snapped, "What business is that of yours?"

"Uh, considering I'm your partner and our company has grown into a multi-million dollar business, I'd say quite a bit." He downed his tequila.

"Well, you can lay your worries to rest. I'm not going into this blind." Chase drank his shot and stepped over to the picture that Sidney had waiting for him to look at. He set his glass down beside it as his subconscious acted like a magnet, pulling his eyes toward the photo.

With every second that passed, Sidney felt Chase's stare as his sharp, invasive eyes intervened in his thoughts. He had to make Chase realize for himself that it's never too late and understand that Heather isn't, nor could she ever be the right woman for him.

There was no mistaking what Sid had recognized. The casual glance Chase had given transformed into a meaningful stare. Sid had seen that look too many times. He knew his brother better than anyone else and it was as if Chase was searching his soul for a rescue, something to impede what now seemed to imprison him. As always, Sidney understood it was Chase's own pride that stood in the way. In that one brief, harrowing, desperate moment, Sid knew he had to tell him, bring it all together and remind him of a better time and a girl he couldn't forget. His last hope in not only stopping this marriage, but a woman that just might secure the very job they were celebrating, knowing Chase had never forgotten her. In some ironic, depleted way, reminding him of her might just bring his curiosity back into perspective.

"Remember that guy?" Sid pointed to the picture of Chase and Carly. "Now that was a guy who knew what love and respect was about."

"What are you talking about?" Chase's eyes reflected confusion. "Me and Carly?" He squinted.

"You just seemed a lot happier back then, Chase. I'm worried about you little brother. You took on all the goals and risks that've brought this company to where it is at now. I couldn't have done it without you. You gave up your life for our company…but trust me; this was no way to get it back."

"I know what I'm doing, Sid. You can give me your blessing or not, but this may be my only chance to have my own family. Life isn't waiting for the storm to pass, it's about learning how to dance in the rain. I learned that a long time ago, after my accident. Remember?"

"How can I forget?" Sid shrugged his disbelief. "You've used that phrase ever since you moved here from northern Cali. The only thing was, I think you've forgotten what it means."

A brief silence followed as Sidney reflected on Chase's words. He knew what his brother had been missing and he sensed it for some time now. The obvious came back into focus, Chase would never see Heather for what she truly was, a manipulating seductress who thrived on opportunity.

"Tell me this little brother, you think Heather would even be with you if you were just some poor working stiff?"

It caught Chase off guard. He was no fool. He could see things as they came. The facts were always there no matter what woman he was dating. With money comes power. With power came prestige and, if it was his influence that attracted women to him in the first place then what made them stay was the man he was inside.

"Well, thanks, big brother." Chase gave a resentful smirk. "I suppose the way you see things, I must just buy my women, huh?"

"Now, wait a minute," Sid held up his hands. "I didn't mean any offense towards you and you know it. What I was trying to point out…"

"Spare me the details." Chase's frustrations cut him short. "I know exactly what you're pointing out and I don't want to hear it. I don't have the luxury of being poor like you and Kelly did when you two were married."

"*Luxury?*" Sid squinted, pulling back his head. "Is that what you call it?" The absurdity of what Chase had just said was reflected in his eyes.

"You know what I mean," his tone was firm. "I have to accept Heather for every reason that attracted her to me, and vice versa. But, the fact of the matter is, she wants to marry me, have my child and raise a family with me, Sid. Isn't that what's important?"

A brief silence ensued as Sid saw the stress on his brother's face.

"Well," Sid looked up. His shoulders cocked firmly with pride. "If I knew for sure that's the circumstance, I'd been the first one to congratulate you, bro. Even so," he hesitated. "You ever think of those days…think of her?" Sid pointed to the picture with Carly, conspiring in the thoughts that would bring it all back. "You left Milpitas and never looked back."

"Hell, Sid. What are you getting at? That was a long time ago."

"You aren't fooling me, I see the way you look at that picture...the way you look at her. You may have been just kids back then, but don't tell me Carly Bourque hasn't stayed in your thoughts. I remember those days, you going back just to see her graduate. You thought I didn't know," Sid saw a surprised look on Chase's face. "But, I knew. You came back a changed man though. Agitated, bitter, your entire personality morphed and it's been that way ever since. I don't know what happened, you never told anybody. Never realized anybody knew, up until now. I may be older than you, but I never forgot how you felt about her. I was living in Phoenix already, but our phone calls were frequent enough. Don't you ever wonder what happened to her?"

"I already know what happened to her, Sid. She hooked up with some other guy after graduation. Why do you think I came back so pissed off?" He suddenly caught his ramblings, realized it still hurt, but didn't dare show it to Sydney. "What does it matter now? Why does it matter to you?"

"Because," Sid's eyes widened, "I did something, Chase. I've been worried about you. I don't like this person you've become with Heather. You've succeeded beyond all expectations. You have nothing to hide anymore, you should hook up with some of your old friends, find that guy you used to be. You'd be much happier."

"Who says I have anything to hide?" Chase looked confused, trying to find the relevance in what Sidney had said.

"Every contract you ever signed, every paper I've ever seen your name in, you go by your first name, Chatsworth. Hell, your full name's even written in our ownership that way."

"That's for legal purposes, you know why I go by Chatsworth. It gives me my sense of privacy. Only my close friends know me by Chase. What the hell are you complaining about, you're the one who gave me the nickname when we were kids."

"Yeah, thank God." Sydney's sarcasm spikes back.

"Yeah, well…forget all that. What did you mean you did something?" Chase questioned. "What the hell are you up to, Sid?"

Sid smiled, knowing he had to tell him. Somehow make him get past his own reluctance and see the good that could come out of this. "I started you a Facebook page."

"You did what?" His shock and surprise came all at once. "Not this Facebook shit again. Sid, why?"

"I already told you why, it's going help our business, our company status, particularly with this damn new immigration law. Our state's targeting minorities for crying out loud! We need all the positive exposure we can get. Our largest contract ever is only a month away. People need to perceive us as confident and politically correct, especially since the project's in California. We both know every politician in that state's furious over that law. You're the President and co-founder, authority types want to hear from you…besides," Sydney raised a devious and perceptive smile. "I already sent out a friend request."

"What? To whom?" Chase looked up, as spite and disgust glared in his eyes.

"Who do you think? Carly Bourque," he pointed to the picture.

The grievances of his past and the regrets he still felt all collided the moment her name left his mouth. He saw it in Chase's eyes, the emotions that uncovered all his transparencies, the crippling, dire resolutions in a truth Sidney could never have surmised.

"You did what? You've got some nerve, you know that, Sydney?" His shock wore off and turned to anger.

"Calm down, bro, this is a good thing."

"A good thing?" Chase widened his eyes. "You know who she is, *don't you?*"

"Of course I do. Why do you think I sent her the request?"

"You're a fucking asshole, Sid." Chase's panic took over, revealing through his eyes all he had tried to conceal. Years of endurance he thought had been laid to rest, had come back the moment Sid told him.

"Careful how you word things, Chase, you might come to regretting them later. Besides, what's wrong?" His look remained confused. "I actually thought you'd be kind of happy."

Chase rubbed his eyes and slowly shook his head. All his thoughts in complete turmoil as he gradually looked up to his brother.

"She's the reason for my accident, Sid…why I think I'm sterile." His tone was low, dismay crashing together with every word he pronounced. "I never told you or anyone else the truth about how it happened. It was just too embarrassing. I've been trying to forget it ever since."

"Forget what?" Sid refocused, not sure what he had missed.

"She was a foster kid, you know." All his memories and recollections came at once.

"Yeah, I remember you telling me that on several occasions." Sid opened a look that led Chase to continue. "Seemed to me that was one of the things that attracted you to her," Sid clearly read what was transpiring right before him.

Chase nodded "I just felt this overwhelming need to protect her, Sid. She was such a good person… So beautiful. She never talked about her real parents. In fact, I don't think she had any. She was all alone and she deserved so much better." He held a steady pause as his eyes admitted his failures. "I'm the one who screwed it up."

"What do you mean? What happened?"

"She just wasn't ready, Sid." His tone lingered, crawling with the sorrow that he still felt from that night. The vision so clear it played in his head with the reluctance of a memory that he could never forget. "I misread her, my hormones took over back then," His shame and humiliation were all brought to life. "We were getting pretty intimate, parked in the back alley behind her foster parents house, when all of a sudden…man." His hands helped explain, coinciding with his words as the moment overtook him. "She just freaked out. Jumped up out of the bench-seat of that two-toned Chevy truck I had, panicking and yelling. I tried to go after her but she slammed the car door on my fingers. The knob on my gearshift was missing on my floor shifter with just the rod sticking up. I fell back, and…well," his shoulders pitched. "You can guess what happened after that."

Sidney stood paralyzed. His eyes dimmed at Chase's conclusions and his hand moved onto his crotch. As if feeling it for himself, he realized what had happened. He never knew the truth and could now understand his brother's reluctance.

"That's when you guy's broke up. Isn't it?"

"I was just a kid, man. But, I still regret that night more than anything in my life. Especially, how I acted afterward. I let her think she cost me a baseball scholarship at Arizona State."

"You did what? You were just a walk on."

"I know," Chase raised his hand, nodding at what came across as absurd. "My anger, my embarrassment…hell, my own stupid pride stood in the way after that. It was just never the same."

"Then fix it," Sid demanded, while holding a care in his voice that understood Chase's concerns. "Now's your chance."

"You're crazy, man. Didn't you hear what I told you?" Both Chase's hands opened up, raising his arms as he flashed his palms. "I'm getting married."

"Maybe," Sid scowled at the unlikelihood. "There's still a lot you have to find out. You aren't standing at the alter, *yet*." Sid paused, allowing Chase to think, seeing the look in his eyes, the hesitant, yet thought-provoking stare that came back. "I even sent her a message…well," he tilted his head. "*You* did." He teased a grin as he said it. "Your old phrase, 'Life isn't about waiting for the storm…'"

"Yeah, Sid, I get the picture…just great." His sarcasm swallowed him whole.

Sid blew it off, "Carly's still single you know; says so on her profile." Sid struck a nerve and exposed a deep awareness he could feel across his body.

Whatever it was, intrigue or hope Chase was not the type to leave himself so open. There was still a lot Sydney had to explain. There were just too many unanswered questions. But, as relevance took control, so did his insight and whatever he decided to do. From here on out, Sidney would be kept out of it. He was still left searching and craving love and believing that life could grant us a second chance. Now more than ever, Chase felt that again.

CHAPTER TWO

Carly Bourque couldn't believe her eyes at first. She refocused the tiredness out of them then gazed back to the screen of her laptop once again. There was no mistaking the name, or the face. Chase Bishop looked the same as he did back in high school, only more grown up, more handsome and sophisticated. His strong chin and robust shoulders seized and captured the pure domineering forcefulness of his stature, digging deeper into her conscience. Everything she'd remembered about him now chilled her skin, raising small, excited goose bumps tingling throughout her body. The strong, assertive poise was held in his eyes and a charismatic aura that surrounded him was sweet and pure, yet virile and domineering. At least that's what she envisioned; that was the only thing she could think after all these years.

My God, she thought, arching up her back from a relaxed prone posture, now at full attention as she sat up from her living room sofa. Her bare feet snuggled into the soft, woven carpet as all of her elated emotions tensed up from the sheer memories alone, everything she thought she had laid to rest. Yet she still couldn't forget the one man from her past.

She had been registered on Facebook for only a few months now. Although she had become extremely private through the years, she'd found it an easy escape without revealing too much of her life and was often easily side tracked; catching up with old school friends she hadn't heard from in over a decade. What they do, where they live, most of them married with children, living the American dream, as most liked to call it. Carly, however, put having relationships aside to concentrate solely on raising her son. She was only nineteen years old when she gave birth to Caleb and for the past fourteen years she devoted all of her time to taking care of him, providing for him on her own.

Sure, she'd tried dating. But, in the end it was nothing new. As soon as she became close enough to share her secrets about her son, all of the men saw a greener pasture up ahead. She never gave them any warning at all, always catching them off guard when she finally introduced them to Caleb. In her own justification, just to see their initial reaction, everything that said who they were and how they felt would all become exposed in a naked truth before her. She tested their character by their reaction to her son. Though the blame had never bothered her.

But, now it all seemed different. From the moment Chase's face appeared on her screen it opened her thoughts to her loneliness. Attractive and desirable, yet guarded from the world, she would never allow herself to ever be hurt again. Maybe this would mean something different, for if anyone had needed a sign, any reason at all to still hope and dream, it was Carly in her self-imposed loneliness. Trapped in a world with life passing her by.

Often times when she was alone…*always alone it seems*, she thought of Chase. Thought of searching his name on the Internet, seeing what he looked like now and where he was living. Of course there was the dreaded thought he was married. The one pervasive circumstance that kept her from doing so, the one and only sanctuary she found was in not knowing the truth. Would she always be held under the torment of teenage love and nothing more? Or was it?

Seeing Chase's friend request brought back much more than she ever bargained for. So much more, that it wrestled inside her head, twisting every emotion she had at the sheer thought of accepting his request.

She leaned in closer; hesitant to click the mouse, as if just the sheer thought alone would bring everything back. Though, who was she kidding? She wanted to know more, so much more it begged every sense of her curiosity to seek out the truth. The strength and the courage that grappled inside her as she slowly moved the mouse, placing the arrow over his picture, highlighting his face as it exploded on to her screen. Every grasping, appealing feature pressed vividly before her. As she stared into the glow of his deep, hypnotic, light blue eyes, her mind ceased to exist. Every reality clung to her desires, searching for the past that had come to find her. Lost in the deep realms she had laid hidden for so long. The past yearned to remember and be set free.

There, in that moment, Carly could see it all clearly, the critical moments from her past she thought destined to never touch. The regrets and mistakes she forbade herself to think about, now played out in still-frame shots.

How happy she was when they were dating. Whether it was the sheer weight of his name or the popularity it carried at their school, what she saw in his eyes she would never forget. The hidden passions he carried about, his plans and dreams all layered under a mask of his heavy jock status. Though, to Carly, whenever he confided in her or shared his most inner thoughts, the true Chase behind the scenes was the guy she had fallen for, the man she remembered. A woman always remembers her first sexual experience, and although Chase should've been; what haunts Carly the most, was knowing that he wasn't.

True, there were 'what ifs' always hanging in the back of her mind. Lying dormant for so long she thought she had forgotten about them. They were two kids living in an elapsed era. That one single night, the night of their prom that haunts her to this day. Although Chase never blamed her and to her knowledge, had never told anyone about the truth of that night and the real circumstance of his accident, Carly knew all too well that she was the blame; she was the cause. And because of her actions, she cost him a scholarship to play baseball at Arizona State. It was the one single regret that had torn the two apart and she has been living with it ever since.

In this silence she reached out, slowly, cautiously and moved the mouse over the acceptance button. Just before she could click it, she heard a faint squeak coming from a loose board in the floor.

"Caleb?" She turned, seeing her son standing behind her. A smile rising on his soft, innocent face, his thick, straight blonde hair, tousled from lying in bed. "What are you doing up, honey?" The care in her voice rose to concern. She stood and turned towards him and placed her hand across his forehead.

He's growing so fast that Carly knew he wouldn't be ready for manhood, despite his stature he had the mentality of a child. A small, innocent child who still believed in Santa Claus and the Easter Bunny, reflecting his entire demeanor as he stood before her.

"You don't feel hot." She slid her hand away, resting it on his curving cheek as if cupping his smile in her palm.

"How come you always do that, Mommy?" His words crawled just above a stutter as the lines in his face pulled into a squint. He wrinkled his nose showing the confusion of a boy who could never understand the obvious.

"You know why." She now brushed across his hair. "I'm just seeing if you're hot. Do you feel okay?"

"Yeah." Like every other night, there was the perpetual ritual to get him to sleep, a game to Caleb that had exhausted Carly. Though, to her credit, she never lost her patience. She knew it wasn't his fault, he just didn't understand. He didn't have the capability to see how adults perceived him. He was an adolescent, soon to be trapped in a man's body with a brain too underdeveloped.

"Then what are you doing up?" Though, Carly understood. His trouble at school had become almost unbearable; he couldn't decipher just how some of the kids, as well as the adults, had treated him.

"I don't know." A sudden frown replaced his smile as he held his teddy bear in his hands, his only solace from the darkness of his bedroom.

"Was it school, sweetie? You miss it… I know." Her hand now covered his chin, tilting his head towards her as her caring smile hit his eyes.

"Yeah," he answered as his breath carried the sound of his thoughts. His eyes tried to divert hers. In his timid response held the uncertainty of what had happened, how his world has drastically changed, and to him, for no reason at all.

"Don't worry, sweetie," Her voice soothed him. Feeling his pain wash into all of her senses, she thought of everything that crippled the strides he had taken, which diminished his confidence and broke his heart. "I told you everything's going to be fine. You didn't do anything wrong, honey. We'll fix it, you'll see."

"How come we have to fix it, Mommy?" There was confusion in his eyes, "You always said you couldn't fix what was not broken."

Carly had no answers, anything to explain the temperament of people who judge and expel anyone or anything that was different. In her own thoughts what troubled her most, was how someone with a diminished mentality like Caleb could see things so clearly. How he could see the truth and all the innocence that lies within it, while others with the knowledge and education couldn't see past what has blinded them. To see Caleb for whom he was, not what he was, the most remarkable, openly honest person that God had blessed her with.

"You're right, honey." Her smile widened, looking into his eyes. She concealed all the troubles he would never understand.

"I am, Mommy?" His voice rose up sharing a glitter in his eyes, excited and pleased as if he had just won a prize.

"Yes you are." Carly cheerfully played along. Her voice riding on her playfulness with each word she pronounced. "So what do you think about that? Huh?" She tickled his sides knowing that always made him laugh.

"No!" He yelled, chuckling and buckling as he dropped down to his knees. "Stop, Mommy, stop!" He giggled the entire time.

"Only if you promise to go to bed," Carly kept tickling, trying to find a spot as he held up his teddy bear as a shield.

"I promise! I promise!" His words mixed with his chuckles, laughing uncontrollably as Carly finally stopped.

She gave him a hug and a kiss the moment he stood back up, watching him wipe the moisture off his cheek as his sparkling, bright blue eyes fluttered from her affection.

"What did you do that for?" His tone suddenly lowered, now looking up as if embarrassed.

"Because I love you so much," She smiled with a tone that only a mother could appreciate. "Now, you need to go to sleep, Caleb. Alright?" She said reaching across his shoulders to turn him around. But, with a boy like Caleb it always took some effort.

"Who's that, Mommy?" He now noticed the screen, pointing to it with his hand as his other held on to Teddy.

"No one, honey," She glanced over with him, playing it off as if it were no importance at all.

"Then why do you have his picture?"

It was a good question indeed, igniting Carly's true feelings.

"He's just a friend of mine, nobody you've ever met."

"How come you do not want me to meet him? Was he bad?"

"No, honey, of course not. He's just someone I knew a long time ago, back when I was in school. That's all."

"Wow! He must be old, Mommy. But, he does not look old." His broken speech pulled at her heart with every word.

"Well, thanks a lot." Carly widened her eyes, still keeping a cheerful tone.

"You're welcome, Mommy." He shrugged his shoulders, unable to comprehend what came as sarcasm. "What was his name?"

"Why all the questions?" She raised her brows. "You trying to avoid going to bed?"

"Huh?"

"That means I think you're looking for a way to stay up. You know you have a big day tomorrow, it's the weekend, remember? I wanted to take you to the park and big boys need to get their sleep."

"OK, Mommy, I will. He was pretty, huh, Mommy?"

Carly couldn't help but to let out a slight chuckle. She never thought of Chase like that. He was always masculine and athletic, daring and bold, but seeing his profile picture on Facebook, he seemed somewhat sophisticated. It took seeing him through Caleb's eyes for her to realize that, once again enlightened by her son in a truth that still waited.

"He sure was, baby," she says, walking him back to his room.

The entire time she could hear herself asking a thousand questions, everything she wanted to know about Chase now circling in her thoughts. Who he has become? What he was like?

It was her memories that remained clear, the only thing she had left of him. Chase was always a kind person, strong will and minded, but with a sincerity that reflected everyday they were together. Yet, with the circumstances life had left her, there was one thing Carly had learned through the years; people change, and not always for the better. She thought of Chase, the true man in the picture daring to believe he hadn't turned out like the rest, cold and tainted, selfish and mean, everything she had wanted to avoid. It was Caleb's father who had taught her that.

She poured herself a glass of wine after tucking Caleb into bed. All of her worries from the effects of the day were finally catching up to her and she knew tomorrow would only be worse. As soon as Ross found out what she had done, it would be only a short manner of time before she heard from him again. His kind of response always disappointed her. He never cared about her or his son and he never did anything to help them.

Now with Chase bringing back all the memories she had misplaced for so long, the visions and what she imagined mixed with her feelings, gave her an entire new list of anxieties to reflect upon.

Carly paused for a moment as she took a calm, soothing drink. She never needed a man to shake her up in this way and didn't have anything left, nothing left to give. There was no room for anyone in her life but Caleb. But, as her emotions reflected what her mind refused, she realized it was nothing more than a friend request on Facebook and she was getting way ahead of herself. After all, she had been out of touch with him for so long and she didn't know anything about him anymore. Though, there was one thing that was certain, she would never discover anything if she didn't accept his request. She was still as guarded and afraid, as she was reluctant to seek the truth.

There was one thing that had stuck with her and it helped to build her confidence; Chase was the one who had searched out her name and if he didn't want to hear from her he never would've looked her up. Yes, it was Chase who took the initiative and it raised a smile on her cheeks as she looked at it that way. A happy, relieving smile as she clicked on the screen that brought Chase's friend request back into her sights. Now reading the message he had left for her eyes was the one phrase he said ever since that one night. The words he wrote encompassed her as she read them over and again. Her mind racing to free her from this torment and free the thoughts of not knowing what reality lied ahead. *Was he married and did he have kids?* These questions restored all of her worries.

As each word left her thoughts, each sentence guided her fate. She wrote short intervals of what she had been doing over the years, but nothing too revealing of course. It was way too soon for that. Just enough to answer his message and what it had meant to her. Her greatest expectation was in hoping he would write her back and tell her all the things that she needed to hear. Everything that would draw them back together again as if they were never destined to be apart. She considered endless possibilities that love takes for granted, the insights and the pure jubilation, all now at her doorstep as she accepted his friend request.

From the moment she clicked the icon the anticipation swallowed her whole. As she took another drink she experienced instant glee and spontaneity that released her true emotions. She was so glad to hear from him and now it took over all of her thoughts, her mind overflowing with hope. Though, *the hope for what* brought her a new confusion.

There was nothing on his Facebook page that gave her any insight as to what he had been doing. In fact, when she looked at his friends list, she was the only one on it. It added to her confidence and pulled at her curiosity. He was such a popular guy at school she didn't know what to think. Was he trying to hide something or was he just new? The scenarios raced so fast that it challenged every thought she had, the possibilities and speculations all colliding within that instant.

She logged out of Facebook now and then Google'd his name. What seemed like minutes had turned into an hour. She found nothing that was useful. His name was just too common. But, in a man who had kept his private and business affairs so separate, Chase had never told Carly his birth name was Chatsworth. There were no pictures she could refer to, nothing to single him out. Whatever he was up to, wherever he lived, she would have to wait and see and could only hope that the anticipation of his response wouldn't monopolize her thoughts.

She put away her laptop and gave way to a slight yawn when suddenly she heard a car pulling into the driveway. Her cozy little two-bedroom condo had depreciated so much that she didn't know why she kept paying the mortgage. It had a small front yard and one car garage, in Milpitas, a bedroom community in California's Silicon Valley. Her heart now sunk as her throat took a deep swallow, hoping and praying it wasn't whom she thought. Her usual glowing, light sienna eyes turned into a deep, dark brown from the moment she realized who it must be. Had he already received his notice? What did he expect to gain by coming here? She moved over to the curtain to see for sure.

There was no doubt about it. She could see Ross stepping out of his car. The shadowy wrinkles on his face outlined his demeanor; every single crevasse that exclaimed his purpose for being here. His hard, driven strides that led him up the walkway to her front door defined his animosity.

The lamplight in her front room outlined her silhouette in the window, so it was useless to pretend they weren't at home. The restless beats of her heart mixed with fear and anger, afraid of him making a scene and waking up Caleb, and even more spiteful for him being here now. She only wished she had some kind of warning, even though she always knew he would be showing up one of these nights. But, now he was here and she knew she wasn't ready, always held captive to his threats and his disregard for Caleb.

She held the chain on the door as she opened it before his knock. She could feel his beer breath come through the crack filling her senses. Her anxieties were in a race with both her nerves and her thoughts; trying to control a bad situation that only promised to get worse.

"What are you doing here, Ross?" Her tone held firm as her eyes seized her hate. "It's late, if you want—"

"You got some fuckin' nerve!" His voice so strong, it was as if Carly could feel it pushing through the door. All of her bodily functions were now at the mercy of his intimidations. "You know Goddamn well why I'm here. I can give a shit what time it is."

"Keep your voice down, Ross." Her courage now strengthened. "Caleb's asleep, I don't want you dragging him into this."

"Why not?" He shook his head, his temper mounting. "He dragged me into this, didn't he, you and him?" His audacity exposed nothing but hate, everything she despised about him including needing his help. "You're crazy if you think you're going to get me to pay for some special school for that idiot!"

There, he said it, the way he always described Caleb. Everything that determined exactly how he had felt, hanging in the air like a thick, black cloud pouring his resentment. His hateful deprecations and everything Carly loathed.

"Now, let me in, Carly, we need to talk about this."

"I will Ross," her voice tried to remain calm. "Tomorrow…at a decent time…when Caleb isn't home and when you haven't been drinking."

"No, right now or I'll bust this door down and tell Caleb what I really think of him." His eyes squinted, knowing her weaknesses and just how to influence them.

Carly paused for a moment, wishing she were holding her cell phone to dial 911, wishing she had never answered the door. But the fact always remained; she did everything for the sake of Caleb, never wanting to expose him to his father's cruelty, his aggressive animosities that were sure to bring damage. Instead she took a deep inhale, collected her courage as well as her thoughts, and gave in for now, realizing if she didn't it would only get worse.

"Only if you're willing to talk reasonably, Ross, I don't want you waking Caleb."

"What the hell do you know about reasonably, Carly? Huh? I got served this summons when I was at the union hall looking for work. I wanna be the crew to build that new Veterans Hospital, and I got served this thing in front of everyone? You could've warned me. You know how embarrassed I was?"

"I did tell you Ross, but you just yelled at me and blew me off," she answered in disbelief, raising her brows and tightening her jaw. "What do you expect? For once in your life, do what's right. Help your son, for God's sake."

"Just let me in, Carly. I promise I won't wake Caleb."

She paused for a moment and then slowly closed the door. Her eyes scanned across the front room to where her phone sat on the coffee table, unchaining the latch as she went to retrieve it.

Ross immediately pushed himself in, a bit calmer now, though his face still showed his anger. As he watched Carly take her phone in her hand, he stepped over to where she was standing and the moment he reached her, she led him into the kitchen. It was the farthest room away from Caleb's bedroom, sure to give them privacy. She feared Ross and what he was capable of, but in the event of any physical violence, her safe guard was having Caleb in the other room.

"Now, are you ready to talk reasonably, Ross?" She said as she turned to him, taking a seat at the kitchen table as Ross stayed standing.

"What the hell you expect, Carly, the way I got served?"

"You left me with no choice, Ross; I don't think they're going to let him back in that school. That means he would have to go to a private school. I can't afford that on my salary."

"Well, tell him to quit kissin' up on girls, Carly. What the hell ya teaching him anyways, Huh? You raising some future rapist here?" The fury of his words crawled on her skin. Everything she hated about him and what he had done to her brought back all her recollections and how much she despised him.

"Girl! Ross," she quickly defended. "It was only one girl. And it wasn't his fault; she had to have tricked him."

"Yeah, well that isn't hard to do, is it?"

"Does that make you feel better, Ross?" Her tone comes in disgust, shaking her head and pivoting her shoulders. She wished she could just strangle him as her tone pulled sharply once again. "It's cruel and he doesn't deserve it."

"He can't hear me," Ross snapped back, waving his hand out in front of him as if what he said was nothing. "Even if he did, you know damn well he still wouldn't get it. Face it, that boy's as dumb as a box of rocks."

"He's a lot smarter than you give him credit for, Ross. He just needs more help than most kids his age, that's all, on account of his condition."

"Condition?" Ross snapped. Was that what you're callin' it now? I told you a long time ago not to have that…that kid. Especially after you found out what he was going to be. I still don't believe that's my goddamn offspring."

"Well, you can believe it, Ross. Remember? You're the one who insisted on blood tests when he was born, and you've been forced to do very little to help us, up until now."

"Then why the hell start now?" His smugness continued as he slowly walked towards her propelled by his intimidation and sarcasms. "It was a goddamn one night stand, that's all. Now you're tryin' to hold me to this?"

"Oh," she spit back. "And is that what you're calling it nowadays…a one night stand?"

Ross hesitated for a moment, reading her clearly. All the innuendos she used in the past and everything she misinterpreted had come back again. Though, Ross had never seen it that way. What she refused, he saw as shyness, never believing Carly's rejections. In his eyes she had wanted him.

He began a slow, daunting stride as he made his way towards her, free of shame, his devious rules of engagement knew exactly how to hurt her.

"You know I'm going to fight it." His bitter words invaded her thoughts, waiting to steal her soul. "Or... better yet," his mocking, despising smile rose. His eyes opened wider, livid with sarcasm, swimming in a mind of retribution with each word that followed. "Perhaps I *will* pay for his school."

He had the features of a man that didn't care for anything or anybody but himself. His stomach was growing and his face showed the signs of his rough lifestyle. He was a man built on fabrications and it was all catching up to him. But, with those words, those painstaking, sarcastic words, the tone he reflected was far from a compromise.

"What are you up to Ross?" Her eyes held her spite, alive with the sensations that tore into her heart.

"Up to? Whattya mean?" His sarcasm floated, clinging in the air with every word he pronounced. "Isn't that what your court order wants?" He paused, concentrating solely on her. He stood right in front of her, leaning in as his hands braced against the oak tabletop. It was time to call her bluff and he knew just what she feared. "Of course, seeing how I'm being forced to support the young, disturbed lad, I think it's only fair that I get half custody now, Carly. Do the boy some good, spend some time with me, don't ya think?"

Her head pulled back, repulsed, enraged. Instinct without thought took over as she dropped her phone and immediately shoved him away. All of her fears were exposed in that one single moment, everything she protected Caleb from now had become a reality.

"That will never happen Ross! Never! Not as long as I'm alive!"

Ross regained his balance as rage now infected him, the effects of the alcohol mixed with his adrenaline. Power and control, and hate ignited his fury.

"You stupid bitch!" His horrid, antagonistic eyes scoured across the kitchen. He eyed the meat cleaver resting in a holder on the counter. Quickly, he knocked her phone off the table and it flew across the kitchen. Within that instant, holding the cleaver in his hand, he saw the panic and fear across her face. "You just don't get it, do ya?" As he raised the cleaver above his head, his steps brought him on top of her, sneering with the sins of a thousand Devils and all Carly could do was to raise her arms for protection. "I'll put you to sleep right fuckin' now! You don't think of that shit!"

Within that instant Carly could see her end, her demise like her life, unfair and so unprotected. All she could think about was Caleb and if he was next. Though, in the world of the unguarded, life always held hope.

"What are you doing to my Mommy?" Caleb's frightened voice called from behind.

Ross quickly turned as Carly raced over to Caleb, who was holding Carly's phone in his hand. He immediately lets go of the cleaver.

"911 help! Daddy is hurting my Mommy!" He shouted over and again. Agitated and brave all intertwined.

Carly shielded him from Ross. Her arms formed a barrier as they backed out of the kitchen, tears running down her face. She was seized by horror.

"You get the hell out of here Ross! Now!" She screamed. Her voice cracking and pitching while her nerves trembled uncontrollably as Ross followed them out.

"Shit," Ross spit. "That idiot don't have the first clue how to use that phone."

"You willing to risk that, Ross?" Carly kept backing away, still shielding Caleb. "Now who's the idiot?"

As the tension mounted, Ross gained some composure. He could still see the bigger picture. If after tonight Carly didn't call this off, he would make good on his threats and he knew Carly would never risk it.

"This isn't over, Carly." His teeth ground hard. "You hear me? I mean what I said. You go through with this, and then I'm fighting for visitation rights. See how smug you think you are then," He mocked, heading towards the door.

Carly didn't say anything as she continued to shield Caleb. In all her worries, the thought of Ross unsupervised with Caleb was what she had feared the most. What Ross threatened and what she had succumbed to, all coming back to haunt her in his trail of lies and deceit.

"Don't worry my boy; me and your mom were just playin' a game. We were testing ya, seeing if ya knew how to use the phone for help. That's all." He stopped as he reached the door, slowly turning towards them as he cracked it open. "I'll be back real soon, Caleb. I think it's about time we started spending more time together…don't ya think, Carly?" He grinned, mocking and spiteful all in the same smile.

Carly stood petrified as she listened to his torment, feeling a relief come over her as she watched the door close behind him. The anxious beats of her heart shrouded her worries, incensed and afraid, acting on pure instinct as she rushed over to lock it. Watching through the window, her fear mixed with regret as she confirmed his departure.

It was always just she and Caleb, the milestones they've overcome and the progress they've made were now in jeopardy due to Ross' cold heart. She risked everything to protect him and if Ross stood by his threat, she knew she'd do anything to stop him. Regardless of her fears, that would never be an option.

CHAPTER THREE

Carly thought about the weekend and nothing brought her any closure. It was now Sunday night and what Chase's friend request brought to her, left an entire new sentiment she would have to acknowledge.

Not even Ross' threats could expel what she was feeling, an uplifting emotion that empowered all of her splendor. Majestic and soothing, warmth and inviting, with every bit of awareness that told her Chase would write back. It was the only thing she could allow herself to think. As the weekend closed into Sunday night, she still hadn't heard from Chase and the anticipation weighed heavily in her heart.

She hoped she would hear from him and he would be just as happy to hear from her. She thought about it so hard, checking her Facebook wall so many times that she made it the homepage on her laptop. Once again, finding herself enduring the inevitable as she checked it before she went to bed. Though, in the appeals of her heart, what imprisoned her again was the one thought that kept repeating, telling her that he would.

Sleep was now her enemy as Carly pulled back the covers on her bed. The comforts of home with the despair of silence, of living her life alone with no one to share it only brought back the compromises she made. It was a deep, relenting cycle that never seemed to end, filled with passions lined with guilt that she couldn't wash away. Thinking about it so many times that each time she did, it brought a familiar pain into her soul with emptiness left searching, wondering when love would truly find her.

Sure, she'd had relationships but nothing ever meaningful, nothing to withstand what always stood in the way. Caleb was her life and she declared it to him. Her devotion and all her care held every bit of her personality and kept her guarded and protected. No man could ever stand up to Chase's standards, and he was the only man she would ever be willing to trust again.

Of course, I have regrets. Who doesn't? Lying underneath her covers with the thoughts that would not leave her alone, she thought of the life she had made and what she gave up to secure it. How she defended Caleb from a world that would only devour him. Would this be all she would ever know?

Was it that important? Could there be room for a relationship in her life? These tormenting questions came to invade her thoughts. What it brought to her heart had paralyzed her soul and abandoned every belief that it was always a possibility. She'd been way too guarded, and her own sense of protection was what kept her apart forbidding any man to pursue her.

With everything that played out over the weekend, her hopes stayed with Chase, relying on her instincts even though it remained a fantasy. As she put out the lamplight beside her bed, the silence that followed echoed in the darkness. The thoughts that wouldn't release her no matter how hard she tried, kept tugging on her soul hoping Chase would answer her back.

She could feel pleasing, drowning, stimulating sensations sooth over her, teasing and tempting her desires and imagination as she reached into the top of her dresser drawer. Always having it ready, knowing its place and where to find it. She used it so many times before; that what it brought to her could never be mistaken. Her passion overcame her fear, as she craved to feel Chase's touch.

In the dreamscape her mind created, she saw every bit of Chase's naked, steaming masculinity, pulsating right before her, his chest flexing strong with a six-pack forming his torso. She could feel his weight lying on top of her as if every bit of his body heat seduced her senses, touching her skin and igniting every erotic sensation that quivered throughout her body. Moans became her breaths, arching her back above the sheets as her thumb turned it on.

The muffling sound it made was deaf to her ears, shutting out its reality as it vibrated in her hand. For this moment, her mistakes and regrets were all erased. The only thing that mattered was what she'd imagined about Chase. He's pure, sweet, tantalizing splendor that had swept through her body. A man as strong and virile as in his picture, giving her this new light, clinging in her memory, holding him up as her prize as she caressed all the warmth of her pleasures like nothing she'd anticipated. The arousing, speeding fantasies that soaked into her pleasure, excited every bit of her wetness as she rushed to pull off her panties.

There, in that moment, her thoughts were suspended as she briefly shut it off and fumbled for the extension, twisting on the end as she imagined the true Chase. The last thing she envisioned was him penetrating her beauty and giving her all he had to offer. With every inch inside her Carly's moans gasped from the sensation. Stroking and pleasing her in an erotic fantasy. It was pain mixed with pleasure. Dominate and submissive, and the further inside she pushed the more her wetness accepted its full penetration. She could feel her moans give in from each inch he had to give. Every single lasting desire that brought her this escape, secured every desperate, awakening pleasure to this point of no return.

***

By the time the weekend was over, Chase had so much time to think about Carly, that to deny it any further would mean to deny his own piece of mind. Their beauty was so striking and similar in appearance that every time Chase caught himself staring at Heather, he could no longer mistake the reflections that came back. Like an echo, his thoughts could not fade away and the pounding in his heart released his worst fears. Recognizing and discovering what it brought, he wondered how he would pursue it.

Sidney had opened a new door and Chase's curiosity was set on fire. Every last detail that thrived inside his memory promised him no relief to what he had forsaken all these years. He remembered every relationship he had ever been in and lived not to repeat the same mistakes. Yet, Carly's influence kept pulling at him.

His bathroom light clicked off as his eyes followed Heather as she made her way towards him. Even though with each step she took into his bedroom his thoughts remained elsewhere. However, with a manipulating mind such as Heather's, nothing would escape her. Ever since the party, she noticed Chase's reluctance. They still hadn't picked out a wedding ring set. There was so much planning ahead but she could sense his hesitance.

Tonight would be special. Whatever held his reserves or whatever distractions corrupted his thoughts, she would seduce his desires and control him.

Although the two still lived separately, she coerced her way into sleeping over tonight. They had to discuss the plans for their wedding and the date had to be set, but ever since their announcement Chase seemed to block it all out. Whatever her motives, she wanted it to be soon, before speculations on the truth. She had her own closet in Chase's bedroom and throughout their months of dating she'd built it into an entire wardrobe. Like everything else, she was taking instead of borrowing and on an evening such as tonight, the attire she'd chosen reflected every bit of her physical gifts.

A soft white, see-through negligee draped off her body and revealed her lacy, French teddy lingerie underneath. The smooth satin fabric glistened with her skin from the soft glowing light of a crystal chandelier that hung above his grand king bed. Every suggestive curve of her body called upon his fantasy, every appetite she fulfilled redefined what pleasure was.

"Do you like my new gown?" Her head posed above her shoulders with a seductive, alluring tone so exquisite and soft that to mistake her intentions would mean to be a blind, deaf mute.

Chase's eyes stayed on her as her appealing features brought him out of his thoughts. Watching as she slowly turned around, showing him every revealing curve of her body that craved to feel his touch. She was absolutely gorgeous, stunning and elegant, possessing everything a man could ever want in a woman. But, as Chase's eyes kept on her, what invaded his vision crept into his thoughts once again. Everything Sid told him was now coming to the surface.

Did he confuse Heather for Carly? Their features and likeness were so close it astounded him. *Could Sidney be right?* Was it his own way of never forgetting a past that kept repeating no matter how hard he pushed it away?

"Well?" She persisted, wanting to hear him say it; wanting him to feel every waiting pleasure that would be his now and forever.

"Since when do you need me to tell you how ravishing you look? You know how I feel about you." His eyes tried to replace his thoughts, yet seeing Carly standing in front of him left him confused and numb. Everything he remembered about her blocked out everything he'd refused, crawling inside his conscience and closing in with doubt.

"Well, I'd still like to hear it, darling." Heather licked her lips as her head gave way to a slight shudder, still feeling his reluctance; she put all the blame on his brother. Whatever Sid told him, Heather would have to make him forget. Her thoughts stayed clear and her appetite strong as she crawled towards him on the bed, like a tigress prowled for her prey.

"I can assure you, my love," her tone craving to have him, feeding on a hunger he could never pass up. "Whatever it was that troubled you this weekend, I'm about to erase every last worry from your head. It's just us tonight, darling." She paused in temptation as she looked into his eyes with all she could instill. Igniting this plea of passion for Chase to surrender and be her prisoner throughout time.

"I'm going to give you a night that you'll never forget."

"*Oh?*" He played along. As he tried to refocus, he searched all his strength to block Carly out. "And just how do you plan on doing that?"

Yet, Chase was unable to clear these thoughts that beckoned him once again. He just couldn't help it, a man so virile, so strong-minded and confident; left weakened from a truth that had finally given it merit. Regardless of Sid's intrusion and how it came, if Chase resisted any longer, it only promised to suffocate him.

"What's wrong, darling?" Heather noticed his missing bulge. She didn't know what was bothering him. She brought temptation in a body that promised to deliver, so she climbed on top of him as her legs straddled his sides.

Deep, unbridled lust now ground her smooth, firm bottom into his pelvis while she touched her ample, mesmerizing lips to the cheek of his warm, hypnotizing face. Her cleavage exposed the bare skin of her breasts, perky and firm, with every appealing feature that captivated a beauty that not even Chase could understand.

"What's wrong?" she whispered. The supple touch of her lips still caressing his cheek. "Don't you want me?" Her desires fanned her insatiable flame. The inside of her thighs rode against his hips as she glided her delicate beauty on top of him. She wanted to feel it, craved his long hard erection that had never before refused her.

Chase closed his eyes as he felt her lips press on to his. His imagination reached full bloom, as he remembered a moment he was never allowed to have, searching his heart for what he had never forgotten. In this fantasy he allowed, what has always came to dismiss him, now flooded all back. He pretended it was Carly who was on top of him, riding on all of the pleasures that seduced his very soul.

Carly had been like a dream to Chase, an escape and a prison that twisted his very existence. This girl from his past he had thought about his entire life could never go away no matter how hard he willed it. Although the moment Chase closed his eyes everything else evaded, imagining the woman she had become and the feeling had now left him breathless. In this one coherent thought, he now realized whatever this friend request has brought to him he owed it to himself to discover what remained.

CHAPTER FOUR

From the moment Chase woke the next morning, the thoughts that had hounded him, throughout his restless night stayed just as demanding. He hadn't even looked at his Facebook page. His curiosity became so overbearing that to put it off any longer only promised to continue to haunt him. He was a man of habit. His usual ritual would have found him rising before dawn and having his morning workout before he headed to the office. But, as he lay in bed beside Heather, he recalled every last detail in what he remembered about Carly, only confusing him further.

He couldn't let her memory go and it drove him crazy, every thought persistent. Thoughts of her overcame all reasoning, begging to know more, wanting to learn everything he could about a woman he didn't know and a girl he couldn't forget.

But, that's just it, *where would he start?* Carly *was* a woman now. He missed so much of her life, he didn't even know what she looked like anymore, and who she had become or if she was still the same. As a strong, proud man with confidence and dignity what bothered him most was how it all affected him. He was lost in the transition of love's last escape, trapped in the shallow destitution of his own mistakes. If there was any cause or purpose, or any reason he could think not to explore this chance, than there was absolutely nothing that had come to mind except his fear of the unknown.

His reaction immediately took over as he recognized the musical note playing on his phone. He turned to the sound and could feel Heather waking to the noise. Crawling out of bed, he retrieved his robe from the closet before stepping over to the dresser to answer it. He was sure Sid was already in the office by now. He could already feel and sense it with every note that played, knowing what Sidney must be calling about. Sid texted him numerous times since the party, but the last thing Chase wanted to hear, especially with Heather in the room, was anything about Carly or Facebook. It was just another complexity that wouldn't go away and as he felt his reluctance grow. Staring at the phone, he didn't want Sidney to keep hounding him about it.

But how could he guess what life would have to offer? In the unexpected anxieties that carried new dilemmas, Chase was about to discover that nothing was certain. Like so many times before, life brought contingencies and how you chose to resolve them defined the real you.

"Morning, Sid." He held his cell to his ear as he looked across to Heather, lying awake and staring back, causing Chase to lift a smile as if giving a morning hello. "Don't worry, I'm running a little late was all. Heather spent the night…they did what?" His tone suddenly rose. "Ground breaking's only a month away, they can't do that." Disturbing wrinkles crowded on his forehead as his face expressed panic.

"I'll sue those bastards and put a lien on that project so fast they won't know what hit'em!" His anger immediately flared, so he tightened his jaw and clenched his fist, causing Heather to jump out of bed the moment she heard him screaming. "I want to see Jerry Roth with our signed contracts in my office in one fucking hour, Sidney! This is bullshit, goddamn it! What the hell does our company have to do with Arizona's new immigration law? They can't hold us liable for that!"

The more he yelled, the more incensed and outraged he became. He was a man bent on principle, pride and honor, reduced to fight for integrity with the high standing reputation that he sustained. He immediately took the offensive and knew there was absolutely no foundation they could stand on. As far as he was concerned, it was an ironclad contract. The project created jobs. It was important for the veterans. With the Iraq and Afghanistan wars taking its toll, the old facilities couldn't possible take on the new patients. They were outdated and inferior to any of today's standards. Plus, Chase was in the position to make tens of millions of dollars on one single job. And nothing was more important to Chase than the success of his company.

As he took a quick shower and got dressed, he left Heather to fend for herself, telling her she'd have to pick out her own wedding ring set today as he headed out the door. Before he knew it, he was maneuvering his way through the busy streets of Phoenix, feeling like Moses parting the Red Sea. An hour felt like minutes. He didn't even park his Cadillac Escalade in his space, leaving it at the entrance as if there was a valet attendant waiting to park it for him.

Chase noticed his employees watching him as he made his way up stairs to his office. Without even a single 'good morning' or 'hello' from his secretary Jennifer, he realized the news had already spread. He felt like a thousand eyes were piercing him, embedded in his thoughts, wondering what he was going to do to save the company.

His stride depicted his anger, though he tried to keep it restrained. He pushed open the door to his office where Sidney and their attorney were already sitting.

"What the hell's going on, Jerry?"

"Now, just take it easy, Chase," Jerry said, as he held up his hands. "I just arrived myself. Sid and I are going over it right now."

"What's there to go over?" His tone still enraged. "The money's in escrow, permits are approved, contracts are signed and subs are lined-up. What kind of shit are they trying to pull?"

"You're in a sticky situation here, Chase," Jerry explains. "This was California's reaction to our state's new immigration law. That entire state's legal staff, all the way up to the Governor is trying to stop all Arizona based companies from doing business their state. It's racial profiling to them. In a state whose minorities are actually the majority, they are trying to amend every contract they have with Arizona, including privately owned companies like yours."

"Can they actually fucking do that? Tell me they can't do that, Jerry."

Jerry Roth lifted his shoulders, confused and dumbfounded. He'd been their attorney ever since they first needed an attorney, cunning and persuasive, well respected and even revered at his job. His matured features and likeable personality completed a distinguished appearance. He carried all the accomplished characteristics that Chase recognized in himself. So whatever advice he had ever given he knew that Chase always listened and trusted his opinions.

"Well, they're certainly trying." Jerry tipped his head as a lock of his slightly graying hair fluttered across his forehead.

"Goddamn it, Jerry! That's not what I asked. What're our fucking options here?"

"Just take it easy, bro." Sidney finally intervened. "We can't rush into anything...Jer's got his associates digging through the contracts now. We need to know all the legalities of it first. This is unprecedented, Chase."

"*No shit!*" He shakes his head to the obvious then finally taking his seat at his desk. "This project's important! It's for people who've fought for our country. You know what this means to me. I want to be the one to build it, and I want to do what's right, for them goddamnit! Don't those political pricks know it's the veterans that are at stake here?"

"Hear me out," Jerry said, trying to calm him. "Because I think a lot of this is going to be riding on you, how they perceive you, how you conduct yourself. It all comes into play now."

"And just what in the hell is that supposed to mean?" Chase's eyes flicked between Sid and Jerry. He sensed where this was leading. "If I hear one accusation about how this is my fault...then I'm gonna fucking blow! You two hear me?"

"You mean worse than you are?" Sid raised his brows, giving a shake of his head to Chase's furious behavior. "You need to calm down bro, this isn't helping, we need to be rational about this and look at all of our options first. Going off half-cocked isn't going to help."

"Well, what fucking will help Sid? Huh?" Chase was livid as he pounded his fist against his desk. "Because if this is their only reason for trying to cancel our contract, then they're fucked! There's no way they have any legal ground to stand on!"

"You know we weren't the low bidder on this project."

"So what, Sidney," Chase shook his head. "Master Builders Management was the only one with the financial stability to complete it, that's why we got the contract. There's got to be more to it than this stupid Arizona immigration law."

"That's what I'm trying to explain now." Jerry remained the calm professional, using rationale and logic to replace disorder. "Your constant outbursts during the negotiation talks, your aggressive demeanor towards the banks to get the financing might be the building commissioner's reason to pursue this in the first place. I think he's getting pressure from the higher ups."

"You're losing me here, Jer. Can't you legally force them to live up to the contract?"

"Sure," Jerry straightened. "I can sue them; put an injunction on the project. But, by the time we get a court date, it'll be costing you six figures in legal fees before it's all over. In the meantime, the project will already be underway with a new builder, or the delay will be too far-gone to ever catch up. Liquidated damages will come into effect. Whichever the scenario, I can assure you, none of it is promising."

"Goddamnit, Jer, what the hell do you suggest I do to fix this?"

"First thing you guys need to do is franchise there, open up an office somewhere in the Bay Area. Let them know you're not just an Arizona company."

"With those taxes? You gotta be kidding me!"

"You have no choice, Chase," Jerry confirmed the obvious. "The state's claim will appear unfounded if your company holds a California license as well."

"Why do I get the feeling there's more to it than that?" Chase felt the tension mounting, studying both of their expressions the moment he asked.

"You have to go up there Chase, meet with the city councilman." Jerry lifted his chin, widening his eyes, as if asking instead of explaining. "He just got elected. You need to get on his good side. I have a feeling he's the one that pressured the building commissioner to do this. But, I can tell you right now, bribing him or buying him girls, exotic vacations, whatever precedes your reputation, isn't going to work on this guy. Jesse Montoya is a Boy Scout. You have to use your charisma and finesse to get this resolved. Otherwise, you two are in for one hell of a fight. You need a major PR campaign Chase, and it all starts with you."

Chase couldn't believe it. Everything he'd strived for and all his hard work was at the mercy of a politician. The very same people he'd expected his campaign contributions had bought. Never having been in this position before, he had always had control and always held the power to bend the rules. But this was totally different and what disturbed Chase most was not knowing what he was going to do to fix it.

It had come at the worst time. Their business had been in a slump since the recession and the residential, commercial and industrial departments had all taken a hit, being forced to lay off hundreds of workers over the past year. His company needed this job, if anything for survival. Not to mention all the planning for the wedding, Heather's condition and everything that had come to life over this weekend had now begun to implode. For a man who always stood at the top, his mountain was becoming a molehill.

"I have a personal life here too guys." He looked to the both of them, "Have you forgotten, I'm getting married?"

"No, I haven't forgotten." Jerry grinned, always the man of reason. He was used to Chase's antics over the years and he wasn't intimidated by him. Chase's bark was far worse than his bite. He always knew just what to say and how to phrase it so Chase would understand the importance. "I congratulated you at your party, remember? But unless you get this resolved, planning for your wedding is going to be the least of your problems."

"Well, why's this all on my shoulders? Goddamn it! Why can't you go, Sidney?'

"You know that's not my role. You're the front man of this company. You've always been the 'go to guy'… and all by *your own* choice."

As Chase just stared, his eyes held his thoughts, hating to admit it but he knew both of them were right. He would have to be the one to fix this. Regardless of the bad timing or the implication of what this would mean to their company, Chase was the front man and he would do whatever it took.

"Damn it!" He looked away then abruptly and angrily stood from his chair. "Fine, I want a complete profile on Jesse Montoya. His likes, dislikes. More than what's in the fucking media," Chase demanded. "I want our usual investigator on this guy too, Sid. I need know what he eats, where he sleeps, when he pisses and how big his shits are. If there's any dirt on this prick, he'll be my bitch before the week's out."

Jerry shook his head and Sidney rolled his eyes.

"Don't look at me like that," Chase demanded. "I have a certain way of doing things and it's never let me down."

"Hey." Sid flashed his hands. "Didn't you hear what Jerry just said?"

"Sure, I'm listening. And I am not bribing anybody. I just want to use all the tools at my disposal. I'm sure as hell not going into this blind."

"Well," Jerry closed his laptop. "I can see I'm done for now." He rose from his chair. "Just make sure you get that office opened up with all the proper licenses and try to get a meeting scheduled with Montoya this week. Keep me informed. If I find something in the contracts, I'll let you know." He shook both of their hands before heading out the door.

Sydney remained seated as they watched him leave, his eyes focused on his thoughts. He looked over to Chase, calm and collected, a moment of repose as he gestured for him to sit down.

With his stress and anger left exposed, Chase took the empty seat Jerry had left. The very foundation that separated the two was the reason Sid wanted to talk to him now.

"Why the hell you looking at me like that, Sid?" Chase could see his plotting brewing. "Now what kind of surprises you have for me?"

"No surprise," His voice remained calm. "We still need to talk about this weekend."

"What about this weekend?" Chase tried to play it off.

"Oh, come on." Sidney pleads. "I've been thinking a lot about what you told me."

"Oh, go figure." Chase's sarcasm reflected what he wanted to avoid.

"You can play it off all you want to, bro, but this is serious."

"You think everything is serious when it comes to my personal life, Sid."

"Well, someone needs to. You didn't answer my texts all weekend and when I checked your Facebook page I saw you still hadn't been on it."

"First thing I need to do was learn how to change my password." Chase stiffened in his chair. "Just stay out of it Sid, haven't you done enough?

Don't you see? This is your chance to fix it."

"Fix what, Sid? What the hell are you getting at?"

"What happened between you and Carly, of course. Everything happens for a reason Chase. Luck or karma, whatever you wanna call it, you've been on the wrong side of it ever since your falling out with her."

"Shouldn't you be concentrating on more important things?" Chase's frustration grew impatient. "This veteran's hospital is a five-hundred million dollar contract over two years, Sid!"

"You don't think I know that?" Sid stressed the importance through his eyes. "But, if we lose it, we'll still survive. You, however, are what concerns me."

"Well, let me lay your concerns to rest because I'm fine. My personal life is in complete control. Everything's exactly how I want it."

"When it comes to the women you've had in your life, how come you keep making the same mistakes over and over?"

"What you see as mistakes, I see as success."

"Fine Chase," Sidney pointed to him with both hands. "This is the last thing I'm going say about it, until you make amends with Carly Bourque." He leaned in towards him. "You're always going to repeat the same mistakes. You'll never find happiness, Chase. I'm not talking about a relationship, that's all farfetched. I'm just talking about fixing your regrets. Not a lot of people get a second chance and if they do, they're just too stubborn to recognize it."

The very instant Sid said it Chase knew he was right. He had been fighting it all weekend. Every last detail from his past dared him to act. He felt he needed to press on to fix his mistakes.

From the moment Sid left his office, Chase's nerves fed his conscience. He starred at his computer for so long it blinded his view to anything else that had mattered. *What was Carly like after all these years? What kind of life has she been living?* All the related questions came the second he went to his Facebook page, all of the answers before him as he read Carly's profile. Her face and beauty were the same that he remembered as his eyes and thoughts consumed what she wrote. She was so glad to hear from him and missing him all these years. He finally relinquished his gloom and gave birth to a smile. It filled his senses, knowing at that very moment, he had missed her just as much. No more confusion about what he needed to do. His imagination had found him and the reality was his. As his fingers began to type, his worries went away, telling her how glad he was to hear from her. Thinking of her so vividly now, he found a place his heart he could never forget.

CHAPTER FIVE

Time controlled Carly's entire life as it consumed every detail that outlined her day; her time that was specifically put aside for Caleb and keeping up with his routine. She was now left to seek a compromise in a ritual that had been broken. It was all happening so fast that she had to scramble to get it on track. She found suitable care for Caleb during the day, but what he really needed was to be back in school. It was unfair. Since his suspension from class, she endured the troubling emotions that came from her son. But, what disturbed her most was not knowing what she was going to do to fix it.

With the events of the weekend closing in, her fears about Ross pressed in her thoughts. *Did he really have a chance to get partial custody of Caleb? Was he just bluffing in a blind drunken rage?* Whichever the case, Carly needed some help to guide her through this dilemma. If only she could get the principal to reconsider, she could finally get Ross out of her and Caleb's life forever. Though, after talking to the principal this morning and setting up a meeting for later on today, the probability of that happening seemed to be hopeful at best.

She'd been employed at ChromeNetFusion for over a year now, a security software company based in Sunnyvale, California. She had a minimal position in the marketing department, and although the pay was low, she took the job because it was a short commute. Raising a special needs child on her own, she needed to be close to home in case there was an emergency with Caleb. She had transferred to the marketing division and had been there for only a few months now, the low person on the totem pole in a company that employed hundreds.

She considered all the risks. Though the pros outweighed the cons, she needed to leave work early today in her last effort to hopefully convince the principle to let Caleb back in school. What bothered her now was that she had to ask her boss Andrew, who was less than perceptive to the needs of his colleagues, if she could leave early. Considering only a couple of friends at the office knew about her circumstance, she felt vulnerable and hated to expose it to Andrew. Though there wasn't anything she wouldn't do, or compromise for Caleb's well being.

As she sat at her cubicle, what hounded her thoughts for most of the day had finally relinquished with the understanding that there was nothing she could do about it now. She had to put it aside and concentrate on her work. Even though Carly struggled with uncertainties, she couldn't get Chase out of her thoughts, knowing she had to look one more time to see if Chase had answered her back.

She kept her worries in the back of her mind. However, trying to focus on her work seemed hopeless. She had to restrain herself from opening her page. She hadn't checked Facebook all day, and what kept her from doing so was her recurring disappointment. Maybe it was just her or this age of social media, but what seemed to be most important to people was building up their friend list.

Carly hardly ever messaged anybody and people rarely wrote on her wall. She was dying for Chase to write back, though the probability of that held an entirely new reality — Chase seemed like the rest, only wanting to build up friends. A ridiculous assumption considering she was still his only one. But there was nothing she could think of to excuse it, he hadn't written her back and it didn't seem like he was going too.

She still believed and hoped, bringing all the distant reminders that when love becomes instilled in ones heart, it can never be washed away. She realized that now, that she had never gotten over him, and if dreams are meant to be caring, then hers would shed some light. Once again she went to Facebook.

She saw the message note immediately and clicked on its red icon. Seeing that Chase had finally written her back the anticipation swelled for her to read it. Every word from every line soaked into her heart, and every worry she ever had relinquished brought a thrill the moment she read what he wrote. This man from her past who held all her deepest regrets, now empowered the girl who was now a woman hoping to correct them.

I'm so sorry it took me this long to write you back. I have thought of you too over the years, Carly. You still look the same, just as I imagined you would. I'm new to Facebook, as you can probably tell, but I'm so glad to be on it now, because I found you. It's so wonderful that we'll be able to keep in touch now. I'm not married either. Just never found the time, I guess. More importantly, I just never found the right person to share my life with.

I'm glad you remembered my saying, 'life isn't about waiting for the storm to pass, it's about learning how to dance in the rain.' I hoped you've tried to live up to that theory, though at times I have forgotten it myself.

I'm in construction now and I've been living in Phoenix ever since graduation. Even though work's been slow, it's been a good life. I have a chance to work on a job in Frisco coming up on the new veterans' hospital they're building. It would be nice to see you after all these years. Maybe we'll have a chance to catch up then. I really don't know what else to say right now, other than I'm looking forward to writing you some more, and that I'll be disappointed if I don't hear back from you.

I wish you all the best Carly.

Chase

It was short and sweet. But, what it brought was a long lasting elation that held open promises. When she read what he wrote, she pictured him speaking directly to her. What she imagined and what she felt opened all the doors that she would never close again. She felt so happy and free, so hopeful and honest. Her deepest peace had come to soothe her and the escape left her breathless.

She enlarged his picture on her screen again, wanting to see his face, wanting to imagine being with him. A heart left circling with her imagination in a race; opening up a truth she couldn't walk away from.

"Andrew's done with his meeting now, Carly." Pam suddenly appears at her cubicle.

Carly looked up, startled, broken away from a world she didn't want to leave. She was so deep in her thoughts that she never saw Pam coming. Then she noticed Pam's curiosity drawing her eyes to the computer screen.

"My," her tone flirtatious. "Who's that hunk?"

Carly hesitated for a moment, not wanting to reveal too much of her privacy. She trusted Pam. But, her personal life was all she had. It was the only safe security that kept her apart from the rest. She noticed Pam's expression, inquisitiveness so apparent that Carly couldn't dismiss what Pam held in her eyes.

"His name's Chase." Carly's smile spread even wider, her elation growing stronger just from saying his name.

A clearly, painted picture spread across Pam's face, her thoughts more intrigued, feeling every bit of Carly's excitement for a woman who never shared anything. Then she suddenly noticed, "Oh, you're on Facebook. Who is he, a friend request?"

It all echoed out as her thoughts and emotions tangled a reply. *Was Chase just a friend request or was he something more?* Whichever it was, it pulled her hesitance and caused her to blush knowing her answer ran much deeper than just a simple yes.

"Just someone I know." Carly's joy reflected in her tone, intriguing Pam even further.

Pam couldn't help but to analyze her. For over a year, she'd been Andrew's secretary, the boss in their division and she knew everyone pretty well. Carly, however, was new to the company and the chance for Pam to find out more about her held her absolute attention because Carly had always remained so private.

"And what are *you* smiling about?" Carly kept a playful tone; trying to hide the embarrassment she couldn't help but to show.

"You, for one," Pam's chin stretched as her red hair fell across her face. She leaned down towards Carly. "The way he has you smiling, there has to be more to it than that."

"And what if there was?" Carly tilted her head. "Think you can handle it? Or is this something I'm going to hear all over the office?"

"*Carly*, I am honored… but no." She held up her hand. "Privileged you would bring me in on this. Nothing ever escapes these lips," she tried to reassure her. "I'm a vault." She twisted her fingers at her mouth as if turning a lock.

"You know, this is hard for me." Carly's smile now dissipated, talking in a more caring tone, totally deviating from her professional persona.

"I know Carly," Pam settled her nerves and gave a response that showed she completely understood. "Just tell me who he is." She lowered her hands to the sides of her skirt. "He must mean something to you; why else would you have his face covering your screen?" Her head gave a subtle shake.

"He's an old friend of mine back from my days in high school," Carly let it out, subtle and brief as if prying for a response.

"Hmm," Pam played along, knowing obviously he meant more to her than that. She struggled with all her instincts wanting to just stand there and scream, *liar!* "He sure is attractive," she flirted with her eyes. "I mean, really, really—"

"Yeah," Carly stopped her. "I can definitely see the obvious." She reduced the size of his picture, seeing the distraction. But a distraction for whom? That was what she now considered. Feeling a certain impairment creeping into her thoughts, jealously or regret, desire or passion, whatever it was, she didn't want Pam to see it.

"So, what's the story with this guy?" Pam's curiosity grew. "What's his last name?"

"Bishop, his name is Chase Bishop." Carly heard herself say it again, a name she hadn't spoken for so long it seemed that just the pure sound aroused her senses.

"A very strong name," Pam raised her chin, her hair bouncing with every nod and gesture. "Mystical," she said sharply. "Handsome even..." she paused as searched for the right word. "Debonair. You sure he isn't more than just an old friend from high school? The way this guy has you smiling there has to be more to it then that." Her brows highlighted her curiosity once again, staring down at Carly with her anticipation gleaming; she waited, and wanted to know.

"We dated in high school," Carly explained. "I went to his senior prom with him. I haven't heard from him or seen him since I lived in Santa Clara. Now here he was on Facebook sending me a friend request...caught me completely off guard. Don't know why..." She paused in a haze, caught herself drifting, and suddenly refocused. "Guess, because I never thought I'd ever hear from him again."

"Well," Pam resumed her smile, which helped to build Carly's confidence in whatever she was feeling. "It's obvious he's thought about you since then. He wouldn't have found you unless he searched out your name. Is he married?"

"*No,*" Carly answered as her embarrassment showed in her tone. "Why would I care anyway?"

"Are you kidding me?" Pam placed her hands on her hips. "If that's a current picture then this guy's pretty hot."

"Yeah," Carly nodded as her cheeks widened back to a smile. "I'm pretty sure it was and yeah, he always has been."

Pam narrowed her face as if to say, *good for you girl.* "Well, whatever's going on with this guy, I want to know what happens. I like seeing you like this."

"Sure," Carly held her smile." I will, as long as it stays between us."

"Of course," Pam winked again. "Right now though, if you still want to talk to Andrew, you better catch him before he goes to lunch. I'm heading out myself."

"Sure," Carly logged out. "Thanks for letting me know he's free, Pam," Her eyes looked behind her, towards his office. "Didn't happen to notice what kind of mood he's in, did you?"

Pam smiled. "His meeting seemed to go well, if that helps." She lifted her brows and tilted her head.

"Not really," Carly smirked. "But, I guess now's a good time as any."

"Anything I can help with?"

"I just need to leave early today."

"Oh," her expression suddenly changed. "I don't know why you have to leave early. But, if I were you, I'd just tell him that you have a doctor's appointment."

"You think he'll understand?"

"Of course," Her eyes gave reassurance. "He can't hold that against you…and Carly," she paused. "If he calls you into his office, I'd leave the door open."

"OK," she nodded, although she found the comment curious. "Why?"

"Let's just say," Pam searched her thoughts. "He responds better when he's under public scrutiny."

Carly watched Pam leave, thinking no more about it, feeling more secure and confident with herself. It actually felt good being able to share it with someone. If she kept the news about Chase in any longer, she would've burst at the seams. Considering it was Pam and not someone closer, what it brought to her was a subtle relief. Perhaps that was why she told her in the first place, to help build up her confidence from another woman's perspective. To feel what Pam had seen and convey what she thought, someone who didn't know much about her, though an opinion she needed to hear.

She stood up from her desk as her mood took a turn. Her reluctance about having to ask Andrew to leave early now set precedence. She felt like everyone was watching her as she made her way to his office. With every click of her heels striking against the tile floor, what echoed in her thoughts was just how he was going to act. She was fairly new to this division and was already behind in her work. He's a demanding boss that would only hold it against her.

The subtle taps of her knock defined her reluctance, a woman too proud to beg. No matter what happened, she wouldn't let Andrew make her feel guilty for leaving. She was a mother first and duty had called, trusting he would understand.

"Yeah, it's open." She heard him answer.

Her eyes rolled back as her head tilted in caution. She opened the door slowly and peeked inside.

"You have a minute, Andrew?" She lifted a smile from her cheeks, trying to feel his mood.

"That all depends on how long it's going to take. I'm pretty busy." He sat behind his desk in front of his laptop.

"Not long," she kept her smile. "I just have a favor to ask."

"Yeah, you and fifty other people around here."

It was like a game to him. His practice of self-importance and the intimidation he imposed. He made the employees feel inferior. How he perceived his employees held the dark secrets with what he could get away with. He was a man in a powerful position who used it to his advantage and today, without warning, he wanted Carly as his prize.

"I promise, it's nothing big," Carly tried to remain pleasant, still holding on to her smile and all the fabrications that came with it.

"Sure," Andrew winked, waving her in.

He noticed Carly many times before. How could he not, she was absolutely beautiful. What shared in his fantasies, in a man who has many, was what an easy target she was. With every gesture that had come from his eyes, what stayed in his thoughts twisted more for him to have her. He studied Carly; the curves of her body, the color of her hair, every radiant, striking feature that aroused him gave birth to his desires. In an office full of women, she wasn't the first one that he chose to pursue and in the mind of a deviant, she wouldn't be the last.

She stepped inside his office remembering what Pam had told her, but then heard, "Please, Carly, close the door behind you." Leaving her with no alternative, she slowly closed it before stepping up to his desk. He was much older than Carly, with gray highlights in his hair. He was a bit overweight, which made him look awkward in his brown polyester suit. His cheeks were pudgy and he had a roll of chins around his tight shirt collar. But with a man in his position and the power he controlled, he wasn't the type to let his lack of good looks stop him.

"Now, what's on that beautiful mind of yours?" He said pleasantly enough. He winked up again at Carly. It was subtle and smooth, tempting the improbable, all conveying a message that he wanted Carly to know his interests.

It was a side of him Carly hadn't seen before and it began to make her feel uncomfortable. His small gestures and persuasive expressions gave merit to her alarms. Her instincts and reasons had all come to life, her paranoia's and unrest now awake in her conscience. Not even her thoughts of Chase's message could help her escape what she was feeling, and if it felt like the walls were closing in, when in fact they had already collapsed.

"I was hoping I could have the afternoon off today, Andrew."

"Wow." He widened his eyes, pulling back his head. "And here I thought it was going to be something simple."

Carly said nothing, not sure if he was serious. With a man like Andrew, humor lacked trust. Her hesitance and doubt mixed with her insecurities, and caught her off guard when she should have been prepared.

"I'm sorry I have to ask, Andrew," her tone was apologetic. "And if it wasn't important, I wouldn't be asking."

"Well, Carly, What you consider important, I may consider futile."

She could see the calculating reflection in his eyes and the impatience in his tone that wanted her to explain.

She wanted to say it, just come right out and say it, but what her fears rejected, her thoughts restored. So she arrived at the conclusion that Pam was right. It was best to just lie and make this as painless as possible with little explanation.

"It's for medical reasons, Andrew," she quickly blurted out. "I have a doctor's appointment." Her deceit thickened, trapped in a device meant to simplify her excuse.

"Oh," Andrew's eyes narrowed in on her and he gave her his full attention while his corrupt, indecent mind considered other incentives. "I trust it's nothing serious?"

"No." The subtle shake of her head denoted privacy. "But, I am uncomfortable talking about the reason for my appointment."

"Well, I don't want you to feel uncomfortable, Carly." He let a moment pass, feeling her nervousness feeding his control. "I understand you're still behind in your work."

"I'm almost caught up."

"Have a seat," He gestured with his hand; still sitting behind his desk as his eyes wandered to where she sat. "I'm worried about you, Carly," He stood up; stepped around and sat on top of his desk right beside her. "You've been so behind in your work, I don't know if you ever *will* be able to catch up."

It disturbed her again. The expression on his face and that look in his eyes held all the menace that Andrew was getting at something and whatever it was, she was reluctant to find out.

"I'll catch up, Andrew, even if I have to work through my lunch hour for the rest of the week, I'll catch up."

"Perhaps I can help you." His grin emphasized his mood and projected his expectations. "We could stay late one of these nights, just the two of us. See what *we* can get done. "He paused, curving his brow upward and lifting his chin. "Or, better yet, see what can come out of it. You never know, it could be a *very* productive night." He reached down slowly, seductively, touching her bare arm.

Carly quickly pulled away. She didn't know whether she should laugh or cry, whichever the scenario, Andrew had crossed the line. It caught her off guard, but it also repulsed her. She wished she could do something, tell anyone who would believe exactly what he was up to and was reminded of Pam's warning.

"Are you implying what I think you are, Andrew?" Disturbed lines formed down her brows as her tone became sharp and abrasive. Regardless of what Andrew thought, Carly wasn't the type to let any man use her that way. She'd been through too much in her life, and what he viewed as weak, passive and submissive, had turned into a mistake that Carly would correct.

"Take it easy, sweetheart." His nickname for her revealing what his tone defined. "I'm just trying to help you. I didn't mean anything by it. All I'm saying is, I know how demanding your job is. But, if you can't keep up, I'm going to have to let you go. Your inadequacy reflects on me and our corporate office expects results. I know how difficult it is for a woman to succeed in a business that's monopolized by men. A woman as beautiful as you, it breaks my heart." His lips pulled and his voice became soft and suggestive. "I'm sure there's something that can come out of this. I can help you, just as I know, *you* can help me. Maybe even give you a promotion as our…special relationship progresses. It can't be easy for a single mother…the only income in the house."

Carly's eyes widened, catching her completely off guard. It repulsed her even more, knowing Andrew had been snooping about her. The lengths it seems he would go to try to corrupt her in his own obscenities represented everything that Carly despised. The fact that he knew what she had never told anyone only proved her theory that Andrew was a creep. "How do you know that, Andrew?" Her anger and resentment came all at once. "Have you been profiling me?"

"Profiling," he sneered. "Googling, searching, whatever you want to call it. I know what I need to about the people who work underneath me. And you, my dear, require the kind of discretion that I find attractive. I know that financially your condo was mortgaged to the hilt and it's only worth half of what you owe. I can help your career in this company tremendously, Carly. All you have to do is let me."

He repulsed her even further and had shocked her way beyond fear. He was a predator hunting prey and Carly wasn't about to become his rabbit. What incensed her worse was how he had seemingly investigated her. His stalking tactics and meaningless threats gave way to a compromise that Carly would never surrender to. She refused to let him have her body and mind, mistake her as weak-hearted and revise it with contempt. In all she had despised, hated and refuted, what she now came to loathe about Andrew, made him her worst enemy.

"I'm going to Human Resources." She quickly stood up. "God only knows who else you've been doing this to."

"What? Help?" He smiles deceptively, knowing that there was nothing that she can do. "You're the one who's behind in your work…and by the way, Carl Muller's head of Human Resources and a good friend of mine. We play golf twice a month," he mocked, keeping a candor in his expression that held all of the advantages.

"This meeting's over," she barked back with all the animosity that took her out his door.

"If you're leaving early, I'll expect a doctor's excuse…and don't make any hasty decisions, Carly. It'll only go against you."

It was the last thing she heard as she slammed the door behind her. She couldn't believe it, she felt outraged and cheap, vulnerable and insignificant. Pam should have warned her. Carly would never trust her again. It was just another one of life's cruelties in a world that Carly had wanted to be so different. Another omen that her life would never change.

CHAPTER SIX

It was an hour before the final bell at Milpitas High School, a campus in a town small enough to be considered a community. Every ethnic race flooded the crowded hallways as each group of teenagers formed their alliance. The higher performing academic students wore backpacks and sweaters, ignoring any distractions as they headed to their next class. The Odd Squads and Gothic's have existed just to shock, while the Preppies and Jocks mingled and flirted. There were the Hispanic groups and Asians, Black's and White's all coinciding in existence in a fast paced chaos that had taken Carly by surprise. In all of her thoughts, what stood at the present was how well Caleb had managed to be a part of it all. He always talked about the kids here and she knew he missed it, but Carly could never have surmised the extent. Her next-door neighbor, Rogine, had been watching Caleb while she tried to get him back in school. When she picked him up he found out that he was coming with her today, his jubilation only made her more desperate.

There were 'hello's' from boys and gracious hugs from girls. All the kids who cared about Caleb, missed him and wanted him to come back to school. *"Where have you been? Have you been sick?"* Their curiosity was open and their questions were plentiful.

Carly had no idea that he was this well liked, that there were so many kids who actually noticed he was gone. She realized that her protective attitude towards her son was preventing him from experiencing normal school life and that wasn't natural for a teenager. She had to find the perfect balance of restraint and freedom. To keep it all intact seemed to be her only answer.

It brought her some hope in a day that had been so disparaging. From the stigmas she felt to what now replaced it brought encouragement and pride if just to see it for herself. She knew Caleb was special, incredibly good- natured, innocent and pleasant, but those precise attributes were what made him vulnerable. He knew right from wrong and was trustworthy and good-hearted, perhaps that was why he had been so lost in all this, being unable to comprehend how people could turn or how they could mistrust his own caring nature. If anything would come out of this or whatever lesson could be gained, Carly could only hope that Caleb would somehow understand it.

She had to give him credit though because Caleb never blamed anyone. He took it all remorsefully, but hatred or anger never came into play. It was another unexpected example she was taught by her son. She wished it could be that easy for her. Every time she thought about Andrew, her anger burned. The disdain she felt and the disgust it brought buried another promise to herself; to remain private and distant, place her trust in no one and only rely on herself.

She had to look past that now and concentrate only on Caleb. The last thing she wanted was her own misplaced feelings to affect his good mood. She tried to keep a smile and an open honest mind. The closer they got to Mark Johnson's office, the more she felt her stress building up inside. She could feel each beat of her heart reconcile with her conscience, searching for the rationality that would get Caleb back in school. In a mind so determined to fight for her son, what she had overlooked would only come to haunt her. Carly's child wasn't the only one involved in all this, nor was she the only parent willing to fight for their child.

***

The parents of Shelly Blake, the girl that Caleb had kissed and the event that started this entire situation in the first place had arrived well before Carly. The principal informed them that he had a meeting with Carly today and wanted to talk to them first. Though, his rationality to put a resolve to this conflict had only met a dead end, Justin and Kathy Blake weren't bending and in fact, they had been the entire reason for Caleb being suspended.

"There's no way I want my daughter going to the same school as this boy" Justin Blake's anger exposed every animosity that glared on his face. "He's dangerous and he don't belong here." The tone of his voice reflected his deep hate, a prejudice whose only justification came from Caleb's circumstance.

"I understand your concern, Mr. Blake." Principal Johnson tried to plead his case. "But I think Caleb Bourque has learned his lesson. His punishment seemed fair. I don't think there's any legal need to expel him permanently. He does have a right to attend our school. I'm sorry folks, but the law is very specific."

"Rights?" Kathy Blake interrupted. "Shouldn't your concerns be for the real students at this school…their safety? Not for some boy who shouldn't even be going here in the first place. I'm shocked you're taking this position, Mr. Johnson and I'm quite sure the other parents with kids in the school will feel the same."

"Now, I don't think that's going to resolve anything, Mrs. Blake. I've gotten to know Caleb since he started attending our school. He's actually a very good kid. Most of the students love him. He hasn't shown himself to be mean tempered or violent at all."

"What the hell do you call what he did to our daughter?" Justin takes his turn. "He practically attacked her!"

"Now," Principal Johnson raised his finger, trying to find a reassurance that, to them, didn't exist. "That hasn't been validated."

Justin and Kathy Blake stood there shocked and appalled. They fought this from the beginning, judging a boy they'd never met, fearing a situation that they didn't understand. They were as protective of their daughter as Carly was of Caleb.

"Mark," his secretary's voice suddenly came over his speaker. "Caleb and Ms. Bourque are here."

The hostility of the parents came across as an angry silence. Tense anticipation combined with their contempt and ill will preceded their thoughts. They had already accepted who's to blame, and it only added to their prejudice. As Principal Johnson gave his approval for Carly and Caleb to enter, what he'd seen in the Blake's eyes would only get worse.

Carly had experienced the hatred and prejudice in the past. To believe in herself and the love of her son meant she stood as a testament that no one could ever break. Not even the eyes she was met with when they entered could elude what she had felt. It was all a setup, why else wasn't she informed that the Blake's would be here?

"Principal Johnson," she nodded. "Thank you for seeing us." She purposely avoided the Blake's and their four burning eyes.

"Of course, Ms. Bourque—"

"Carly… please," she assured him.

"Fine," he politely nodded back. Carly realized they were already in mediation and she was cautious to whom he would favor. "Please, have a seat…you too, Caleb." His eyes could not help but stagger back and forth from her to the Blake's. "Carly," He continued. "This is Justin and Kathy Blake, Shelly Blake's parents."

"Oh." Carly lifted her chin, stern and cautious, locating the strength to bear their hostilities. "I wasn't aware they were going to be here as well."

"And the problem is?" Justin quickly snapped. "Shouldn't we have a say in this matter?" His aggression pointed right at her. "Our daughter's the one your son attacked! Do what's right for everybody and get him the help he needs, because if he ever touches our daughter again, nothing will be able to save him."

"Who's attacking who, Mr. Blake?" Carly's resentment took a hard stance. "You have no right—"

"Please folks, please." Principal Johnson tried to clear the atmosphere and sustain a more tolerable mood. "I didn't agree to this meeting for it to turn into a shouting match. Restrain any hostility for the sake of your children."

If looks could kill then Justin and Kathy Blake's exceeded the limits. Each of them refrained from speaking, though the expressions on their faces needed no words. They resented Carly and her son, and worse they resented Mark Johnson for trying to find a solution to all of this. To them it was abundantly clear. Set Caleb up as an example and expel him permanently from this school.

"Thank you," Principal Johnson continued. "Now, if I may speak to Caleb for a moment, I'd like to get his understanding in all of this." His eyes shifted between both families as if for approval, watching as Carly gave an agreeable nod while the Blake's just glared in disgust. "Caleb…" He looked directly at him. "Do you understand why you haven't been allowed to come to school?" The ease in his voice, the tone of his experience, the calmer the mood, meant better results.

Caleb slowly nodded, keeping to his silence as his lips folded in a pucker. His hands rested in his lap while he rocked back and forth in his chair. He was anxious and confused; his lips set in a pout and ready to cry.

"Can you tell me why, Caleb?" The principal kept a soothing tone, coaxing Caleb to explain.

"Because kissing girl b-bad," his voice cracked as he stuttered.

"Sometimes," Principal Johnson said pleasantly, ensuring an understanding that the Blake's didn't like. "That all depends on who wants to be kissed, where you're at when you kiss them, and how you kiss them. Do you understand that, Caleb?"

"Yeah, my mommy told me that already. Was that why you are mad, because girls are not supposed to kiss?"

"Not boys like you!" Justin breaks his silence. "You got me, bud? Shelly don't like you, and she don't want you kissing her."

"I know," Caleb's eyes swelled up; finally releasing the tears he had held back. "Kissing girl bad, kissing girl bad, I tell Shelly that." Rocking even faster, pouting even stronger as Carly calms him, wrapping her arms around him as her anger flares at Justin.

"You yell at my son one more time, Mr. Blake, and you'll have a lot more to worry about than some innocent kiss." Carly ground down her teeth while still hugging Caleb.

"Yes, Mr. Blake, please," the principal quickly intervened. "That isn't helping anything."

Justin once again refrained, appalled and astounded that he was the one being reprimanded in all this. In a man so bent on anger, so judgmental when it came to someone so different, what stood in his way was his own drowning arrogance.

"I d–d–don't like him, mommy, he is mad." Caleb rocked even faster, stuttering even stronger as Carly tried to comfort him.

"I know honey." Carly's securities got him under control. "But, I won't let him hurt you. It'll be alright."

"Your mom's right, Caleb," Mark helps to put him at ease. "We just want to talk, ok?"

Caleb nods, feeling the security of Carly still hugging him.

"You said you told that to Shelly?" The principal continued, trying to give substance to a matter that should never gone this far. "That you were sorry?" He planted the words for him, and in doing so, gave Caleb an opening to secure his place at school.

"I told her kissing girl b-bad." Caleb stuttered.

"When, Caleb? When did you tell her that? Have you been talking to her?"

"I told her kissing girl bad. Then Marshall got mad. He scared me, Mommy."

"Who's Marshall?" Carly's eyes were vigilant as she looked at the principal, anticipating as she suspected, that there was more to it than what she knew.

"He's dating our daughter." Kathy now spoke.

"Yeah," Justin added. "And thank God he showed up when he did. Who knows what would've happened if not."

"You know, Principal Johnson." Carly's tolerance was worn out. "At least my son had the courage to be here. Where's Shelly in all of this?"

"Hasn't our daughter been traumatized enough, Ms. Bourque?" Kathy couldn't help but to focus the blame on Caleb.

"She's still too distraught to even look at your son, let alone be in the same room as him." Justin added his own degrading insults.

"Well, she should at least be here to defend herself. If she's accusing Caleb as the aggressor, then she should be—"

"Please folks," Intervened the principal once again, holding up his hands. "The facts are, Mr. & Mrs. Blake; I think Caleb understands that he can't act on his feelings in such a way. His condition and his ability to prosper at our school have already been evaluated by our counselor and the special education team. He has never shown any violent or aggressive behavior in his past, or since he has been a student at our school."

"What are you getting at, Johnson?"

"I think Caleb's been punished enough. Caleb attends our special education classes, while Shelly's a teacher's aide in his final class of the day. I think for all concerned, he can continue his studies here, with the exception of that class."

"That's your solution?" Carly's disbelief sounded. "Can't she just tutor another class?"

"Our daughter shouldn't be the one to sacrifice anything here." Kathy snapped at Carly.

"Nobody's sacrificing anything folks. Your son can either go to study hall or take the early bus home, Carly. His last class was an alternative course; he doesn't need the credits. He's only in it because of your work schedule."

Carly didn't like it. But, at least it was a solution. In a life full of compromise, so unfair, what eluded her and Caleb were the contingencies that people had always placed on them. They were at fault no matter what the stakes. They didn't belong. The simple fact of who and what they are, infringed on people like the Blake's and their own rigid morals. To accept was to understand, to allow was to encourage and what Carly had always found, was that people never did.

The halls were empty now as Carly and Caleb made their way out of the school and back to the parking lot. She didn't appreciate being surprised by the Blake's and the disgust soured her thoughts, once again she found herself on borrowed resentments. In a day that had been so distraught and dire with consequences, the facts that were there eluded her once again. To see the truth, as it was, plain and simple, would mean sharing the same innocence as Caleb in even the most hardened and strong willed minds. And it was clear the Blake's were incapable of compassion.

It actually brought a smile to Carly's face when she and Caleb left before the Blake's, hearing them immediately argue with Principal Johnson from the moment she closed the door. What it brought to her then, stayed with her now; Caleb had won his freedom again no matter how partial the victory or what others thought, for once there seemed to be a light in a tunnel that had no end.

It still bothered her how the Blake's looked at Caleb. The blame they projected and the degradations he sustained, held all the principles that blinded them from the truth. If it weren't for Principal Johnson, there wouldn't have been any reasoning or rationality at all. At least now she had some options, and yes Carly understood them. She could drop her suit against Ross and get him completely out of the picture.

She knew there was something Caleb was trying to say, and she had prayed for some clarity that would help her understand. She felt Shelly had tricked him some way and that the entire situation had been nothing but a set up. When she and Caleb reached her car, Shelly Blake was waiting for them in the parking lot. Caleb recognized Shelly Blake right away, speeding up his pace as he rushed to see her. Surprise mixed with delight on his face. She saw an obvious affection that could be witnessed from a mile away. If only Caleb could understand as she did, see through the girl and the root of this trouble, his innocence could finally understand a person's true value. What appalled Carly most was that this girl actually had the nerve to keep leading Caleb along as if they were still friends after all this.

"Shelly!" His happiness sounded. "Look, mommy, it is Shelly."

"*Caleb*," Carly stressed. "Slow down, honey. Stay away from her. She'll just try to get you in trouble again."

"No, I won't, Ms. Bourque. I promise I won't." Shelly's assurance sounded sincere. "I'm so sorry, Caleb," Her voice distraught, fighting back her tears. "This was all my fault, Caleb. Please forgive me."

"Okay, Shelly." Caleb reached her with a hug. "Do not cry.

Principal Johnson's not mad anymore."

"What do you mean, Shelly, this was all your fault? What happened... the truth," she demanded, now pulling Caleb away.

Shelly wiped her tears. Obviously she was remorseful and as scared as Caleb. She was just a teenage girl. Though, regardless of the circumstance and what was yet to happen, Caleb deserved her loyalty, now more than ever.

"This was all my fault, Ms. Bourque. I should never have let it get this far. When Marshall came in and saw the kiss, he just exploded." She pulled back as her anguish and dismay all poured out at once. "I didn't know what to do...I." She waved her hand into the air. "I just panicked. Marshal just assumed it was Caleb trying to kiss me." Her cries plead as she tells her. "I let Caleb take the entire blame, even when Marshal told Mr. Johnson he attacked me."

"What are you saying, Shelly?"

"Don't you see? I kissed Caleb, not the other way around."

Everything Caleb was saying now made perfect sense. *'Kissing girl bad'* sustained an entire new tolerance. It was Caleb's way of saying: Shelly was a kissing girl and she was bad for kissing him. It all made sense and Carly only wished she had realized it sooner. But in the end, fate had a way of securing life's uncertainties, knowing that the Blake's would never stand for such a scenario. They were already decided about Caleb long before they ever met him, and they would not be deterred.

"What do you mean, you kissed him? Why?" Carly demanded every detail.

"Caleb made me a papier-mâché flower," There was sorrow and

remorse in her words. "I told him he was sweet and kissed him on the cheek. That's when Marshal walked in. He saw it, or..." She paused, "saw what he wanted to."

"It was nice, mommy," Caleb's smile interrupted her confession. "I made it for you, but Shelly seemed sad."

"It's okay, sweetie." Carly touched his cheek. "That was nice of you."

"Thanks, mommy." Then he turned to Shelly. "I get to come back to school now Shelly, but no more kissing, okay?"

"Okay, Caleb," she sighed, returning his smile.

"Why didn't you just tell him?" Carly shook, "Tell everyone what happened. Do you realize what you've done? How this has hurt Caleb?"

"I know, Ms. Bourque. I'm so sorry," Shelly pleaded again. "But, my parents or Marshal wouldn't listen. They didn't like me tutoring the special needs class so they thought I was just trying to protect him. They didn't want to believe it."

As Carly listened to her cry and heard the remorse in her voice, she understood the pressure that came from people like the Blake's. She felt sorry for her in that moment, a girl held captive to her parent's beliefs and prejudice. The girl seemed caring enough even remorseful for what happened, but she was just young and scared, naïve to the situation that had exploded in her face. Carly was once young and had lived through such regrets. Perhaps that's what brought her understanding now, seeing the girl as herself and all the regrets that came with it, a circumstance to remember for a lifetime. If anything had come out of this, at least Carly knew the truth. However insurmountable, Carly would take a lesson from Caleb and allow peace into her heart. Forgive the unforgivable and in a pleading way, find the power to forgive herself for her own past mistakes.

CHAPTER SEVEN

Chase fought every emotion and finally his conscience persuaded him to answer Carly's message. When the moment came to push the send button on Facebook he began to experience remorse. He was spoken for now, engaged to a woman who carried his child. In his moral agenda, the facts were always present staring straight back. He could never look at himself in the mirror again knowing he had other alternatives in mind.

No, he would have to forget about Carly, confide in himself that they were never meant to be. No matter how hard his emotions and curiosity had pushed him, he had to refrain and concentrate on a future with Heather. The one elating promise that he was going to be a father and the one conflicting pain he would have to fight off if their marriage would ever had a chance to flourish. He had to accept that the baby was his and that God has allowed him to be fertile.

He wouldn't allow himself to believe anything else and forbade himself from knowing the reality of his condition. What Chase was feeling inside harbored every bit of his own speculations, and to get tested and know the truth about his fertility, to him, would have decide the fate of his manhood and Chase just wasn't ready to commit to that yet.

He wanted to believe Heather so bad, that to hear anything else was what kept him from getting tested. Though, in the end, the result gave him the excuse he needed in not knowing. It's as if he had kept his own sense of manhood, if indeed she was pregnant. Chase never went with her to the doctor and Heather never showed him any documentation showing the positive results of her pregnancy. All Chase knew, was that from the moment she told him, his thoughts were racing with the endless possibilities.

It was Friday in a stressful week. He read the report on Montoya so many times that he knew it word for word, and there was nothing there that he could use against him. Their attorney, Jerry Roth, was right. He would have to accept the verdict. It appeared that Montoya was exactly who he seemed, a Boy Scout in a cause fighting for his own race, a man on a mission. He would have to build Montoya's confidence in him, befriend him and get his trust if he ever had a chance to secure his place and this contract.

He knew everything about him now; his entire life story was in the file he held in his hands. Montoya had been elected in a landslide. He had a large and proud Mexican-American family. His office was active on all the social media sites and he was a liberal that had fit the Bay Area like a glove. For Chase to break through, Montoya would have to see him as a constituent. If anything, it gave Chase a reason to keep his Facebook account open, using it to his advantage in getting to know Montoya and his inner-circle better. He wanted the Montoya office to see him and Sid as allies, not as a threat. Chase had already 'liked' the Jesse Montoya fan page on Monday.

It was clear to Chase that Montoya was a family man and he fought for human rights. He was for gay marriage, pro-choice and affirmative action. Though, what stood out to Chase most, was Montoya was the father to a Down Syndrome child. It explained his entire demeanor, who he was and how he lived, the very dominance of his standing in how his district perceived him.

Sure, Chase found himself in these situations in the past, being a man that was always able to play on people's emotions but this was different. Chase had always felt uncomfortable being around the mentally challenged. He never knew how to act or what to say and always found it repulsing when he would witness some pretentious ass, baby talk to one of them. As if somehow and in some way they would be better understood. No, Chase didn't like it and he felt for Montoya. With a man who always had to hold blame with doubt, what Chase saw in Montoya was either bad genes or terrible luck. Whichever the case, what Chase had to do now was structure circumstances to his favor. He had to reflect on his beliefs and feed from his instincts.

Chase could see Montoya vividly through the file pages. It was as if he could sense his entire demeanor strictly through what he read. How it made him feel and how his emotions had come to react, all played a significant role in his plans for Montoya. Surely a man with such influential power had a place and the means to fight for human equality. But, what confused Chase was why he targeted Master Builders Management at fault in all of this. They had always donated to charities supporting the less fortunate of the world. Earlier in the week Sid had taken the initiative to donate ten-thousand dollars to Montoya's own charity organization; The Cheer for Hope Foundation, an organization that not only helped fund medical research for Down Syndrome, but it provided financial aid to their parents as well.

He arrived in San Francisco alone that afternoon, already setting up a meeting with Jesse Montoya at his Mission District office. His attorney didn't want to get involved as of yet and any appearance with Chase and Roth would only set a precedent that they were on the offensive. Roth felt it had to be up to Chase to rationally resolve the situation first and explore all the reasonable options before they could ever make their case in court.

Chase hadn't gone in blind. Of course they went over all the strategies and being a man that always came well prepared, today had come with no exception. All day yesterday Roth had his own team of strategy analysts coaching Chase on how to act and what to say, predicting Montoya's entire demeanor and how they would counter it with their own tactics if Montoya stayed on the offensive. Their details ran so deep and precise; they even dressed Chase down for the meeting, trying to give him the appearance of a down to earth, blue-collar worker. It removed every intimidating feature about Chase and made him more approachable, especially when it came to Montoya.

Sure, it was a far cry from Chase's usual three-piece suit and polished shoes, but he liked the fit. His straight-legged Levis covered the tops of his naturally tanned leather boots, with a white-buttoned cotton shirt covered by a gray blazer. Respectable and honest, a generally sincere look without giving away the obvious. As an acceptable man, they had hoped Montoya would acknowledge this and come to them with reason.

With all the open business space available in California and the bargains to be had in the city, Sydney leased a very nice warehouse with a front office not too far from Montoya's downtown office; purposely making sure it was in Montoya's district. Chase had insisted at the very least, considering all the time he would have to be spending there. Sydney had the company provide him with his own transportation, thus his reason for the detour before the meeting. There was to be a brand new Chevy Silverado delivered by the dealer waiting for him in the parking lot. Of course, what Sydney would find out later couldn't hurt him now and Chase saw no reason why he should be the one to sacrifice everything. After all, he was used to a certain custom and that had already been tailored down. There was no way he would have to give up everything just for the sake of what Montoya perceives. For his own selfish exploits he made the switch and had the dealer deliver a Cadillac Escalade instead, just like the one he had at home. Chase wanted to use the drive over to Montoya's as a test run.

Sitting in the back of a cab on his way over to their new office, he couldn't help to think about Carly. Every recollection he tried to wash away only came to surface the moment his plane landed. He was back in California and more precisely, back in the city by the bay as memories crowded even further inside his mind. He hadn't looked on his Facebook homepage since he decided to cancel his message to Carly and what it had brought to him now was an entirely different perspective. He was so close to where Carly had lived that there was no use in trying to fight off this curiosity that kept hounding him. Everything that reflected what she had once meant to him dared to form an alliance with the true feelings that he obscured. Life was a boundary held captive by vices and to explore the unexplainable only opened new horizons.

It tore at his conscience and ripped at his soul. So much

importance was riding on this meeting, that to let anything else distract him, only inhibited his chances to succeed. The consequences of that held a dire resolution. Too much money and too many lives were riding on this. This veteran's hospital was important to so many people and he knew he couldn't let them down. He knew he was the right company to build it and he truly cared for our nation's heroes. Their company was the only one with innovative design to benefit veteran rehabilitation. He had to make this work, regardless of the means, regardless of the sacrifices and any deterrence from that would mean failure.

The sites of the city had taken his full view. Steep, climbing hills made up the city landscape with a towering and impressive array of earthquake-proof skyscrapers that reached into the heavens. The sidewalks were crowded as electric trolley cars and buses filled the roadways, each packed with commuters and tourists. In the distance, the murky waters of the bay opened up wide as his driver reached the top of the next hill, slicing through the peninsula that divided San Francisco and Oakland. The Golden Gate Bridge stretched grand across the bay and just as mesmerizing as he remembered. In fact, everything was just as he remembered. As a man trying to forget, starving with temptation, what fed him once again was this curiosity of the unknown.

He thought of everyone now, not just Carly, even his high school friends that he hadn't heard from since grad night. The crazy shit they used to do and the trips they would take, all intruding deep into his conscience collecting every last remembrance of what it all meant to him. Perhaps Sid was right. Whether it was karma or circumstance, fate or irony — the path that led him here now brought an entirely new enlightenment. Regardless of all his success and all his accomplishments, Chase missed those days and it took being back in California for him to realize that. No matter how hard he tried to push it away or try to refuse his own suffocating reluctance, what always returned was his own self-reliance. He was too strong willed, too young and ashamed back then to let Carly know he had come back for her graduation.

He realized now that it was the coward within him back then that he despised. The disinclination he carried throughout all these years sheltered him from a truth he had been hiding from his entire life. Perhaps that was why he chose to make a life in Phoenix with his brother. It was the only way he knew of escaping regrets as well as sorrows. But in the end, what Chase was trying to escape from was a memory, not a life and memories like dreams have a way of following you. Chase could feel it once again, the 'what if's' and 'have not's' shared every bit of his thoughts about how things might have been different.

He wanted to see Carly and maybe get to know her again, but it all seemed so frivolous now, all a fictitious scenario to a man who was recently engaged. *Could he actually see her, talk to her? What if he did? What would it mean?* Every crazy scenario circled with his questions and every refutable voice told him it could never be.

He heard his phone ringing, which pulled him out of his daze. It was Heather's tone that was playing and he felt guilty in a way; thinking about his 'what if's' with Carly when was engaged to Heather. She didn't know much about his past. He had shut Heather and everyone else completely out of that that part of his life. Those who know him, know how he is now, not who he used to be. To Chase, he had never changed, only adapted. Yes, he had come a long way and Heather, at least to Chase's consideration, would never understand the person he was back then. She wasn't the type of woman to get caught up in the past because she only lived in the present. She couldn't possibly comprehend what Carly had once meant to him and, in fact, Heather would view her as a threat. Yet, in life's stolen promises and with concern to hearts that have been broken, do any of us ever share the details of our past loves with our new lover?

Arizona

Heather sat across from her friend Kat, at Rufo's Café. Her delicate, thin, French manicured fingers held her phone to her ear as the two of them sat at an outside table up in the Colonnade deck overlooking the city. It was one of their favorite places to go, a very popular downtown lounge and bistro resting in the heart of Phoenix's restaurant row catering mostly to the upper class. Of course what waited in the wings were women like Heather, the stubborn underachievers that wanted to be a part of high society.

Temptation was all Heather knew. The cold weather in Indiana was a far different lifestyle then what she had become accustom to here in Phoenix. She had come from a working-class family and their moderate means and selfish behavior only fueled a fire that she could never put out. She had to rise above what held her back, take her place among the wealthy and live in a city where her reputation didn't precede her. She had to start fresh again and leave her past behind, which was what brought her here to Phoenix, that and a simple transfer of her Job at Sears.

She was good at manipulation and her standard came well disguised. The moment she set her eyes on Chase he became fair game. For a women like Heather her past remained reserved. She had always told Chase as little as possible. The less he knew about her brothers and her family's poor education the more Heather could distance the truth.

It brought a comfort to her, knowing those days were over. Her relationship with Chase was built by seduction and if she ever wanted to keep him she had to manipulate her fate. It was the one standing motive she kept all of her life. Money, not people, made the difference. Influence, not truth set her goals. If looks yearned for passion, then attraction set her stage. It was the only thing of importance within her, but with Chase she had them all.

"Hi, baby," came her soft, pleasant voice. "I miss you already..." She paused, winked at her friend Kat, and twirled a lock of her long auburn hair in that conniving way she always did when getting at something. "Noise? It must be the people in the lobby, darling..." Her eyes glanced over, feeling a faint deceiving smile slowly pulling on her cheeks.

"Yes, sweetie, I'm at my appointment now...I will, darling, of course." Her tone played along, gliding on all her falsehoods. "Well, that's how important you are to me, honey. I always have time for you." Her chin pulled down, giving way to a smirk. "It shouldn't matter if I'm a few minutes late, Dr. Swallows has adapted to more outlandish challenges than that, I can assure you. After all," her eyes teased back to Kat, "Her name is Margaret Swallows. Could it get any more outlandish than that?" She scoffed, "Besides, it's bad enough I had to pick out my own wedding set." She gestured to Kat as her thumb and her index finger rubbed together, displaying the extravagance of how much it cost. "But, you still haven't committed to a date and I prefer to have our wedding announcement in the paper next week. With all this nonsense in California occupying your time, I'm taking it upon myself to hire a wedding planner. The only problem is, we need to set the date. And you know how I feel about that. The sooner the better." If Chase needed a push, then Heather didn't mind shoving.

Ever since their engagement announcement Heather had been insistent on setting a date. She had been rushing him as each day pressed on, wanting to get married before any signs of her pregnancy. She was a conceited, want-to-be debutant, inflated with her own self-importance. Make no mistake about it; this entire wedding was going to be all about Heather.

They didn't talk for long. A few 'I love you's' and 'I miss you's' sounded the air and with every one Heather never missed a note in this tune she was playing. She was so persistent in getting Chase to commit, that before their conversation had ended, she accomplished just that. It would be less than two months away. From the moment she heard him say it her flamboyance came alive. The prestige of wealth made her cocky and when it came to boasting Heather loved to flaunt her new jackpot.

"Ok, darling, I will." She winked at Kat and teased her with a mocking smile. "I will, darling, I'll handle everything. I can assure you.

And thank you, honey…thank you for understanding—*Love you, sweetie.*" She rolled her tongue. Her tone seductive and suggestive, her long artificial eyelashes fluttered with her words. "I'll have a wonderful surprise for you when you return. I'll let myself in, you can unwrap me when you get upstairs…I can't wait either, sweetie. Ciao for now." Her breath crawled through the phone as if floating through the airways, clinging to every sense that would enhance his imagination.

"What was all that about?" Kat said confused. She held a Virginia Slim in her fingers as she placed it between her Moulin Rouge lips. One of the pleasures of taking a table up in the Colonnade deck, other than the spectacular view of the city, was that you were outside and thus the privileges of smoking were granted.

"Have to keep the lion fed and build anticipation that keeps them starving for more." Heather lifted up a smile, taunting every bit of what she was holding back. So much so that Kat couldn't help but to inquire.

"Mmm-hmm," Kat pulled back on a long drag of her cigarette. Her puckering lips exhaling a steady stream of smoke above them as her flirtatious eyes peeled back to Heather. "You going to tell me what's going on or am I going to have to pry it from you?"

"What Chase knows and what he thinks he knows are two different things, Kat." Heather straightened in her chair, her back stiff and tight, pushed out her chest as the fabric from her blouse exposed her revealing cleavage.

Kat tilted her head. "What appointment are you talking about?" She exhaled smoke. "*Dr. Margaret Swallow's*, is that even a real Doctor?"

"Of course," Heather smiled, "Margaret Swallows, I found her on the net. I couldn't resist not using her when I saw her name. She has an office ten minutes from here."

"You mean *you do* have an appointment?" Kat's intrigue suddenly turned into surprise. She watched in awe as Heather took a drink of wine. She had wanted to say something when she ordered it earlier, but didn't dare.

"Of course not." Heather waved her off. It was as if she lived two lives, the proper and unemotional woman that had trapped Chase into this marriage, and the outgoing, party-girl whenever she was out with her friends. Of course, the latter was the reality while her times with Chase were spent strictly in defining the woman he preferred to be with.

"Then, why the charade?" Kat's cigarette waved in front of Heather again, while her free hand brushed her dirty, blonde hair over her ear. Her designer blouse hung low as her augmented breasts bulged even more dominated by her push up bra. She exposed every prevailing trait that made her and Heather the same, every measure and principle that her demeanor had given away. If looks portrayed the significance of how people perceive you, then what Heather and Kat portrayed, devoured everything that was considered common, as if everyone else was inferior.

"I have my reasons." Heather pulled back as a devious, self-important grin hung on her face.

"And give me one of your cigarettes," she added, while leaning in towards Kat. "It's been drivin' me crazy watching you smoke."

"Of course," Kat politely snickered. "I can't believe you've been able to hide it from Chase all this time."

"It's getting harder to hide it. I'm definitely going to have to quit sometime." Heather placed it in her mouth. "He thinks it's a turn off." She lit her own cigarette, looking around as if insulted that a waiter didn't come running over to light it for her.

Kat just stared, as she watched Heather inhale the smoke. *Really?* She thought. *Wine, and now cigarettes, has Heather gone completely mad?*

"You know I'm never one to interfere," Kat couldn't hold it in any longer, "but in your condition, do you think that's wise?"

Heather said nothing and only lifted a grin.

"*Something's up*," Kat's tone dragged out. "What's going on Heather? Are you really pregnant?"

"What makes you imply that I'm not?" Heather's narrow, petite shoulders shrugged up above her neck.

"Because, I know you. I know that look." Kat's eyes demanded an explanation.

"OK," Heather gives in. "What if I'm not?"

"Oh my God Heather!" Kat gasps out loud. "How can you lie to him about being pregnant?" The moment Kat said that she quickly looked around, cautious of anyone hearing her.

"You think he heard?" Heather's concerning nod gestured to a man sitting a couple tables away.

"I don't think so." Kat quickly glanced his way. "He's been chatting on the phone ever since he sat down." Her eyes peel back; shock and disbelief hold her reflection. "I would just worry about me for the moment. Don't hold anything back. I wanna hear every detail."

"Don't look at me like that", Heather smacks. "It was the only way I could get Chase to commit to me fully. Otherwise, it just seemed like he was never going to ask me." She finished off her smoke. "I'm not going to work at Sears my whole life."

"Well, honestly heather, this seems desperate." Kat shakes her head. Unwilling to give approval was something that made her feel awful. "Why don't you just go off the pill? Honestly, I don't know how you're going to get yourself outta this one."

"Believe me," Heather sighed. "Don't you think I've tried to get pregnant? I haven't been on the pill in months and nothing," her tone was discouraged. "This seemed like my only option."

"Still, Heather, how are you going to pull this off?"

"I'm no one's fool Kat; I've thought it out," Heather smirked. "You were listening. We just set the date; it's only a couple of months away." As far as the rest," She effortlessly expelled it. "All I have to do is fake a miscarriage"

"*Ooohhh* my God," Kat's shock expelled all the breath she had in her. "Can you really get away with that?" she gasped again. To Kat, this just kept getting worse and worse.

"This trouble in California couldn't have happened at a better time even if I planned it that way. Even better when he does start the project. Why, it's got him so busy now he doesn't know which way was up or down. *You* heard," she flaunted, "I'm completely in charge of all the wedding plans. Hopefully he'll be spending a lot of time in Cal. Whatever the case, we already made the announcement at the party. He could never dump me after suffering a miscarriage. Image is everything to Chase. He couldn't bear to face the scrutiny of people talking behind his back. Besides, and you're not going to believe it…"

"What?" Kat hangs on her every calculating word.

"He hasn't even brought up a prenup yet." Her confidence and arrogance stood as belligerent as her soul.

"Unbelievable," Kat's jaw dropped.

"My only worries now are how I'm going to excuse my family from attending."

"Are you kidding me? Why?" Kat's head pulls back.

"My brothers will probably get drunk and my parents will undoubtedly start fighting during the ceremony."

"That bad, Huh?"

"Worse." Heather answered, shaking her head. "Maybe I can tell Chase they all came down with the flu or something."

"It *is* that time of the season." Kat reluctantly agreed with a nod.

Though, how could Heather surmise just how bad Sidney had wanted to stop this marriage? To be so open in public is what he had been counting on. To show Chase the proof would finally expel Heather forever. Each of them had been enthralled they had never taken notice of the gentlemen sitting alone who wasn't using a phone at all. What they overlooked put everything in jeopardy and now there was nowhere to hide.

***

The detour to their new office took longer than Chase had thought. The traffic was worse than Phoenix and the tall, steep, endless hills had taken their toll on him as he sat in the back seat of the cab. But, it would all be worth it, just as soon as he sat in his new Escalade. He hated taxis, their smell, the drivers, all dirty and obnoxious, trying to spark a conversation in a language that was supposed to be English. Perhaps it was their way to preserve a tip, or their self-taught understanding of what English was supposed to sound like. Whichever the scenario, Chase refrained from talking, keeping it strictly professional when he did, only telling them where he needed to go. Which brought him to where was now, arriving at a downtown stretch of complexes off the beaten path, a strategically chosen location only a couple of miles from Montoya's office.

The drive seemed endless. His thoughts had been somewhere else when he should have been concentrating on this meeting. Hearing from Heather so soon after he landed only brought a torment that had been persistent all along. At times he felt backed into a corner, trapped in confinements and enduring his own fate. A man of his caliber, creed and standard, reduced and torn by a woman he knew he wasn't truly in love with.

Sure, he cared for Heather, but there was always too much friction when it came to his family. Even on the occasions when his parents would visit from Lake Havasu, their chosen retirement, it seemed as if they tolerated Heather instead of welcoming her. He knew the look and seen their stares so many times with different women, that for once, Chase would like to see a change. Perhaps when he committed to her in marriage and when their baby was born it would bring an entirely different response. He hoped it would shine a new light or open a new door to an endearment towards Heather he had never felt himself.

Though, he never talked to Heather about it, he assumed a woman of her understanding should already presume that marrying the wealthy would come with sacrifices. Jerry Roth told him yesterday that he would courier their prenuptial marriage decree and obviously from her mood, she had not received it.

It just seemed so odd to Chase, building a relationship with love, devotion and respect, yet here it starts, ready to divide two lives on the probability that they would divorce. Perhaps that's why Chase agreed to let Heather plan the wedding the way she wanted it. He would give her the prestige of extravagance as if was just another reward he had to hand her in a relationship that had come with standards. Whatever the circumstance, he understood her wanting to get married before her pregnancy started to show. If setting the date eased her thoughts, he knew at the very least it would occupy her time and give him some peace of mind.

"Which one?" The driver asked, referring to a row of driveways Chase wanted him to turn into.

"Um...I don't know." Chase shuffled for the address as he awakened from his thoughts. "Suite 369".

"No, which one," His voice came a little harsher, pointing as they passed another parking lot.

"Great," Chase mumbled. *Where do they find these people?* Finally feeling the frustrations himself, he decided to make it as simple as possible. Surely the name 'Cadillac' was recognized in any language. "The one with the brand new Cadillac Escalade sitting in an empty parking lot," Chase spit it out.

"No Caddy, just old truck...see," He pointed, looking back to Chase as if he's crazy.

"What?" Chase looked, matching the address to his. "That can't be it."

"Turn?" The cabbie gestured, approaching the driveway.

Chase just nodded, lost for words and puzzled at what he saw, telling him to wait while he makes sure this was the place.

This was it all right. He took the envelope that was taped on the windshield. His eyes and thoughts all rushed to read it, which only made him furious. This *was* his truck, a ten year old, half-ton Chevy Silverado, tricked by Sydney once again. It appeared as though Sydney wasn't about to spend eighty-thousand dollars for Chase to ride around in his old stomping grounds just so Chase could feel better about himself, *'Besides, who tricked whom first?'* Sydney wrote. *'As soon as the dealer called for approval from a Silverado to an Escalade, that's when I thought it'd teach you a lesson. You shouldn't hide things from me, bro. You know I'm on my game. Get this contract finalized once and for all and you'll get your Caddy. Just think of it as an incentive.'*

He paid off the driver who was obviously mad and mumbling to him. It must have seemed to the cabbie that Chase was actually crazy so he hastily sped off. Chase shook his head as he watched him peel away, feeling like it was all just a bad dream. But when he looked over his shoulder, the truck, along with all of his problems laid bare before him. It seemed like forever since he had driven a vehicle that was more than two or three years old, and if Sydney wanted to start teaching lessons, then the one he had coming would be far worse than this.

He took his phone in his hand and texted his brother. His fingers punched in every vulgar thing he could think of as he told him exactly what he thought about the truck and his note. What he wrote made him laugh as he pressed the send button. Then he headed over to their new office knowing none of it would bother Sydney and it would change nothing at all. Chase would still be stuck with the truck.

The keys were supposed to be in the mailbox, which he could see was attached to the wall by the front door. Before he could even reach his hand inside, he received a text back with nothing but a frown, displaying Sydney's displeasure.

Chase shook his head again, purely disgusted as he paused for a moment before stepping inside their new building. Compared to their main headquarters in Phoenix, the office was moderate. The entrance held a space for a receptionist's desk. As he searched around, he could see that the place needed a little work, but considering it was last minute and Sydney leased it at a bargain, he didn't do too badly. Though, as far as Chase felt, Sid had to do better than this to get him off the hook. There was a single office in the back with a door at the end of a hallway, which led to the warehouses outside. It was certainly adequate for their purposes and Chase felt that once they remodeled it to his specifications, it could be quite nice. Nothing too elaborate of course, but enough to bring the influence that Master Builders presented. As Chase looked it all over, he knew he would be the one coordinating the work, while Sidney in all of his comforts stayed back in Phoenix with his family.

It just wasn't fair to have all this put on him right now. Sure, he had to be on the road before, overseeing projects in other states, and he had the personnel to put in charge of this project if it ever got off the ground. But, to be stuck here now like this, dressed the way he was and driving a truck he would never be seen in, only added to the complexities that drowned him in its wake. After all, what kind of marriage would he have, with it starting out like this? What kind of husband would he be, abandoning his future bride before they were even married?

What have I gotten myself into? He thought as he reluctantly walked back to the parking lot, as the dread of having that truck crept into his thoughts. That question cohered to him even further, knowing that it pertained just as much to the mess he had here in California as it did to the one he had back home. Chase realized now more than ever that he must free himself from his own self-doubts, his doubts in a woman and her pregnancy, and his doubts within himself in getting Montoya on their side. It all came imploding in on him at once and he couldn't decipher the difference. With a man so prominent, so poised and confident, what overtook Chase now were his own anxieties in knowing that they are one and the same.

He set the GPS on his phone that showed him how to get to Montoya's office. He was never usually nervous before a meeting, but then again, this wasn't ordinary. Even with all the practicing and the different scenarios Roth's team coached him through, none were really helpful, not right now. There was nothing there to give Chase any hint or reference as what to expect, and who would actually be there when he went in to see Montoya. Though, even in life's uncertainties, fate had a plan to guide the unforeseen and what Chase was soon to find out would contain Sydney's biggest surprise of all.

The drive over to Montoya's would only take a few minutes and Chase knew he would be arriving right on time. Surprisingly, the truck in comparison to similar vehicles this age, hadn't been that bad. It drove nice, had new tires and a modest appearance. The interior was in good condition and the body showed no signs of rust, but it had over 100,000 miles on it. Chase hated the trucks two-tone colors and he knew Sydney had known that. Whether he was trying to be spiteful or careless, it was just like his brother to do something like this. He compared the existing with the imaginable and threw it in Chase's face. Whether it was for the memories of Carly or the doubts of Heather, Sydney knew damn well that the truck Chase had in high school, the very same truck he had his accident in with Carly, was a two-tone Chevy as well. Two different, yet comparable women tied to the same fate that had come from that night. Two women, trapped in different eras, yet competing for the same space that his heart couldn't seem to decipher. If Sydney's purpose in all of this were to bring back recollections, then what was colliding in Chase's thoughts could be counted as a victory. An outcome to follow that could never be erased, for in life's modest reflections, fate had a way of finding you. When you least expect it, circumstance and coincidences would become one and the same.

    It happened at that moment. Chase's eyes followed his GPS when they should have been following the road. As Chase found out, the steep hills of San Francisco were never streets that should be traveled by the novice driver. His eyes caught a glimpse of yellow as he suddenly looked up. Instinct and panic forced his reaction as his foot crunched with his brakes. If Chase could ever find a way to screw up this meeting, it all started now with the cab he just rear-ended.

    It was his entire fault, being out of practice driving in a city like Frisco. He remembered how the steep hills were and he needed to use more caution. Other than the cabbie yelling at him in some mish-mash of English, he was glad it was this piece of crap instead of the new Escalade he was supposed to be driving. Either way, Chase knew he didn't need this, not now. As a man built on schedules, dominant and persevering, he didn't know what the hell would happen if he missed his meeting with Montoya.

It all came closing in now; everything that consumed him took its toll on what was to come. If Chase ever needed a reason to lose his temper, what just happened gave him every reason to scream. Surprisingly, he collected himself as he stepped out of his truck. The driver's insults deflected off his ears and for once Chase was glad he couldn't understand a cabbie. Though, even in life's excursions, Chase could never have surmised the events that were destined to follow.

CHAPTER EIGHT

The feeling that calmed all of her fears stayed with Carly all week. A passion and loneliness that yearned for excitement had awoken anticipation the moment Chase began writing her back. What it had brought to her then stayed with her still. This sweet, tantalizing anticipation that restored memories to hope, forfeited dreams to reality and gave the past a second chance.

It was all she could think about as the week progressed. Every message he sent her rejuvenated her once again and with every message she sent back, she only wished there could be more. She thought of him so much, yearned to hear his voice and what he had brought to her now clung to all of her senses. Even at work, it was her thoughts of Chase that kept her going, his touching endearing words that repeated to her still. Every single prayer seemed to find her the moment they reconnected. She found herself telling him stories about her life that she never thought she would ever tell anyone. It was as if Chase was the same person, wiser, but the same. He had the same attitude mixed with, what seemed like, compassion. And if there was anything Carly wanted to know, more than life itself, it was what he had been doing in Phoenix for all these years?

He didn't seem to like writing about his life much. Every message he wrote intended to be strictly about Carly. Whether he was modest or hiding something, ashamed or embarrassed about how his life turned out, the questions that surround her, broke free from any worries. After all these years, she looked forward to seeing him again, no more words instead of voices, no more reading instead of hearing, he would be standing before her in the flesh and she knew that the moment she seen him, every sensation would find her, would come alive in her destined heart.

It seemed so unreal, so impossible and astounding. To believe after all these years, she would finally get to see him, touch and hold him. See for herself if she still felt the same. Though, exposed inside her thoughts, she knew it would take something drastic to ever change that. The one true revelation, of course, would come when she would introduce him to Caleb. A truth set before her that would likely play in slow motion and depict every obscurity in that moment. Yet, Carly knew the likelihood of that was the least of her concerns. He just didn't seem that way. It was entirely his idea for her to bring Caleb and meet him at the center's opening.

Was he trying to impress her, show her his compassion? Or, was it all just a strange coincidence that opened a new door? Sure, Chase knew about Caleb. All week long, in their Facebook messages, they talked about the basics, but Carly never told him that Caleb was special. Even though Chase was evasive at times, he did come across as caring. She wanted to exchange their cell phone numbers just to hear his voice. However, what Chase had inspired touched deeply in her heart. Chase wanted to wait until they were able to meet in person, find each other in the crowd and hear each other's voices for the first time in the flesh. The anticipation it brought her, swelled with every remembrance that tinged throughout her body. She knew where this could lead. Chase met her criteria; he would be everything she expected. Carly felt that today just very well might be the beginning of her life.

***

"Please," Chase flashed his palms as the frantic shaking from his hands exposed his desperation, explaining and pleading with the receptionist to keep his appointment. "I'm begging you. None of this was my fault. As I told you on the phone…"

"I understand your disappointment Mr. Bishop, but Councilman Montoya has a schedule to keep." Her shrewd eyes showed no sign of a compromise.

It seemed that not even Chase's charm, should he choose to even use it, would be able to pull him out of this one. She was despotic and belligerent, older, appearing to be pushing into her sixties. Her entire appearance reminded Chase of his old junior high principal Mrs. Harwich, which the children had renamed, Mrs. Horror Witch. As Chase stood there pleading, feeling it all slipping away, he understood that's who was in front of him, a woman of the same caliber, arrogant and cocky, showing no compassion or understanding as to what was at stake, someone he could buy a million times over. It was obvious to him the very moment he talked to her on the phone that she didn't like him. He had already been judged by her long before he got here and she was more than determined to stand in his way.

"I'm well aware of Mr. Montoya's schedule," Chase took a more affirmative approach. "And if I'm not mistaken, I still have ten-minutes left on time that was supposed to be going to me. So you either announce me or I'm going in half-cocked. The choice was yours, Miss. *Either way* he will be seeing me today."

"Those minutes were forfeited the moment you were late." If Chase thought she didn't like him before, what became so vehemently exposed to him now, was how much she had instantly come to despise him. "There are other obligations the councilman has to attend. If you like, I can reschedule you for some time next month. *Either way,*" she mocked him back, "I'm getting ready to call security."

"Security?" Chase pulled back as his eyes open wide, unable to believe what was actually happening. "You have the gall to threaten me? Schedule me for another appointment a month away? Well, I'm well aware of the councilman's obligations." His frustrations enraging him more. "And believe me, you're not going to get away with this, he's not going to get away with this!"

"Get away with what, Mr. Bishop?" A calm, yet firm, slightly accented voice came from behind him.

As Chase heard it, he realized that this just kept getting worse. He slowly turned around, embarrassed and caught off-guard as he saw Jesse Montoya standing in the doorway of his office. Everything he prepared for and all the different scenarios Roth's team had gone over; who could ever have surmised that it would've all begun like this?

"Mr. Montoya?" Not knowing what else to say, or what else to do but to finesse his way out of it. "I was just explaining to your secretary–"

"What, Mr. Bishop, your reason for standing me up? Your hostilities towards Audrey here?" His hand gestured over to his secretary. "Well, I can assure you it's out of Audrey's hands. It's out of all of our hands now, you'll just have to reschedule."

"I got in a wreck on the way over here sir, that's why I'm late."

"I'm well aware of that. We all are Mr. Bishop…"

"Please Councilman," Chase interrupted, trying to come across as sincere, "I'd feel more comfortable if you called me Chase."

"*Chase?*" Montoya tilts his head. "What is this, a scene out of a movie? I thought your name was Chatsworth?"

Chase looked past his sarcasm, Montoya was mocking him more than taunting, but what lied underneath, Chase had caught right away. How would Montoya know that if he hadn't done some investigating of his own? It opened an entire new door, an entire new format hearing him say that. Chase always had a way of making things personal, shining a light where darkness dwelled and for Montoya to expose that to him, left him with the clear understanding that Montoya operated under the same M.O.

"That's right sir," Chase humbly stepped over and reached out his hand, hoping Montoya would oblige. "It's a nickname I got from my brother. He couldn't pronounce my name when we were kids. It's nice to finally meet you, even under these embarrassing circumstances."

It was just as Chase had hoped. Montoya took his hand, firm and assertive, nodding in a gesture that accepted his perseverance. Chase could read it in his eyes, stamina and virtue, intrigue and contempt, all clashing before him as Chase tried to pull himself together and figure a way out of this. Montoya was a man held on an entirely different platform that even Chase wondered if he could subdue. He made his living off of reading people, controlling circumstances and manipulating the outcome. After all, he was a politician. A first term of course and Chase knew from this moment on, he could read Montoya like a book. The two of them were so alike. It was obvious they each had their own agenda and competitive streak.

"I wish I could say the same, Chase." Their hands let go as Montoya looked directly at him

"Excuse me, Councilman?" Chase caught his remarks, a harshness in his tone that measured respect as nothing more than manipulation.

"What do you expect me to say?" Montoya shuttered his eyes and shook his head, obvious in his disapproval and frustrations. "You came to my office nearly an hour late. You not only stood me up, but also the mayor and building commissioner as well. We all have a say in this matter."

"It wasn't on purpose, I can assure you," Once again Chase was quick to explain. "Like I said—"

"I know all about your accident, Chase, I can't help what happened."

"Neither can I, sir." Chase desperate, felt his fears rising. It was all just a setup; the Mayor, the building commissioner, all here to impose their sanctions and to deny him any clemency. Chase wanted to explode, wanted to scream, feeling it all slipping away until he heard him say it, confess to his scrutiny and admit blame.

"Perhaps you should have taken a cab straight here from the airport instead of picking up that old truck at your new office?" Montoya let it slip out as he saw the look in Chase's eyes, catching him completely off guard and exposing him to uncertainty. For Montoya it made all the difference. Yes, Montoya knew all about Chase, or so he had thought.

"I see," Chase raised his chin. "Well done, sir," Chase said, trying to keep his respect from turning into disgust. If there was anything that Chase wanted to do now, it was to call him out on his deceit and twist it all against him. "It appears the only way you could know that was if you had me followed. Not exactly the way to start a meeting where honesty and candor come as the highest priority, not to mention respect, sir."

Silence now impeded that one brief moment of distrust, so he looked the councilman straight into his eyes. Chase didn't know what hand he was playing, but whatever he's up to or whatever he held against him, Chase wasn't about to go down without fighting.

"Well, good for you Chase Bishop." Montoya's smug approval gave way to his tolerance. "You just bought yourself ten-minutes."

Arrogance more than respect assembled every compromise, for Chase knew he was on borrowed time. It was no way to start, but at least he had ten-minutes. Given to him so directly and precise, Chase could move mountains in ten-minutes.

"Thank you, Councilman." Chase's voice came as a sigh of relief, reaching out to shake his hand once again. And make no mistake about it, Chase could read every curve, every denial and curiosity that showed through Montoya's eyes. He was intrigued by Chase, his contract and his company, but, more than that, Montoya had wanted to use him as a steppingstone. An Arizona company he could denounce in the media, fight for equal rights and put an end to Hispanic profiling. And in his jurisdiction, Hispanics were the majority. Regardless of whom the contract was rewarded to, the hospital would still bring jobs in his district and Montoya wanted it to be a California based company.

Chase read from Montoya his adoration of the secretary who he placed as his most trusted and dedicated employee. Chase comprehended this all too well, having a secretary himself, and if anyone ever came into his office barking at her he would've had them escorted out. The best thing to do was to make amends. "I'm so sorry, Audrey," Chase's tone swallowed every bit of his pride and arrogance in his admission. "I never meant to disrespect you in any way." If there was anything Chase was looking for now, it was the compassion he hoped would come from Montoya. "It's just the week has been so–so stressful. I've been worried about–well–what will become of my child–" he stuttered purposely, drawing on the magnitude, "–my fiancé. Everything that's been building up to this misunderstanding with this state, particularly with your district and Councilman Montoya." Chase briefly turned with a sorrowing look. "There're lots of people counting on me for jobs in a time when work is scarce. And now this, my accident keeping me from getting here. This is an important project to me, the Councilman, and it needs to be done right…for every war hero that's served to protect our freedom. Our staff is certified to meet the criteria these veterans need for rehab. I know my outburst is no excuse, and I do apologize for my rudeness. In fact, I'm embarrassed about my behavior. You seem like a wonderful person and you certainly didn't need to hear me raising my voice. It's an ugly side of me, Audrey." He smiled, teasing with a wink as his charm worked. If Chase was expected to deliver miracles, then it all started with her, calling on her sympathy in a time when leniency was scarce.

Audrey reached out with a smile across her face. Chase took her hand into his. It was that look he held in his eyes, that somber, grieving expression that brought sincerity back to light. As Chase looked into her eyes and saw the glow upon her face, he felt the inherent admiration that he drew from her the moment she shook his hand. Once again calling on his finesse, charm and sincerity, hoping Montoya would be just as easy to subdue.

Though, if Chase was ever able to win over Montoya, it would take much more than an apology and go way beyond words. Chase would have to earn the respect that he demanded for himself. If Montoya had a weakness, Chase figured it laid with his son. Why else would he have started the Cheer for Hope Foundation in the first place? It had to come from his son.

It was the only thing Chase could warrant, looking for Montoya to give him some compassion. Surely a man with a Down Syndrome child understood compassion. Even with the lessons Roth's team had coached him on, Chase already knew that to be certain. How could he not?

Montoya followed him in as he told Audrey to have his driver pull around up front. His words calling out, "This won't take long," before closing the door behind them. He stepped around to his desk and gestured for Chase to sit as he adjusted his cufflink before gradually resting in his chair. Considering his office was on southeast corner of the lower income, Mission District, it still remained quite nice and respectable. Obvious to Chase, it had been remodeled since Montoya had been elected. Everything was new and modern in a building so old it seemed like a historical site left over from the big quake in 1906. The outside seemed defaced and showed signs of structural damage, while the elevators remained inadequate and slow, having gates instead of sliding doors.

Montoya himself looked out of place. Reaching into his late forties, he was a dark skinned Hispanic with jet-black hair, and Chase could only assume that he dyed it that dark. He was medium height and slender with a body that fit his narrow, proud head. His cheekbones highlighted the entire outline of his jaw, structured; yet refined. Each line on his face carved his endurance, a man that depicted some wear, though kept a respectable appearance and was actually quite handsome.

It all came as a package; decided and judged. His three piece tailored suit, polished shoes and gold wristwatch, represented his entire demeanor, while Chase looked to his own attire and saw how he was dressed. Chase knew it was all for a good cause and that Montoya was obligated to make an appearance, as was Chase. He knew Montoya's schedule and Chase was already planning on attending the councilman's opening ceremony for the new Cheer for Hope Center. After all, Sid had already donated ten grand to the cause, but that was all this was to Chase; an obligation, not a reward. And for Chase to ever conceive it as endearing and prominent as Montoya had, he would have to live it for himself.

"Well, Chase…as you prefer." He tilted his head as his dark brown eyes affirmed Chase's touching plea of emotions and he wasn't buying it. "I don't know what that turn of events was with Audrey, but I can assure you, I don't think you'll be as fortunate with me. I don't know what we could possibly accomplish in ten minutes without all the proper figures being present. But," he said as he pulled back in his chair and interlocked his fingers, "I'm listening." The lobes of his ears pushed through the ends of his hair as he sat and waited for Chase to say something, anything that could actually contradict what he had learned about him, his brother and their company.

"I just don't understand how this has all come to be, Councilman Montoya. We've a signed contract with the state, the city and your district, not to mention the federal government." Chase paused for a moment, as if giving Montoya a chance to respond, though, when he didn't, Chase became cautious, feeling that Montoya was conspiring to lead him into something he wasn't sure about. Chase continued, sure he was about to find out. "Our company has no control over some ridiculous Arizona law that is so outlandish and unjust. It'll likely be going through appeal courts and injunctions probably till the end of time. The fact that I'm here to discuss this openly and honestly, without any representation, should go to show you my company is still dedicated to the city of San Francisco, California and all its veterans who need this new hospital. Your district's injunction, particularly you sir, has no bearing in this. It's like you and the state have been waiting to attack us, waiting for the last minute to file this motion and surprise us. Like today."

Montoya grinned as Chase finished, taking in every word; every syllable. Chase's foot had been put inside his mouth. He knew Chase was supposed to be so ruthless and cunning, yet, here he was exposed to the lies he had tried to pass off. He couldn't help but to bury him now, cast off all of his assumptions and provide reasons as to why he wanted him out of this contract and out of his district.

"You arrogant ass." Montoya leaned forward. His assertive tone lost all patience as he caught Chase completely off-guard, seeing him flinch as he pulled back in his chair. "That contract was signed by my predecessor. Who you think you're talking to here, *Mr. Bishop*?" His accent digging deeper the more his anger flares. "Chase or Chatsworth, or whatever name you choose to hide behind, I can see you for who you are. A conservative deviant, whose only care for this project is the millions you are guaranteed to make. You have the nerve to actually suggest this was all sprung on you…well," he mocked, "What kind of company do you run if you don't even know what concerns you?"

"What are you talking about?" Chase's confusion and frustrations began to flare.

"This injunction to amend the contract was sent out months ago. It required a signature upon delivery, which I was informed by the state's attorney was received as delivered."

His words echoed. *What the hell was going on? What's he talking about?* Chase had thought.

"Months ago?" Chase's confusion sounds his alarms. But I just received–"

"No, no, no *Mr. Bishop.*" Montoya's finger waves out in front of him with each 'no' his choppy, yet assertive accent pronounced. "You don't come into my backyard under false pretense." His angered finger now taps on his desk. "And Sit there and tell me about contracts when you're in *my* state. California does not condone racial profiling! The morality clause in your contract clearly stipulates that!"

"Morality clause?" Chase sneers.

"There you go again, *Chase,*" Montoya's accent hissed with the sound of his name. "We have every right to contest this contract under the sheer liability in that. Your attorney should've already informed you of that. I just assumed he'd be here with you. That's why I invited the mayor and building commissioner to join us. Not to mention our legal staff as well."

As Chase heard him confess that, he thought, *way to go Roth, another brilliant move.* All of his team's insights and predictions carried no bearing at all. His worst fears came to life, as he realized he was taking a beating in this meeting, instantly wishing he had never even listened to them at all. Yet, with every prison Montoya jailed him in; Chase stood his ground, refusing to yield. Unfortunately, this meeting only guaranteed ten-minutes and the councilman had more to add.

"You're an Arizona based company whose state just passed a law to legalize racial profiling," He shook his head and continued to spit his disapproval.

However, this time Chase was prepared, because they had already set a plan in motion for that. Though, with every hint of success and every stipulation of progress, the councilman only found a way to contradict him again.

"Not anymore, Councilman," Chase still tried to feed him respect for his title, his name and his influence. "We're a licensed California company with an office right in your district, Sir. Even though we both know you're already well aware of that, it should at least give you some sort of confidence that we are in this for the long run. Far after this project is over, we still plan on being here with jobs for people in your Mission District, Mr. Montoya."

A long pause ensued as Montoya contemplated Chase's proposal. It's everything he wanted to hear, though considering who it was coming from, he knew there are no guarantees. His recent scrutiny over Chase and his brother's company proved that to be certain.

"Yes, Chase," Montoya now contemplated. "What took you and your brother a matter of days to accomplish, usually takes other companies months to achieve. I can only imagine under what influence you persuaded the licensing board to grant such a quick request. Your office is just a small little shell down the road you leased for pennies."

"And your meaning in all of this, sir?" Chase not only took offense, but he could feel Montoya getting at something he wouldn't like.

"Pardon my reluctance if I don't congratulate you and your brother on your new franchise. But, it appears to me a company with the capability to be granted such a quick request is able to pull out just as quickly. You're a union construction company whose jobs are already spoken for. Tell me this, Chase, when you're doing all of those water treatment plants, grabbing up all of those Presidential Stimulus bucks in Tuscan or New Mexico, or even in Nevada, did you stick around those communities and provide jobs?"

Chase didn't say anything, for the first time in his life he was totally unprepared in a time when he should be overloaded. He sat there listening, and watching every gesture and obstructed premise Montoya had for him, his brother and his company. He was a man so despondent with his denial and stale reasons, profiling on his own and he didn't even realize it. He didn't even have the decency to distinguish the legalities this would all ensue.

"Well," Montoya continued, "I can see by your reluctance to answer that, that your answer is no. Correct me if I'm wrong here, Chase?"

Montoya gets no reply.

"Like I say before, who you think you dealing with here? Your company was several million dollars over the next bid for this project. The suspicions of that alone were cause enough for an inquiry."

"What are you suggesting, Councilman?" Chase barked back. "There are stipulations for that. No other company had the certification or the bonding to finance such a figure."

"That was then, Chase." The continuous shaking of his head a solid reminder that Montoya had no intentions, now or ever, to grant Master Builders this deal. "Times have changed. As far as I'm concerned, Municipal Constructors, *a true* California based company, will be awarded the amended contract and I highly doubt there's anything you can do to stop it. This may be a federally funded project Chase, but we both know it's on state donated land in my district. Under that stipulation alone the clause in our contract can override you as our management team, and deny you this indenture. You came in here hoping for some plea of sympathy, over some cockamamie, ridiculous story about a fiancé, your conniving worries over her child. Really Mr. Bishop, how gullible do you think I am? I know all about you, how you operate. Your type of greed sucks the life out of communities instead of nourishing them. The only stimulus you provide is for your own bank account. Now, if you'll excuse me, I believe your ten-minutes are up and I have a charity opening to attend."

Chase took a moment, trying not to glare, trying to keep some self-respect. "Well, I guess at the very least, I'm glad I was able to meet you in person, not to mention get your clear understanding on how you feel about all of this." Chase kept his composure when he just wanted to explode. But, considering what Roth's team had coached him on, he knew that wouldn't be helpful.

"Admirable of you, Chase." Montoya holds his dignity, lowering his chin and pushing down his brows. Chase's entire demeanor and attitude was nothing like he expected. He had done everything he could to try to mock him and provoke anger. But, it seemed Chase wouldn't bend or he misjudged him all together. It was hard not to feel for him, he seemed like a regular guy trying to make it, even though Montoya knew he was worth millions, the man that stood in front him was nothing like he had ever encountered. Everything he'd been briefed on and read about told him he was cunning and ruthless, a man capable of outbursts, yet he came across as calm and collective. In the end Montoya knew he was just trying to turn a wrong into a right. As much as Montoya wanted to despise him, there was something about Chase the councilman liked. Whether it was his persistence or candor, or the fact that he came to this meeting alone, what Chase instilled in him now was every bit of a reflection he imposed upon himself.

"I must say," Montoya added, "although it doesn't change anything, I find myself pleasantly surprised by how you represented yourself here today. My intern informed me how–" he stumbled on the word, "let's say…humbling you were after your unfortunate accident. Even when that taxi driver was screaming all of those obscenities at you, you remained apologetic and calm. I am glad to see your conduct in my office isn't just an act."

It was the opening Chase was waiting for, hearing him say that, a small glimpse of acceptance that promised to shed some light. If there was one thing that Chase recognized, it was when he should yield and when he should tilt, and right now seemed like a moment to charge.

"Life isn't about waiting for the storm to pass, Mr. Montoya, it's about learning how to dance in the rain." Chase used old faithful, the words he depended on that had never let him down before.

From the moment he said it, he could see his phrase immediately catch Montoya's attention.

"I only wish we met under different circumstances," Chase continued. "You talk about prejudice, sir, profiling, when here you are unjustly perceiving my company in the same way. A company, I might add, that employs sixty-percent Hispanics. Perhaps you should take that into consideration before you reach your final decision." Chase kept his eyes directly on him. "In any regards, it looks like it's up to the attorneys now. Shame, really." Chase cocked back his head. "They're the ones who end up with all of the money and still nothing ever gets accomplished. We're the right company for the job, Mr. Montoya." His stare was firm and confident as he raised his index finger, as if conveying to an awareness that appealed to his sensibilities.

Chase continued, "We're financially stable and sound in a time when most companies are being forced to close their doors; I only hope you realize that before it's too late." Chase stood from his chair; his eyes never leaving Montoya as every bit of his self-esteem and pride rose up with him. He came all this way for what had appeared to be nothing but an impossible waste of time. But, from the moment Montoya told him that, Chase could feel the odds dipping back towards his favor. However diminutive or implausible they were, Chase's thoughts were guided by intuition, which had always compelled him to succeed where others had failed. Before he left California he would have to see it through, deny all of the sanctions and see if his intuitions were founded.

He kept Sydney in the back of his mind for now. He knew whatever he was up to, whatever Sydney was hiding from him; he had some explaining to do when he got home. What possible reason could he have to keep this from him; pretend he knew nothing, when all along he was informed months ago? Chase knew, that for now, thinking about it would get him nowhere; his focus had to remain on the councilman. He was the entire reason this project was being held up and denying him any satisfaction in seeing him lose his anger, was the best Chase could do at this point in time. However, approaching him at the opening was an entirely different aspect, an option that Chase would use as opportunity, intending on pursuing Montoya at his most vulnerable time. If anything at all, Chase knew, that for now, holding his anger would insure his respect. Whatever Montoya's true reasoning, what consolidated in Chase's thoughts conspired to see it through. The councilman didn't know with whom he was dealing. Chase never lost before and he wasn't about to now.

"As far as the rest," Chase added, still holding his composure and touching on the single most important issue that he knew Montoya held endearing. "I would like to take this time to congratulate you on your opening of the new Cheer for Hope Center on 16th Street. It's an admirable and very important cause, sir. I'm planning on attending it myself."

As Chase finished, he looked him straight in his eyes, keeping all his composure and sincerity that hid his contempt. Everything underneath that conspired deceit lay dormant, for now and in the words that could only backfire, there's no use trying to explain or take it any further. Montoya was already set in his way of thinking, had already decided to judge Chase and his track record. Though still, if there was any way this could ever be rectified, Chase didn't want to make any enemies. Not here, not now and especially not with him. A man so well liked that he could set demonstrations in the streets. Even if Chase was able to get a court order blocking his injunction, he knew he would still have to deal with him later. Even now when Montoya called him out, Chase had touched on a nerve.

"Yes, I'm well aware of your donation, Chase, and in fact," he conceded, "You should come by, see what *your money* actually did for our community. But, don't sit there and act as if you care for these people, their suffering or their future. You just thought you could buy your way in with *me*, the same way you did with the licensing board. Well, you're highly mistaken. So, take a good look around when you get there, Chase. Those kids and their parents, the people who donate their time, that's what life's all about. Now, if you'll excuse me, sir, I don't want to be late."

It was everything he rejected that Chase had heard right then, the animosity in Montoya's tone delivered such a harsh reality. Chase had definitely struck a nerve, but just how to curve that into his favor was the one true obstacle he hadn't overlooked. Could Montoya see through him, feel his contempt for the mentally challenged? Or was it all just his stubbornness refusing to yield? Whichever the case, whatever the enlightenment, what stood between them now was the one true mark Chase hadn't overlooked, he would be at the opening surrounded by his worst fears, having to be mixed in with what he'd only imagined to be a sea of Autistic and Down Syndrome people. To Chase, it was the one conflicting obstacle that brought him the deepest concern: *how he would react and how Montoya would perceive those reactions?*

CHAPTER NINE

The streets of San Francisco always remained a challenge whenever Carly ventured into the city. On a day like this, with the Center's opening, it only added to the chaos. It drew some attention in the press and Carly had seen it on the news last night, drawing her own sentiments, knowing who had invited her and why she came. It touched on every nerve and awareness, filling her with hope and releasing all her distant worries as if they were never even a thought at all.

As she turned the corner down Valencia Street in the Mission district and headed towards sixteenth, she immediately saw the crowd with their flags, ribbons, and banners decorating the Center. The press was making an appearance as everyone assembled out in front of the entrance. And, as she drove past and found a spot to park close enough to walk, her eyes couldn't help but search through the crowd as if every tall, dark haired, slender man was the one she had been looking for. It was a silly concept, considering how long it had been since she last saw him and then she suddenly wondered what *he* would think of *her*, a notion that had struck much closer to home. *Would he be disappointed? Would she be able to see it in his eyes and read it on his face?* A haunting question she forbade herself to answer. To give it any rational thought at all only held her to accept that it could always be a possibility.

No, Carly was determined to seek those answers from him and let his expression and entire demeanor speak from his heart. To believe in anything else, would be up to Chase to ruin. The only thing she had to go by were her memories. The fact that all these years had passed them by, now pressed into her thoughts and swelled into her conscience of just what this all meant and exactly what will become of it.

"How come you picked me up from school mommy and drove me *here*?" Caleb's restless confusion mixed with excitement the moment Carly turned off her car.

"I told you silly, this is a special day." Carly awoke from her thoughts, pulling a smile the moment she looked at him, her eyes sharing every bit of intrigue he inspired for himself. "I want to show you someone. Besides, I think you'll like this place."

"Sh–sh–show me who, mommy…*who*." Caleb tilted his head, smiling the entire time, then paused from his crackling speech looking out his window and then back to Carly. "How come I like this place?" His brows come together and inquired thoughts that only Carly could understand. "What is it, mommy?"

"You'll see soon enough, Baby." Carly smiled back, sharing in his excitement. Her eyes, a twinkling glow, felt for the first time in forever that this was what happiness was supposed to feel like.

"You dress pretty, mommy," Caleb's inquisitive thoughts sounded. "Was that why you dress like that, because this was special?"

Carly widened her smile and nodded, keeping all her elated, joyous feelings from erupting in front of Caleb. As bad as she wanted to show and exclaim how happy she was and why, to share such things with Caleb would only trigger more questions and confusion in a time when she couldn't exactly explain it, not even to herself. With every breath she took, Carly stood on that conviction. If anything were to come out of them reconnecting like this, she knew what remained most important was how it all affected Caleb. She could never let that get away from her no matter what happened today.

She wanted to make an impression of course, so she played hooky from work while Caleb was at school all day. She had her nails done, along with her hair and even bought a new outfit and of course no new ensemble would be complete without a new pair of shoes. She'd been looking forward to this moment and all day she fantasized about what it was going to be like. What she was going to say and how would Chase react when they finally did see each other, held the anticipation of what was to come. Each moment that pressed closer and each elated breath that she took, mixed with her anxieties of not knowing what to expect. The beats of her heart raced with her thoughts, all drawn from her own conclusions in an outcome she could see in no other way.

She took Caleb's hand as they crossed the street. The center was engulfed with people and a bit chaotic. At first as her eyes peeled around, searching; however, there was only one person she had come to see. And there, in that brief moment she wondered if she would even recognize him at all. It had been so long and all she had to go by was his Facebook profile picture. But, as the moments approached, Carly knew that time would hold no prisoner. She knew she would know and recognize Chase whether he was thirty-four or sixty-four, strictly because of his eyes. And that provided all the strength that had brought her here; to believe if only for this moment, that life does have a purpose and hers had found her.

It was a pretty impressive attendance from what Carly could see. Her eyes scanned through the crowd, tracing the outlines and silhouettes of each figure, feeling it all coming to approach her now. Her anticipation and curiosity, her pride and excitement, all sharing in this moment had come to claim her emotions. And the hope that there would be no more searching and to see him now, raw and in his element, excited her even further. Now, if only she could find him.

***

"God damn it!" Chase blares, catching his blazer on the sharp, crunched in metal of what use to be his fender. "Oh, that just takes it all, right there." His eyes reflected his anger as he looked to the torn pocket lying open like a battered wound, peeled and exposed to the very nature of his day. If Chase didn't think it could get any worse, he had to realize the day wasn't over yet. Just as he turned around from inspecting his damaged front grill, the heel of his boot caught on a hole in the street and he fell to the ground, lying on his back in an old, dried up pool of oil.

He felt like an idiot, laying there shaking his head and looking like a clumsy, awkward fool, completing this revolting day he'd been having. If everything and anything could go wrong today, then it all slid in a slow descent the moment he found out that Sid had replaced his truck, to now, everything imploding on him at once as he reached his final plateau.

He stood back up and dusted himself off, scowling embarrassment, looking for a reprieve from any passerby's that had seen him. Considering he was late and parked over a block away, he felt relieved. Though, on a day like today nothing was for certain. As Chase turned around, his eyes met with a middle-aged, Down Syndrome man, staring at him with a half-lit smile and choking up gurgling bursts of laughter the moment their eyes met.

Chase stood there paralyzed for a moment knowing that he must look like, *one of them*, he thought. As much as he wanted to scream and tell this guy to hit the road, he just couldn't. It *was* funny, *he* was funny. The entire, incredible, unfortunate situation was funny. The more Chase stood there and stared, the more it all came out. A grin turned into a giggle. A giggle into a chuckle, and before he knew it, his chuckle had climbed into an uncontrollable, hysterical, breathtaking laugh. He just couldn't stop, he was losing it and he knew it, and worse yet, he didn't know what the hell he was doing here. Of all places, his kryptonite, his weakness, all bound in the shell of the mentally challenged. To Chase, it stood as his one true test to show compassion and open his eyes to what his heart neglected. For once, he had to see things from a different perspective, feel its essence and confide in himself to never look back.

"Come along now, Benny," an elderly lady, that Chase assumed was his mother, said as she took the man's hand. "Leave this—person alone." She looked Chase over as if he had lost his mind or worse yet, as if he was some dangerous deviant antagonizing her son, wanting to get as far away from him as possible.

Chase could feel her reservations and resentments, thinking he was making fun of her son. And that was just it, this was all making him so uneasy and upset. He knew that no matter what; however he came across, people would see through him. How he felt and responded, no matter what his reaction, Chase had no room for what they perceived in their hearts. There was nothing in him that could help them understand or feel his sympathy and explain to them what purpose he served even being here at all. Montoya very strongly stated his position, regardless of any foresight his brother or Jerry Roth had perceived, there were ways of getting around difficult politicians and Chase knew everyone.

He continued to dust himself off the best he could as he kept vigilant to every motion within his view. He wasn't sure if he should even attend the opening now, looking scuffed up, a bit ragged and dirty, reflecting to him that things had the possibility to only get worse. He was determined to see this through. Regardless of what Montoya thought of him Chase was a man that kept his word. He was cunning, spiteful and able to make opportunities where it seemed none existed.

He was definitely in a rundown neighborhood where the homes showed lots of wear with everyone's laundry hanging out in the open. He hoped by leaving his keys in the truck it wouldn't be there when he returned. He still had several hours before his return flight back to Phoenix, so what else could he do but bide his time here? Besides, he knew it was important. He had to at least make an appearance and show Montoya and his constituents that he truly did care.

Chase saw them all standing out front as he approached the last house on the corner of the block where the center was. A group of Hispanic men were joking and laughing, pointing at him as he made his way closer and the closer he came, Chase could hear and understand everything they were saying. He didn't live in Phoenix all these years without learning Spanish, a trait he always kept secret around his workers. The less they thought he knew, the more he would hear what they were saying about him. A man always cautious, filled with suspicion and today held no exception.

They were making fun of him alright and Chase couldn't blame them, he refused to let them intimidate him though. In an area where most would feel threatened, Chase was used to such encounters. After all, he was in the construction industry and he had seen and heard it all.

"Hey pendejo!" called one of the five men standing in the yard. He stood up and started walking towards Chase. "I can fix that for you, you know."

"What?" Chase stopped. "The truck or that big crack in the street?"

They all burst out in Spanish, laughing and name calling with Chase as the butt.

He let them have their fun of course, understanding every insulting word they threw at him. However, Chase took it all in waiting for the moment he would throw it all back.

"They laughing at the joke or they laughing at me?"

"Both, amigo, both," The man held up his palms, still chuckling the entire time. "You ain't the first one to do that. Why you think that spot's open? No one likes to park there, there's a chunk of street missing."

"Why don't the city fix it?" Chase looks back towards his truck and when he heard their laughs again, his eyes immediately returned. "I say something funny?"

"Where you think you at? Beverly Hills?" He turned to his friends and they all laughed harder. His Spanish said what an idiot this White man was. Just another outsider coming to their barrio in an attempt to pay homage to the underprivileged, as if they cared in the least about what happens here.

Letting him finish, Chase took it all in, his cheeks pulled a taunting grin as the man looked back. His eyes read straight through him. Chase said in Spanish, "Who's the idiot? The one watching it happen or the one waiting for others to fix it for them?"

Their looks had said it all, every notion that he brought out into the open had caught them completely off-guard. Chase felt satisfaction in seeing their expressions after they realized he knew Spanish. If anything at all, Chase knew he had struck a nerve and how they would handle it, still held no threats to him.

"I see." Chase cocked back his head. "Not so funny anymore, huh?" He waited for some smart-ass reply, but when nothing came other than their silent smirks, Chase turned and walked away.

"Oh, come on amigo." The man called out. "Don't go away mad."

"Yeah, just go away!" Another one yelled out. But Chase kept walking.

"No, really," he called out again. "I'm Hector. Come back, I can fix it for you...your truck I mean! Do a good job too, you'll see! What'chu say amigo?" He yelled out louder as Chase reached the corner.

Chase stopped abruptly and turned, admiring the man's perseverance. But then again, he's no sucker. "We'll see," he yelled out. "I'll be back." He then turned and headed toward the gala. If he had any luck at all in a day that had been such a nightmare, when he returned he hoped he could get a cab to get back to the airport.

His thoughts conceded why he was here and Chase knew that if he had any chance at all to salvage this weekend, he would have to get Montoya alone for just one last try and one more encounter. If only for the dignity of knowing he made an appearance and he knew Montoya would know it too.

With each step he took, another repulsive thought crept up. He felt awkward and insulted that he had to be trapped here with the all of these people in need. It was an instant phobia that he had no control over. These restless invading nerves that exposed his distrust, reinforced every inclination that he should've never even come here at all. There was no looking past it, his fears and uneasiness all began to collide all at once. Knowing what he must overcome was his own unjustified scrutiny. The deceit that brought him here had finally come out into the open and with the more mentally challenged he had seen, the more it challenged his heart. He saw it before him, raw and exposed, holding him in his own contempt to deny what he truly felt. Was it his misunderstanding or his ridicule and shame? What appeared before Chase stood as his one true chance at acceptance, if only he could feel it. If compassion and empathy stood as awareness, then just maybe there was hope to get him through this, to see past his failures and understand how others struggle. But how could Chase have ever surmised what Sydney had planned? To feel it and capture it was something he could never have anticipated even in his most trying times. Chase would come to understand that now, having it so close to him and touching on a nerve, would teach him one of life's most precious lessons; the faults that he observed in some, might just very well be his own.

CHAPTER TEN

The ceremony had already started by the time Carly and Caleb found an open place in the crowd. It was all so fascinating and exciting to Caleb, and whether he knew what it was about or not, he clearly understood it was something important. Carly found it a welcoming surprise, watching Councilman Montoya, respectfully in her view, as he stood behind a standing microphone making his speech, a large teleprompter faced he crowd, converting his English to Spanish. His arm draped across his son's shoulders with his wife and the rest of his kids standing to their side as the entire staff of the Center stood proudly poised behind him. It was all quite remarkable actually, a grand presentation with a large, yellow ribbon tied across the entrance, waiting for the finale when Montoya would do the customary honors of cutting it in two. The symbolic gesture that was sure to bring cheers commencing the Center's opening, and Carly was glad just to be a part of it all.

How could she not? After all, it had everything to do with Caleb, feeling and understanding everyone's struggles with families of a similar nature. Even though Caleb was only mentally slow, she considered it a blessing that his thinking skills were far better than most of the others here.

She didn't like looking at it that way, of course, comparing her son to others worse off. But from the moment they arrived, the truth couldn't help to expose what lied inside her. She felt weird, odd and accountable when she looked at it in such a way. But still, she knew Caleb didn't belong here, no matter what struggles he endured. The fact that she brought him here now, at the request of Chase, only encouraged more of her speculations as to why he chose to meet her here, of all places, after all these years. It was an entirely different concept that Carly had completely overlooked. *Did Chase assume Caleb was this badly challenged? Who has he been talking to? What has he heard?* But then again, Carly knew it was all just assumption, and when one assumes, it can only lead to chaos and she already had too much of that in her life.

It was then, when Carly listened to Montoya giving his speech, that a part of the mystery that refused to remain dormant, unlocked. The words in English, vivid and clear on the translation screen, brought all her theories together. The truth about why Chase had chosen this time and place to meet her, traveled through her thoughts as her eyes looked upon Montoya, her ears echoing words that she instilled all her life. She knew who the saying belonged to and what ties they would bring.

"After all, my fellow citizens, la vida se trata de esperar a que pase la tormenta, se trata de aprender a bailar bajo la lluvia!" Montoya's amplified voice came just as proud as his stance, looking over all the spectators as his charisma and confidence, calling out Chase's theme phrase in Spanish, making his own time to dance in the rain. "*Together we can all play a role to what this Center, not only means to this community,*" his eloquence continued, taming their kindred spirits. "But also to what it means to the hundreds of families who need and welcome its opening. I give you the new,Cheer for Hope Center."

With the press cameras rolling, the crowd's applause erupted; constantly gathering strength as he cut the ribbon tied across the entrance, waving everybody inside. The power of Montoya's speech still echoed in the air and had amplified Chase's thoughts the moment he heard him use the phrase. And of all times, what he had expressed shared everyone's thoughts but countered Montoya's blatant arrogance. He knew Chase was going to be here and still he stole his line. Of all the bold, nervy, pilferages and treasons Chase had ever endured, what Montoya did now was a slap in his face. It was as if he was antagonizing him, gloating over their meeting and the beating Chase had taken.

"Son-of-a-bitch," Chase mumbled to himself. "Prick just stole my line." His discouraged head shook, as his brows forming a "v", Chase was clearly disgusted and agitated, his surroundings all a part of what had taken over his nerves. The only defense he'd ever known was to segregate himself from the impaired, the devastatingly challenged and all those he didn't understand. Whether it was mental or physical, it held no deference from Chase. He felt unease with both, seeing weakness in abundance as he looked across the attendees. Chase could feel it all imploding and it now became clear as to why the Center was opened here, *it's the only community or district that would have it*, he thought.

He made his way inside with the rest as his thoughts criticized everything he saw. His mind was in constant turmoil and his expression showed it all, but he couldn't help it. A man who was so used to composure whenever in the public eye, was now victimized by his own unwarranted phobias, which took control the minute he was around the impaired. It's in every bit of his reflection that his expression had given away. Not even realizing what was clearly painted on his face, the hideous infringements that Chase could only feel and the shameless affiliations that tied him to it all. Drowning it out would mean he had to accept it, and yet, to capitalize from its nature was the entire reason he was here. He had to find a common ground and get Montoya alone to pick up where they had left off, if only to seek amends replaced by reasoning when strong-arming wouldn't suffice.

Oh, how Chase wished it could be that easy. But he already knew that Montoya considered him a fraud and if there was anything left, or any hope for conciliation, then Chase would have to overcome his own fears, replace them with compassion and change what was in his heart. If only for a moment, he would put it all aside and treat those in need as if they were his own. Then, and only then, could Chase put it all into perspective, hide the shame of his own awareness and finally get past his weakness. To find empathy instead of disgrace remained his one true test and to look humanity in the eye and treat the mentally challenged as an equal.

His vigilant eyes watched for any sighting of Montoya as he made his way over to the commissary. Tables of hot dishes formed a row, each separate smell filled his senses with their exquisite aroma. The entire feast was prepared in the Center's kitchen as servers stood by their respected, covered trays.

If only he didn't look this way, he felt so grubby and worn and it was hardly the impression he wanted to place on Montoya. After all, the councilman would only assume that Chase was digging for more sympathy. He made his way to the nearest restroom, and after looking in the mirror he felt he could be mistaken for a vagrant just attending for the free food. He cleaned up the best he could but with his scuffed up backside and ripped up blazer, if the shoe had been on the other foot, Chase wouldn't even give himself the time of day.

He felt sneaky as his boldness took over, his wily thoughts conceiving a plan, an assertive yet risky plan that would either bail him out of this mess or sink him even deeper. Surely there had to be a coat rack or something that one of the workers hung garments on while serving the guests? Chase couldn't imagine them coming to work already clothed like a pastry chef. No, there had to be a changing area somewhere and as his eyes focused on a side door of the kitchen he inconspicuously walked through it.

There were lockers and uniforms, white chef jackets and hats, hanging on the walls with a long wooden bench dividing the middle. *This was it,* he thought. He placed his fingers on the first locker he saw in the hopes he could find something, anything else to wear other than what he had on. In a day full of surprises, Chase's had just begun because as he was about to open it, the side door leading out of the kitchen swung open, catching him completely off-guard. His guilty eyes turned alert, his voice a stunned silence.

"You're runnin' late," A man dressed as a server walked in. "No time to change now, food's already being served. Just grab an apron and hat off the wall and follow me. I have a tray for you to push out."

Chase just stood there for a moment, dumbfounded and shocked. He couldn't wait to tell Sydney about this trip and he was going to hear every agonizing detail. The torturous affliction that's consumed him since he landed would play like a broken record to Sydney's resistant ears. Whatever ardent motive Sydney had by not telling him about the injunction, what Chase would soon find out, he would've never have surmised that he had been played like a pawn.

"Come on." The man stressed, his insistence waving for Chase to hurry up.

Why not, Chase now cocked his head. After all, what choice did he have? He couldn't get caught stealing from the lockers. *Oh yeah, that would look good to Montoya*. His eagerness a far cry from acceptance, but considering the spot he was in now, he didn't see a lot of options here. He grabbed the white serving jacket along with a chef's hat from off of the hanger on the wall and followed the man into the kitchen. After all, if he wanted to make an impression to Montoya, a true, honest and compassionate human, being the server to everyone would prove his point.

He kept a grin on his face as he pushed the cart over in line with the rest of the servers. He wore a compromising, ridiculous grin. He didn't know how to act or what to say. In all the banquets he's ever been to he never paid any respect to servers and didn't know how to distinguish what he was supposed to do. For, if Chase ever wanted to fit in now was when he needed to the most.

There was a long line of people waiting to be served, and before Chase knew it, he was already serving his third new entree. With each new plate and every challenged person, whether they were an adult or a child, Chase could see their differences as if he was studying them the entire time. Before he knew it, he was talking and holding conversations with them and their guardians. A lesson he had taken from his own etiquette, using his true voice in a happy and calm presence as if he was actually supposed to be here. His entire expression had changed and he found it intriguing, inspiring actually. He was overcoming his fears and his deepest prejudices, knowing how he'd always felt and the shame it brought to him. *Perhaps*, he thought, *this was just what I needed.*

It was a total turn of events, a deep comprehension that had taken him right there. To see it and finally feel it. This experience exposed every demeaning thought he had ever entertained. Their circumstance and handicaps that life had overlooked wasn't their fault and he always knew that. But knowing and feeling are two different things, and to construe them as the same was something he had always mistaken. He'd been wrong and he now knew it. He still wouldn't want to deal with their problems, but at the very least, today he finally began to accept them and understand his own faults.

He was so enthralled with serving and talking with everyone that he had completely forgotten about Montoya, but he didn't have time to look for him now. Besides, he always knew he would eventually want to eat and Chase couldn't wait to see the look on his face when he found out who was serving him.

"Hey, computer man, what is that stuff?" A young boy raised his plate.

Chase could easily see his hesitance and unlike the rest here, he was definitely distinctive. His voice was calm and polite and he was actually a pretty good-looking kid. He didn't exhibit any physical signs of Down Syndrome, yet you could still tell something wasn't right. His demeanor and entire presence seemed much younger than his age and as Chase looked directly at him he wondered why he had called him that. What did that boy recognize? Chase had no idea.

"It's stuffed cabbage, buddy." Chase kept his smile. "Has sausage and lots of cheese and spices inside."

"*Cabbage*, yuck!" He made a sour face. "Why are you feeding us cabbage? Nobody likes that."

"I know what you're thinking, Buddy." Chase winked, leaning in closer as if telling him a secret, "I thought the same thing. But'cha know what?"

"What," he answers back. Hanging on Chase's every word.

"I ate two pieces and it was so good."

"You did?" His eyes opened wide, intrigued.

"I did," Chase confirmed, "Makes you strong too."

"Like Supermen?" The boys voice rose.

"Like Spiderman and Superman put together." Chase opened up his tongs as the boy handed him his plate.

"Your head looks bigger in real life." The boy squinted at Chase. "Maybe it's that funny looking hat you're wearing. But, I know lots of people with big heads they don't wear hats."

Chase looked down at him puzzled. Embarrassed, he quickly pulled the floppy chef's hat from off his head. He handed back his plate with confusion written across his face, as his thoughts pursue what made no sense at all. "Real life? What do you mean?"

Then he had heard it, a faint laugh growing even louder. A free-willed, stuttering laugh that he'd heard before time erased. It was amazing, he remembered, so distinct that past and present became the same. He would never forget the grunt that came with it. The tiny, little bursts of air that would catch up with a snort, like a calling card or fingerprints. The identity behind the chortle clearly labeled.

But, how could *this be? It couldn't be.* His thoughts and regrets collided at once. Yet even now, after all of these years, there was no mistaking who it was. Her smile was as wide as her cheeks would allow and the gleam and sparkle in her eyes reflected the same heavenly grace that he could never escape.

He just stared for a moment, lost in the memories, confined in this space and all awareness and sanity craving to secure it. He couldn't believe it, or find the words to express what he felt. Joy mixed with anxiety and pleasure all bore the irony that found him in this moment.

Did he will it to happen? Was his heart still enthroned? Whatever came to Chase now grew from his own deep insecurities. It was like the karma Sydney was talking about. The fate that he sealed all coming to fruition before him.

"*Carly?*" He finally spoke. The moment he said her name he was desperate to escape and free his entombed heart.

"Hi Chase." Her laugh now calm turned into a smile. "My, it sure is good to see you." Her elated, captivating voice sounded beautiful. "And look at you." Her hand gestured at his attire. "Helping out the way you are. It's a wonder why you picked the Center's opening to meet us. It all makes sense now," Her wondrous smile never dimmed. "The moment I heard Mr. Montoya use your line, I knew he must've gotten it from you."

It was like a silent prayer that his subconscious had lifted, a dire resolution to tame his endangered heart. His amazement seized his thoughts, seeing but not believing, hearing only the sanctity of her soft, heavenly voice.

"Oh my God, Carly!" His excitement flared. Spontaneity and surprise illuminated that this was real. He took her right there, wrapping her up in his arms before he even realized what he was doing.

She felt so soft, elegant and pure, so tranquil to his touch that he didn't want to let go. This was real, no more assumptions or cowardly regrets. Carly was here, in his arms and hugging him back. With the same affection, she returned a long, hard, grateful hug. So much wasted time yet he had kept her in his thoughts.

Though, what he missed before had surely caught his attention now. *How did she know he was going to be here? What did she mean by us?*

"I can't believe you're here in front of me, Chase," her voice above a whisper.

"Neither can I." He paused, still lost in his confusion, trying to find the answers that his brain couldn't decipher. "I never thought I'd see you again," his words revealed his amazement, but just as he was about to ask how she knew he was here, enlightenment came into effect.

"It's so wonderful to be here with you," she spoke with forthcoming sincerity. "To talk to you in the flesh instead of all the messaging and chatting we've been doing on Facebook. You were right, talking in person for the first time is much better than hearing your voice on the phone. This was a fabulous idea. Having us meet you here like this."

Then Chase realized it and brought it all into perspective. Every thought that required his complete attention now thrived on the one who incited it. *Sydney,* he realized, *and of course Facebook,* all exceeding explanation of just what the hell he had done.

Where deceit conspires, sometimes-good intentions prevail, even when it comes from others aspirations. The promise of love and the guiding hand of fate, regardless of where it had been initiated, all came sweeping before him. No matter what Sydney conceived, whatever his objective, Sydney had no right to set Chase up this way. So unexpected and emphatically persistent that he went to this extreme and when Chase returned to Phoenix he would demand an explanation.

"Yeah, I know what you mean," he said hesitantly. "And *us?*"

Carly just squinted.

"You said, '*us*'." He caught her expression, wanting to know what she meant. But as he stood there and wondered, he couldn't help but to get lost, hypnotized and mesmerized by her staggering, heavenly beauty. Remembering the girl, though now seeing the woman, exposed the disappointment of how much time had escaped them.

"Oh forgive me," Her head shook, "You're right. I suppose 'computer man' isn't the proper introduction." She chuckled, feeling a slight embarrassment as she tried to explain. "It's just that, Caleb saw your picture on Facebook and that's what he related you too."

"Oh, Caleb," Chase nodded. Not having any inclination of what she meant, though apparently to Carly, he certainly should.

"Caleb, honey." Carly had him step over. "This is Chase Bishop, sweetie. He's the one I wanted you to meet."

"I know that mommy, even with his hat on."

"Well, excuse me," Carly blushed. "I should've known, but at least now you know his name. Chase," she looked to him, "This is my son, Caleb."

"*Your son?*" His chin dropped upon his chest the moment the words left his mouth. All his thoughts racing with his heart like an emphatic beat of a drum sounding life's destruction.

"You did want me to bring him, right?" Carly caught his confusion.

"Oh, of course." Chase collected himself. "I'm just a bit caught up in all of this, that's all. I'm glad you brought him." *And his father, where the hell was he?* Crept into his thoughts, though considering the surprise and the predicament he was in, saying it out loud was strictly out of the question. No, Chase understood clearly, that information was either on his Facebook messages he supposedly shared with Carly, or he would have to lead Carly into it and hear it from her. Whatever the objective, Chase didn't like knowing she had a child with someone else.

"Hi, Caleb," Chase turned to him, keeping the same presence and informality in his tone. "Glad to meet you, buddy."

He hesitated as he looked back up, feeling the presence of his mother encouraging him to shake, gleaming a trusting expression across his face as his hand reached out locking into Chase's. His smile washed away doubt, replacing it with an overwhelming feeling of importance that Chase bestowed upon him now, simply by the gesture of treating him like an adult. No rubbing his head or phony, high-pitched talk. What Caleb saw in Chase he definitely liked so far.

"Nice to meet you, Mr. Chase Bishop," They shook hands. A proud, firm handshake as Chase could feel Caleb trying to make an impression.

"Well, thanks Caleb," Chase gave a slight chuckle. "But how about from now on you just call me, Chase. That okay with you, buddy?"

He did it again, asking instead of telling. *This was no accident.* He gave Caleb the same respect he showed him. An encouragement Caleb couldn't possibly understand, only feel. And what he was feeling about Chase, had stood one more test to pass his judgment.

"Yeah, I like." His smile widened. "b…b…"

"That's alright, buddy," Chase saw Caleb's excitement in stuttering his words, so he tried not to embarrass him.

"That's it," Caleb said, explaining what he was trying to say all along. "Buddy, I like that." His head nodded in recognition. "I cannot have many buddies. That means friends."

"Well, buddy," Chase couldn't help but widen a smile of his own. "I can always use a friend."

Without any warning or hesitance at all, Caleb reached out and hugged him, squeezing him as hard as he could, releasing an instant affection. The spontaneity of emotion that only an adolescent could consume all played a part and it caught Chase completely off guard.

But Chase liked it and hugged him back, how could he not? After all, he was Carly's son. With all the women he ever had, he never truly loved any of them, and that includes Heather. It appeared that the one woman he never had was the one that he loved, and he recognized it the moment he found out Caleb was her son. The instant jealousy that took over him and the distinct connection he felt with Caleb, all told a story, which his heart had recited. Even after all those years it never escaped him and seeing Carly now only proved it had haunted him too.

"My, you two," Carly's voice separated them. "You act like you're long, lost brothers and here you just met." Her words pulled a distinct, caring charm that shared all the jubilation of seeing the two of them connected.

Chase couldn't help what took over, shared through his eyes, knowing he was glad to see her and glad that she was here. Whatever circumstance or fate had intervened to bring her, his heart never overlooked what stood the test of time. To see and hold her, feel her breath and embrace her offspring, held Chase to his own standing failures and the sad truth that Carly's life had passed him by.

He never imagined her with a child and a mentally challenged one at that. Never expected to feel what he felt the moment he found out Caleb was her son. When he held him for that one brief moment, he wanted to imagine Caleb as his own and the three of them building a life together, sharing their dreams and fulfilling their future. Perhaps that was why he hugged and accepted Caleb the way he did, knowing it was his only chance to escape. Carly had a son, an entire life here in the Bay Area and even though Chase knew she wasn't married, her life had gone on without him.

Sure, he remembered she was single, but divorce or relationships never entered the equation. If only he knew what she and Sydney had been talking about or what they'd been writing to each other, he could get a sense of what all of this meant. After all, Carly came without an escort. If any man was in her life, then he certainly wasn't here with her now. But then again, if Chase took his own lead, then not even his own life lived up to his theory.

"I feel like I already know Caleb." He suddenly looked down to the young boy, releasing his imagination and inquiring his thoughts. "I just can't get over any of this." His eyes pulled back up.

"Well–" Carly's smile rejuvenated every earnest conception that she felt for herself. "I'm having a hard time believing we're standing in front of each other too."

It seemed so surreal and all came without warning. Everything Chase was feeling and everything that remained all held under the scrutiny that forbade Chase to ask and every presumption that entered his thoughts could see the truth before him. She wouldn't be here to meet with him now if she had someone else sharing her life. No, Chase could feel it and in this sacred line of trust he was about to cross stayed clear in his conscience. Carly had been tricked, just like him.

"God, I've missed you," *slipped* from his lips. Like everything else without warning or any thought at all, just the earnest admiration that came from having been in her presence. It seemed she was the same, kind and innocent, beautiful and delicate, everything he remembered and had imagined over the years. All of those thoughts went spiraling inside his head never letting him forget her.

"I missed you too, Chase." Her soft, inspirational tone reflected what her thoughts had been dying to reveal. He was still devastatingly handsome with the same strong, appealing features that any woman would desire. But what attracted Carly to him most, as it had since they were kids, was the sincerity he held in his eyes. He still had that gracious spontaneity that said he was real, true to his character and anyone else around him. Why else would he be here serving the challenged in such a manner if he didn't care for them? What took her by surprise, now held her warmest thoughts and the way he accepted Caleb, told a story within itself. Chase wasn't like the rest, he showed compassion and resolve, and looked at the mentally challenged, not as a burden, but a reason. Anything she feared before they met had all been washed away the moment she introduced him to Caleb.

"It's just that none of this seems real, Carly." Chase's profound conclusions felt freeing. Yet, he still stared at her in amazement, clinging to a memory and all he had to do was act.

"I have to hug you again, just to know you are real." His sincerity flowed with every forthcoming word, earnest eyes that only concentrated on her. "Just to feel you and hold you one more time after all of these long, wasted years." He let out everything he was feeling now at the mercy of torn regrets.

In that one heartfelt moment Carly knew she felt the same. Everything else around them seemed to fade to gray. The only thing that mattered was what they'd felt and what they still meant to each other after all this time. To be truthful and accepting, careless and enthralled would mean to consider all the possibilities; even if those possibilities seemed to take forever to find. They could never deny what had found them now, a chance to fade regrets and replace the lonely-hearted. It's all within their grasp as they took to another embrace, an embrace so tender and rewarding, they found Caleb joining in.

It was a touching scene that not even the casual observers could resist. The three of them in a hug right there in the open, exposing the very foundation of what love was meant to be. And if people didn't know it, it seemed as if the three of them were a family.

Chase heard the polite grunt of someone clearing their throat. His thoughts collided in a race, seeing Montoya's surprised look trying to break into their moment.

"*Councilman Montoya,*" Chase quickly collected his thoughts.

"Excuse us." His arms released Carly with Caleb still holding on. "We were just...I mean, it's been a long..."

"Please, Chase." Montoya stopped him, lowering his head and holding up his hand. "No explanations needed, it's obvious."

"*It is?*"

"Of course." Montoya stepped closer. "This must be the two you were talking about. Forgive me for the intrusion, my dear." The councilman turned to Carly, holding out his hand. "Jesse Montoya." He provided his own introduction.

"Oh," Carly blushed as her surprise and intrigue lifted with her hand. "I'd have to be stuck on an island somewhere not to know who you are, sir. Carly Bourque," She told him her name and with it, showed her intuitions had been correct. He did know Chase and apparently Chase knew him. What took Carly by surprise most was realizing Chase had brought them up to the councilman.

"And this strapping, young lad?" Montoya's eyes now looked to Caleb, his confident chin poised to meet this young boy. He'd been wrong and he knew it. Worse yet, he was arrogant and defiant, mean and belligerent for validating that Chase was a fraud. But now this woman, this beautiful woman and her son standing here with him confirmed everything and all he had mistaken.

"Caleb, honey," Carly's soft, patient voice soothed as she holds her eyes on him. "This is Councilman Montoya," she said slowly. "Remember how we introduce ourselves?" she coaxes. "How you did it with Chase?"

"*Yeah.*" His feeling of importance stayed prominent, looking to his mother's eyes that help coach him. "Pleased to meet you, buddy."

Caleb stood proudly, holding his hand up to Montoya as he stepped away from Chase.

The three of them looked to each other and couldn't help but to let out a chuckle, easing the tension that had mounted the moment Montoya stepped up to them. Chase knew what Montoya perceived and in this strange coincidence that was quickly gathering momentum, what transpired mentally for Chase, were the things he knew he took for granted.

Sydney, He thought. *Worried my ass.* The outcome of the day brought to light what Sydney had been after all along. It was all just a set-up that had taken place well before Chase ever announced his engagement to Heather. All a miraculous plan that had come into effect the moment he had left for Frisco. Everything made sense now. Sydney was using Carly and her son as pawns in a chess match against Montoya. Playing on any sympathy Chase was sure to get, just by being acquainted. Worse yet, it left Chase hopeless. There was nothing for him to do, nothing for him to consider that would explain his way out of this. He had no choice but to let the councilman presume what appeared obvious. It all fell into place; he was stuck between Carly and the truth, the councilman and his own failures. There was no reason for either of them to believe he hadn't been a part of this. In the eyes of his own justice, he would already have been found guilty.

"Caleb, *honey*," Carly's nurturing tone came to correct him.

"No," the councilman smiled, "It's fine." His eyes just played it off, looking down to Caleb, so brave and proud, standing there so bold, confident and assertive. It was all the councilman could do to hide the shame of his own behavior. Everything he accused Chase of was so abundantly absurd to him that he just knew he had to make amends. "It's nice to meet you too, buddy." He clearly understood what Chase must have been doing earlier, coaching Caleb for when he met him.

In a moment of reprieve, Chase thought he would let it all just play out. Obviously it impressed Carly that Chase was on a first name basis with the councilman. But if she ever knew the extent or the reason behind why she was here with her special needs son, Chase wasn't sure if he could ever repair the damage.

"I hope you're all enjoying yourself," The councilman said as he tried to mend his own mistakes.

"It's very nice, Mr. Montoya." Carly kept a smile on her face. "I'm glad Chase decided to have us come."

"I'm glad also. Believe me. It put everything into perspective." He misinterpreted her entirely.

It all kept digging Chase deeper. And the more groundlessly it had came into play, the more it all made sense. Every blinding notion denied him the sanctity of truth.

"And look at you," Montoya turned to Chase; gesturing with his hands to the serving outfit he was wearing. "I had no idea you would be helping today in such a manner. My," he boasted as his chin tilted up to his surprise, "I can see I underestimated you, Chase. You're a man full of surprises."

"Thank you, Councilman," Chase hesitantly replied. "But if you could just let me explain—"

"No, it's quite alright," Montoya held up his hand. "I am a man that can admit my failures." Montoya suddenly paused giving no inclination to the confusion that appeared on Carly's face. If anything at all, he could tell Chase hadn't told her what had happened earlier between them. Another honorable quality that Montoya completely misinterpreted, because no matter how hard he tried to dislike Chase he couldn't. He's just too likeable and it pained Montoya to realize he'd made such an improbable mistake. "In fact," Montoya said as he turned back to Carly then gave Caleb a quick glance. "Would you mind terribly if I borrow Chase for a moment? There's a matter that I need to clear up with him?"

"Of course not," Carly responded, even more intrigued. "We'll just be eating our food over there." She glanced over to an open table, confirming to Chase they would be waiting for him.

"My God, I feel like such an ass." Montoya wrapped his arm around Chase's shoulders as the two walked away. "I mean, a complete asshole," Montoya whispered in his ear, careful not to let anyone else hear him. "No wonder you were so cool under pressure. You knew I'd be eating my words later. Well, I'll tell you, Chase, I never felt so shamed of myself when I realized you *were* telling the truth. It appears you do have a stake in all this after all. Your donation as well as your efforts here today come with my deepest respect as well as my apologies. I was wrong about you." He suddenly stopped and turned to face Chase. "It appears you're a good man, Chase Bishop, and I know you're going to make a good father to that boy. You shouldn't worry, it's obvious Caleb looks up to you. That's a fine family you're about to start."

Chase stood there for a moment. He just couldn't do it. He was trapped in his old schemes and their empty gains. The temptation was just too incredible to let him pass it by. It was everything he wanted and the entire reason he came was to win over Montoya's trust, but he couldn't resist what he knew was wrong.

"Thank you, Councilman Montoya." Chase's manipulations took over. "It takes a strong, yet humble man to admit his own mistakes. I hold no grievances now, nor when you made them. After all, Councilman…" Chase took a brief pause and in doing so, took in every incredible turn of events that were destined to rise in his favor. He had the councilman just where he wanted him, vulnerable and feeling guilty. "Today's all about the families." He held his head up high. Like before, choosing his words and playing the part. "And the children who face such obvious challenges." He paused again, calculating every timed endearment. It was as if he had a stake in all of this. "You and I understand that more than anyone, don't we, Mr. Montoya?"

"Yes, Chase, I believe we do. It seems the more I learn about you, the more I stand corrected."

"It's like I said before, Councilman." Chase seized his moment. "After all, even *you* agree, life isn't about waiting for the storm to pass, it's about learning how to dance in the rain. It's never too late to correct a mistake. I understand that more than anyone now. As I hope you can too, sir."

"Yes," Montoya said, looking up. "I can appreciate what you're getting at, but please, when we are alone like this—" His eyes peel around, sharing some enlightenment to the respect he feels for Chase. "Call me Jesse." His smile disclosed his consideration.

Montoya's guilt, cocooning into a friendship, caught Chase by surprise for a moment. If the possibilities were there, then Chase had no other alternative then to pursue what he could gain. But could he instill what he'd already favored? In the eyes of cold deceit nothing could be taken for granted.

"Thank you, Jesse." Chase's confidence grew, collecting every bit of fulfillment knowing he's about to succeed once again. After all, what harm could it do? What Chase pursued now even held the most innocent at fault, conceiving the impossible, bargaining for his fate where resolve was left accountable.

"It's just that," Montoya couldn't help but to clarify his mistake. "You arrived here alone and when I researched you before our meeting, there was no wedding announcement to back up your story. What else could I believe?" He shrugged his shoulders as if to excuse himself from his actions and to confuse what was already unexplainable. But whatever the circumstance or the facts, Chase knew there was no turning back.

"That's because Carly and Caleb live here in the Bay Area, Jesse."

An easy explanation that Chase has no problem connecting with the truth. "I meant what I said. I'm in this area for the long run."

It was wrong and he knew it. This time, out of all of the circumstances that allowed Chase to flourish, what he still felt for Carly held him in contempt. Everything that preceded this chain of events, endured the ramifications if ever the truth would be known. To deny it or conceal it, would fabricate its legitimacy that is something he would have to live with forever. If ever there was a time for Chase Bishop to dance in the rain, then his storm was now upon him bringing all of its troubles as well as its rewards.

CHAPTER ELEVEN

Everything Chase hoped for in a trip a promised to be a travesty, came as a triumphant endeavor. He knew there was no getting past it and his success had ridden all on account of Caleb. The manipulations Sydney coerced and the predicaments it left him in all came with the motives Chase would never have agreed too. Yet, here he was, still riding on the examples Sydney had picked up from him. Everything was fair game and no one was accountable when it came to the success of their business. Still, in love as in war, in fate as in life, was anyone ever held accountable to destiny's design?

There was so much to explain and so much to discover. With every second Chase stayed away from Carly he used his phone to get caught up on Facebook. Every message they'd ever sent, every chat they conducted, held all the significance. And Chase wished it had truly been him on the other end. An entire reunion was built on fabrication where lies and deceit replaced what should have been trust.

But, did any of it really matter? Could his life ever be the same? What lay in Chase's heart gave compassion to his soul. He found Carly and she'd found him. Regardless by who or how it was arranged, what Chase realized now was that he would never mistake again anything he was feeling that was in direct correlation to Carly. He wanted something else and just being with her now made him realize that. The fact that Montoya had promised him another meeting on Monday gave Chase the space to provide him with the excuse to stay throughout the weekend.

"*Besides,*" he had told Heather, "*The more time I spend up here now, the less I'll have to spend up here later.*" Though, the disappointment she apparently felt had all been her own. What Chase had been feeling was an entirely different incentive and if curiosities provided the outcome, then at the very least, Chase knew this time away would help put everything into perspective. As far as his concerns for his brother, *Montoya scheduled another meeting on Monday so I'm staying. Pick me up Monday afternoon. Southwest Airlines Flight 502,* was the only text he had sent him. No, Sydney would have to stew on everything, and that included how he played the three of them.

"There it goes again. You should answer it this time," said Carly, referring to the same musical ring tone that kept sounding. "It could be important."

"I seriously doubt it." Chase knowing all too well the sound of Sydney's ring. "Maybe I should just turn it off instead."

"You're making me feel guilty." Her tone pitched up. "Don't put your life on hold just 'cause I'm here with you."

"Don't feel guilty." Chase returned a smile that flirted with her curiosity or just maybe *jealousy* he hoped for. "It's not what you think."

"Oh." Her brows lifted to his bold statement. "Just what am I thinking?" Her cheeks curved a smile, a small, blushing smile that could only confirm what he thought.

"No reason to be jealous," Chase taunted, wanting to stay away from any hint that said he had someone else in his life. "See, he holds up his phone, "It's just my brother Sydney calling again and right now, I just don't feel like talking to him." He tilted his head. "Fact, I am turning it off."

"I forgot all about Sydney. That's right, you talked about him living in Arizona back then." Her head slightly shook, not believing she had forgotten. *But then,* "Why should I care who it was? What makes you think I'd be jealous?" She immediately defended what he had so audaciously mistaken. Or had he?" The thought remained so strong; it took everything within her to keep it from showing.

Chase couldn't help it. He could feel every bit of what she attempted to cover up. After all she was a woman. If she didn't at least have the slightest anxieties about who had been trying to reach him, then to Chase they would have had no hope at all.

"Because," his tone softened, "if you had some guy calling you off the hook right now, I'd be jealous."

The thought had echoed in a prevailing silence. *What exactly did that mean? Where was he going?* All played the role to what she said next.

"You don't have the right to be jealous, Chase." Her eyes glanced up to her rear view mirror, keeping a calm tone, careful not to wake Caleb asleep in the backseat. "Nor do I." she considered all the time and possibilities that were lost. "Just because neither one of us have never been married, doesn't mean we haven't had relationships in our lives."

"I guess you know *that* more than anybody." He contemplated what she said and in doing so, understood clearly that the jealousy had been his.

"Hmm," Carly squinted, puzzled for a moment.

"Caleb," Chase nodded to her sleeping son in the back. "In all of our messaging and chats and even today, you've never mentioned his father. Whatever happened with that?" He pried, touching on a nerve the moment he said it.

Carly had refocused her feeling and knowing all in the same conclusion. Now, wasn't the time to talk about Ross. The less Chase had known about him the better.

"I don't think I'm ready to share that with you yet, Chase." Her calm, soothing tone fights off her anxieties. "In fact, do you mind if we talk about something else?"

"Of course not," Chase caught it immediately. The glow in her eyes instantly dimmed and the blushing smile on her cheeks washed away. If her direct response to Caleb's father was this, then what Chase could never dismiss held his curiosities. It must have to do with Caleb's condition and how his father felt about him. God only knew how Chase would react. Though, considering what he's been exposed to this weekend, he hoped it would be as a caring and loving father.

"Do you know when your truck will be ready?" She changed their conversation to casual and in doing so hoped to elude her own sense of embarrassment.

"Hector said he can have it fixed by the time I leave on Monday. Nice of him actually. Doing it on a promise that the company will send him a check." He converted to humor in an attempt to change the mood. "Though, chances are I'll never see that truck again."

"You don't seem too concerned about it."

"It belonged to the company." His words came cautiously, careful not to include the company as him. "Like I told you, I'm here as a spokesperson. I was supposed to be returning tonight."

"Still," Carly reminisced. "That truck reminds me of the one you had in school." She suddenly realized exactly what she had brought up.

"Yeah, I know what you mean," His stare said it all, everything he wanted to avoid.

Each uncomfortable second they endured tangled with their thoughts from that night, closed in this silence Chase knew he had to break. Seconds impeded his conscience, and in that one heartfelt moment, he wanted to tell her how he felt. The shame and regrets he'd lived with for so long, colliding in an amnesty he just couldn't ask for. He knew it back then as he still knew now, it had all been his fault and no matter how hard he tried to come to terms. What Chase had realized now brought his own humiliation. Sydney was right, the mistakes he had made with women played like a broken record throughout his entire life. For him to accept that now and free him from this guilt opened all the doors his anxieties had kept closed.

"Thanks again for your understanding in all of this, Carly." He released a halfhearted sigh, breaking the silence and all the innuendos that came with it. Avoiding, for now, what he knew would become inevitable. For a future to have any reconciliation at all, the predominance of the past always played a role.

"No problem." Carly returned a smile, trusting her instincts to just let sleeping dogs lie. "If it keeps you here this weekend, I'm glad I could help. It's no bother at all, really. Caleb and I would love to have you as our guest this weekend...we have plenty of room." Her eyes coaxed him further. "My hide-a-bed's comfortable. I should know, I had to use it myself until I saved up enough for the bed I have now."

"Well, that's nice of you, Carly." He conceded, lifting a smile that matched hers. If temptation was an option, then what Chase had considered explored his own doubts. Could he trust himself knowing he had a fiancé at home? Could he expel his desires and keep Carly's innocence intact? What clouded his fate opened his vision and the last thing he ever wanted to do was shame her as his mistress.

"Any credit cards to worry about?" Carly's subtle doubts keep digging. If there was anything Carly had known about it was the excuse of not having money.

"Yeah, but I don't know the numbers so I'll have to hash it out when I get home." He could see the uncertainty in his story reflecting through her eyes. If Chase didn't know better himself he never would've believed it.

Look at me, he thought. His torn blazer and scuffed up backside, his roughed up jeans, all coming to light the moment he took off his white chef's apron. If Chase couldn't have looked more pitiful, now he didn't even have any money. No, he looked pathetic and he knew it. But, from the look on her face when he told her what happened, somehow out of everything the gracious presence and tolerance that Carly had kept, outweighed anything he ever expected.

"I don't know what happened to my wallet, Carly, really." He shook his head condemning his own ineptness and what it must look like.

It was just one more lie piled on a stack of her assumptions, one more reason to fabricate what she already believed. To conceal the truth about his wealth and who he had become was the same kind of deception that brought the two of them back together. But, which was worse, Sidney fabricating the role or Chase playing the part? To decipher between the two of them left no margin for error.

They made it to Milpitas with a quick stop at Wal-Mart. Carly insisted on buying Chase some clothes for the weekend, and considering Chase's dilemma, he had no other choice but to let her. It came as ironic, being on the other side; usually it was Chase supplying someone's wardrobe. But after Carly picked out a pair of pants for him, she and Caleb helped him match some outfits and what came to Chase's splendor, was realizing how much he enjoyed it. Her kindness and sincerity watched over him, reminded him of a person that Heather could never equal.

He picked out his own briefs and even found a nice $20.00 pair of tennis shoes to replace his leather boots. Caleb had stayed by his side the entire time and even insisted on getting the same cotton pajamas as Chase. This was the first time in his life he wouldn't be wearing a pattern that had cartoons on them. It was hard for Chase to imagine off brand names instead of Armani. But Chase didn't mind, he figured Carly was on a tight budget, and the fact that she had squandered on him held all the significance.

He felt proud of her in way. She had defiantly kept her independence like the girl he remembered in school, earning everything that came her way. Her condo was moderate, but in need of some repairs. She needed a mans touch, he thought. But he could tell it suited their needs and from the moment Chase looked around he knew immediately that the entire place could fit inside his bedroom. None of it mattered of course; he kind of liked the presumptions of being of the blue-collar income. But the moment he found out that Wal-Mart had a

Money Gram station, he texted his secretary to wire him some money for tomorrow. There was no way he was going to have Carly pay for the entire weekend. He didn't want her to know he was rich, but then he didn't want to seem worthless either.

He never imagined taking a backseat to his accomplishments. Of course, in all of his years of living in Phoenix, he'd always been a high roller, and what came to impress others only swelled his ego. But that all seemed so trivial now. Carly wasn't like that. He could tell she measured worth in a different way. What clung to his senses as they sat and drank a glass of wine was the one single thought that wouldn't go away. He wanted to hold and touch her, feel her warmth and her beauty caress deep into his soul. He could see on her face and read it in her eyes that she felt the same. With each steaming glance and curve of her smile, it was as if she was waiting for him to take her. But, Chase knew it was forbidden and it pained him like never before. To resist this love, this flaming desire, would reserve Carly's innocence, no matter how bad he wanted her.

Carly could feel it all night and his flirtations had come stronger. Fantasy and desire fed off what remained. Wishing he would just take her and be hers throughout time. Oh how she wanted him to, as if willing it to happen, free his reluctance, carry her off to her room and feel his hard masculine body penetrating deep inside her wetness.

But, with all of her persuasions, Chase refrained. He was proper, yet flirtatious and she could tell there was something that was holding him back. His cautions had a cause and she just wished he would get passed it.

They said their good night's as Chase gave her a hug and her quivers only tested him further. As he lay awake on her front room sofa what Chase felt in his heart came back to drown him. Love and respect, fulfillment and devotion, all united from a friend request Chase had never sent.

CHAPTER TWELVE

Sydney had plenty of time to think as he sat alone in his entertainment room on Saturday afternoon watching the Giants host the Diamond Backs. It was the perfect plan really. In all the scenarios that floated in his head, what gave him encouragement was the fact that Chase was still in San Francisco. He had to piece it all together of course. Chase had still ignored his calls. But the fact that he secured another meeting with Montoya on Monday provided Sydney with the stimulus that everything was intact.

Sure, he played his brother, but the important thing to consider now was exactly how Chase was going to handle it. In spite of everything Chase was a great improviser as far as Sydney was concerned. He didn't put his brother in any situation he couldn't get out of, if he even wanted to get out of it. The momentum had to keep rolling if they wanted to culminate the deal and if it took putting Chase in this position, then Sidney felt it was all worth it.

The important thing was that Chase was away from Heather and hopefully securing a contract. If fate portrayed any fortitude at all, then Sydney could only hope that Carly and her son had played a role in all of this. Why else would Chase be ignoring his calls and texts if he hadn't figured it all out? He tried to open Chase's Facebook page, only to find out the password was changed. Every reasonable theory led him to believe that his plan had been working. In a trip that had meant so much to their company as well as Chase's future, what presided on the facts, Sydney had known about long before now. To expose it all so raw and in the open would have given Chase no alternative but to deal with it, which included rekindling any feelings he still held for Carly.

It was his brother's standing weakness. Sydney had known all about Chase's feelings for the disabled and the guilt from his past that resided in his present. The more Sydney learned about Carly, the more he felt it was the right thing to do. Chase would never agree to it, that much was for certain. Sometimes fate needed a guiding hand and Sydney had gone way out of his way to provide it.

"I see the boys have already abandoned you," said Kelly, stepping into the room carrying a homemade pizza.

"Made it to the third inning was all." Sid looked up. "Can't blame'em, Diamond Backs suck this year, Frisco's already clinched the West. Only we diehards stick with them 'til the end."

"Well, this pizza should bring them back in." She headed over to the intercom already assuming they're outside. "Jacob—Jason!" Her voice amplified in their backyard. "There's pizza in here if you wanna watch the rest of the game with your dad."

"Don't bribe them on my account." Sydney got up to get a coke from behind the bar. "The D'Backs are getting their asses kicked and I have other things on my mind."

"Don't tell me you still can't get hold of Chase?" Her neglect turned into concern as Sydney's head shook a confirming no.

"Do you even know where he's staying?" Her petite, slender body took a seat on the sofa as Sydney took his place beside her.

"No," he said and left it at that.

"Well," Kelly's concerns drew even closer. "Do you think he's alright? Maybe you should call Heather, see if she's heard from him."

But the absurdity of that only focused his eyes, sarcasm and doubt expressed in every wrinkle on his forehead. There was a better chance of the Diamond Backs beating the Giants coming from a 10-1 deficit than there was ever a chance of Sydney calling *her*. If Kelly wanted that to happen, then she better make *that* call herself.

"Oh, right." She refocused. "Well, there must be something we can do." The long, silky lengths of her blonde hair rode across her shoulders with every gesture her body made.

"I wouldn't worry too much." He took a drink from his coke. "Chase can take care of himself. Besides, Jennifer called me last night," He said, referring to Chase's secretary. "Apparently, Chase lost his wallet and he needed me to approve a money transfer to him." He raised a devious smile and for the first time he began to confide in Kelly. He had done it all on his own, not even his loving wife had known what he'd been up to. Kelly wasn't the type to deceive anyone, regardless of the circumstance. He knew she would never approve. But just how much he was willing to tell her stayed as shallow as the deceit he embellished on.

"You're kidding me?" Kelly's amazement sounded, "A money transfer to where?"

"Some Money Gram place at a Wal-Mart in Milpitas." Sydney left it at that as far as he was concerned, the less Kelly knew, the better.

"Milpitas, where's that?" Her brows began to curve with a suspicion that had replaced her concern. She knew her husband all too well, his subtle gestures and quick responses and his lack of concern told her Sydney was hiding something. "And why are you being so evasive?"

Shit, Sydney thought. His eyes moved to the French doors leading to the back deck, watching in his silence as his sons stepped up. A reprieve found him in that moment and he ignored what he would only have to explain later.

"Hey you two," He refocused on the boys. "You come in to watch the rest of the game with me?" He looked for any excuse to drop the subject all together, though, with the mind of a suspicious wife, he could feel Kelly's eyes and thoughts honing in on him the more he tried to avoid her.

"No. I came in for pizza." Jacob was the first one to confess.

"Me too," said Jason, the youngest, as he grabbed a slice.

"This isn't over Sydney." Kelly's eyes scolded. "We're going to talk about this later."

That was the last thing Sydney wanted. If fate had integrity and if life had a cause, then what came to them now exposed the truth he sequestered. From the moment both his boys called out, he could see the shocked expression emanating from Kelly's face. "Uncle Chase is on T.V.!"

There was no hiding it now; the broadcasters replayed it over and over again. Chase was at the game all right and just who was with him, brought much deserved attention. With just the look on Kelly's face, Sydney knew he had to confess if only to clear Chase from any responsibility.

***

The tickets for the game were a complete shock to Chase. After using Carly's car that morning to get his money transfer at Wal-Mart, he arrived just time to see some guy drop them off. And as soon as Chase starting walking over to see exactly who he was, the gentlemen left in haste and Chase had felt jealous ever since.

It was a foul ball hit down the third base line. Chase held up Caleb to catch it, though the only thing Chase provided was a target as the ball had hit Caleb directly in the face. If Chase wanted to give Caleb something to remember then his throbbing, black eye had provided just that. To make matters worse, the guy who ended up with the ball wouldn't even give it to Caleb. And of course, Carly watching it all happen left him in a complete moronic state. What the hell was he thinking?

Yet, Caleb was having so much fun. Wanting to catch the ball so bad, Chase lifted him up without even thinking. But from the moment he was struck the only misgivings came straight from Carly. Her panic of a mother overrode all her instincts and she placed all the blame and guilt directly on Chase.

It was a defining moment that Chase understood. Carly's instant concerns for her son let nothing stand in her way of protecting him. If love and devotion was what Chase had been missing, then what he felt in that instant secured everything. The only thing that mattered to Carly was Caleb, and somehow Chase wanted to be a part of that.

It was a devastating blow and they kept showing it over and over, sure to make all the highlight reels on every sports show in the nation.

Whether he liked it or not, Caleb and Chase's new found fame would most likely stir up some commotion back in Phoenix. *'Why were you there? Who were you with?'* All this had raised a compromise that his explanations subliminally provided. Chase answered to no one and he wasn't about to start now.

From the moment it happened, it was Caleb who surprised Chase the most. He was struck so hard, the vibration shot straight through Chase's arms. Yet, to his amazement Caleb never cried or even screamed. He just covered his face with his baseball glove, shaking his head yes, when they asked him if he was ok.

They took him to the stadium's EMT'S to have him checked out. Caleb was a celebrity by then and Chase could tell he definitely liked all of the attention. His eye was pretty bad but they gave him an official Giants ice pack along with some other team memorabilia. Perhaps the greatest thrill came when the Giants manager stopped by after the game, posing for a picture and giving his condolences along with a baseball signed by the entire Giants roster.

It was everything Chase had hoped for. The fate of a villain now restored as a hero. His compassion and compromise exceeded Carly's embarrassment and if what Carly was feeling was her own humility for yelling at Chase in the first place. She knew she would have to forgive what had happened, even if it meant forgiving herself.

After all, it was an instant reaction of the overpowering alarms of a frantic mother. But, just the look in Chase's eyes the moment she yelled at him reminded her of a time that told the same story. To construe them any differently or recognize them as the same held all the forgiveness that Chase had shown her.

They made it back to Carly's by late afternoon. At Caleb's request they stopped off at Dairy Queen, another ploy of sympathy for what happened at the game. To Caleb, of course, it was all one fantastic adventure that kept taking place. And for the first time in his life he was allowed to explore an outer world. Intrigue and danger along with the excitement of being in the city, all touched upon an awareness he'd never felt before. From the moment he met Chase until now, Caleb could understand that this joy he and his mom felt were one in the same. There could be no mistaking; Caleb wished Chase were his father.

What had once been rejection suddenly climbed to admiration, for Caleb was a hero to the neighborhood. From the moment he shared his signed baseball with the kids on the block what he got in return was the status of celebrity. Kids were actually now calling Caleb the most important thing in the world. They were in amazement just to be his friend and the jubilation that glowed on Caleb's face revealed an earnest respect he'd never received before. For the first time ever, Caleb felt important. If his popularity had come disguised, then its newfound prominence was now contagious for everything Caleb was feeling, Carly had felt it with him.

Carly had been dying to be alone with Chase ever since they had gotten home and they had already made arrangements for Caleb's care tonight. She had surprises for him in the city and she was glad he accepted her invitation to take him out. They had driven into the city just as the sun set, watching the bright lights glare off the hills of San Francisco where it created a view so translucent. To Carly, it was what they needed to finally bring the two of them together.

"Are you always this happy?" Chase's candor and vigilance rode on all the complexities that made her this content.

"What do you mean?" Her blushing smile sank deeper. Her soft, haloing, light sienna eyes, matched the mesmerizing lights of the city as the two of them strolled down Fisherman's Wharf and San Francisco's, Pier 39.

It was all quite romantic actually, a remarkable, surreal dream, perfectly vibrant with emotion and motivating every lasting remembrance of what this day had come to mean. The sights were endless. There was the Aquarium of the Bay made with a beautifully designed, almost hypnotic, crystal clear walk through tunnel housing nearly every aquatic creature that inhabits the sea. Magowan's Infinite Mirror Maze highlighted their fascination with its spectacular lights and mesmerizing scenery. Fine dining restaurants and street show performers provided an atmosphere to the Pier's own unique community. In all Chase could see, the radiance Carly carried overshadowed everyone.

"You've had that same glow ever since we headed back into the city." His observation kept calling what he wanted her to confess.

"It's just that—" She stumbled, trapped in the endearments and every blanketing compromise that had been offered since Chase had arrived.

"What?" His smile coaxed.

As Carly stopped, the lights of the Golden Gate highlighted its silhouette behind her as she slowly turned to Chase. She was breathtaking and captivating like an angel in the night illuminating the heavens and all Chase could see was her everlasting beauty in a heart that held the same. A woman with such grace, such resolve, that compassion and devotion came strictly hand in hand. Chase could see and understand all of it in the same glory. Life was about choices and how you chose to live them and that couldn't be clearer to him than now.

"It's just that, what?" He still urged, knowing that she felt the sheltering prisons that she'd kept Caleb in all his life, bearing all her sacrifices in this sanctuary she'd provided. It all came at a cost and Carly had overlooked that. Chase could see so clearly, how protective she was when it comes to Caleb, yet, the same instincts that kept him safe provided insulation for herself.

"Caleb," Carly explained, as the soft rise in her tone escalated with endearment. "Did you see him? I don't think I've ever seen him so excited."

"It was definitely a big day."

"I don't think you know just what this meant to him, Chase."

With these thoughts, Chase had a good idea. Perhaps even more, knowing it had meant just as much to Carly.

"He's never had such attention before." Her amazement came as wide as her smile. "This was the first time he's been invited to a neighborhood sleepover, you know."

Chase nodded, catching all the significance and realizations that came with it.

"I know the boys he's with are a few years younger than him." The subtle shake of her head denoted Caleb's condition. "But, to Caleb, they're all the same."

"He's a good kid, Carly." Chase took it all in, absorbing every ounce of her openness that freed her to confide in him. "I'm glad I got to spend this time with him…and with you," his own feelings shared in the moment.

Carly could feel the mistakes and regrets, actions and results without restraint.

"I'm glad too, Chase. I've thought about you a lot over the years…perhaps more than I've been willing to admit." Her courage influenced every thought that her reluctant conscience had discarded.

"Of course, the way I acted at the game, you'd never know it." Her apologetic eyes call for his forgiveness, sweet, enduring eyes that felt a shame long before now. "I'm *so* sorry. I didn't mean to snap at you when Caleb—"

"Shhh," Chase whispered, raising his finger to his lips as silence secured his own regrettable fate, enduring a compromise that he never wanted. She deserved to know everything in this inevitable truth that waited and he felt every sensation that forbade him to tell her, monitoring his guilt and shame. If self-motivation came at a cost, then the confessions he's held back tested his very existence and perhaps by forbidding her apology he secured his own admission.

"Well." She realized he had already forgiven her. "I'm grateful you didn't take it to heart and that decided to stick around."

Chase couldn't help but smile. God how he wanted to hold her, take her in his arms and press his yearning, love-forsaken lips on to hers. Every signal he was getting, made him want to act and every recollection left him vulnerable. The probability of just how she got those Giants tickets had never gone away.

"You were just concerned for Caleb, Carly." He finally gave it merit. "I can't blame you for that." His eyes blinked with the subtle shakes of his head and the significance of what he just realized. "I know he has limitations and I should have considered that. But I just don't recognize him that way. Besides," he paused, looking directly into her eyes. "I was more concerned about that Andrew guy you got those tickets from."

What he had said about Caleb was touching and honest and it came from his heart, a moment of clarity that no man before him had shared. Though, what remained on the surface still pulled from underneath and in time as in fate Carly hoped they could get past it. These regrettable mistakes that they'd never confided in one another concerned her, even now.

"What do you mean?" She teased a smile, and as she returned to a walk, she glanced down at her watch knowing the time was approaching and her entire purpose for bringing Chase here.

"If I didn't know any better, it was like he wanted to take you and Caleb to the game. I hope I didn't breakup any plans you might have had."

"*With Andrew?* You're way off track there." The absurdities of his assumptions becoming apparent.

"Well," Chase persisted. "When I pulled up in your car after getting back from Wal-Mart this morning, I felt like I was interrupting something."

"You were." She glanced over her shoulder at him. "Me telling him to leave. I'm mean the nerve of that guy, honestly." Instant disgust her only display. "You won't believe what I told him." She couldn't believe it herself as she lets out an amusing chuckle, giving in to what she refrained from telling him ever since she took the tickets from Andrew.

"What?" He pulled on the anticipation, trying to unravel what was willing to come out: his dire need for explanation and just who the hell this guy was. "Who was he, anyway?"

"Andrew Jenkins is my boss." She fabricated a smile that was sarcastic at best.

"Your boss, really?"

"Oh yeah," her embarrassment followed. "And, let's just say, he keeps trying to compromise me at work."

"You kiddin' me? Are you talking sexual harassment?" His curiosity had been instantly replaced with anger and jealousy.

"Unfortunately." Her lips smack. "Don't worry." Her brows raised with her confidence. "I can take care of myself. I can't believe the creep actually had the audacity to show up at my house the way he did though."

"Do you think you have anything to worry about? Was he stalking you?" Chase's concern had grown more intense.

"I don't think so," Her smile curved with assurance. "Besides, I think he's going to be leaving me alone from now on."

"What makes you so sure?"

"Because," Her grin took on a smile. "I told him I had a boyfriend living with me now."

"You did?"

"Yeah." She looked over, feeling all his reminiscence. "He didn't believe me, of course. Said he wanted to apologize by taking Caleb and me to the game with him. However, he had a whole different attitude when he saw you pulling up in my car."

"What did he say?" Chase found the humor as well, though, the idea of her using him as her boyfriend his ego had liked even more.

"He didn't say anything." Carly's chuckle turned more vibrant. "I could tell he was panicking, that's for sure. Before he knew it, I grabbed the tickets out of his hand and told him if he didn't leave me alone you were going to kick his ass." She suddenly burst out laughing.

"You're kidding me?" He nearly buckled over, his laugh over-dominating any jealousy he had felt. Though, in the back of his mind, the thought of kicking Andrew's ass stayed relevant.

"Now why do you think he took off so fast?"

It was funny and spontaneous, but no matter how much Carly played it off, it all became serious to Chase. Men like Andrew were dangerous, they preyed on women and no matter how much Chase tried to push it away from his overbearing dominance he felt the need to protect her.

"Well, here we are," she suddenly added, pulling on Chase's arm as she led him back towards the entrance to Pier 39. *"And,* right on time," she said while looking down to her watch again.

Chase refocused his attention as she led him to The Bubba Gump Shrimp Company Restaurant & Market which took up a section on the lower floor of the famous pier. It was surprising at best and Chase knew she was up to something when she asked to treat him to dinner tonight but this seemed kind of pricy for Carly's means. The more he kept his wealth from her, the more ridiculous it felt.

"We dining here, Carly? His anxious eyes tried pardoning any embarrassment that might come her way. "I'm not sure if I'm up to anything fancy right now. I mean," he paused, kind of feeling guilty that she had hosted everything, "you didn't let me pay for anything at the game either. I'm starting to feel at fault. I do have money now, you know?"

"*Oh.*" Carly pulls a cheerfully, playing grin. "How sweet, Chase, really. But, you've been the perfect guest up until now. Don't spoil it. I've got everything covered... we all do. He could feel her hand touch him as his eyes followed along wondering what she meant, though no words could escape him. His only sense of awareness was the smooth glide of her stroke comfortably sliding down his arm as her small, soft palm locked into his.

"Are you ready to go inside?" Her alluring lips were the motivation to every beat of his heart. "Think you can handle it? Or am I going to have to end up giving you mouth-to-mouth?" Her seduction and longing questioned all the boundaries that had been built up until now.

Oh how Chase wanted to take her right there, feel and caress every ripple of her body. He could imagine their lips pressing hard in lust. Her breasts and curving buttocks caressed by his hands. She seduced him with her heart and he craved to taste her beauty. His sweet, tantalizing yearning begged to feel her touch. Lust and desire were battling his need to not act. He was a man held captive by integrity in a time when loyalty was scarce. She was everything a woman should be: attractive, spontaneous, compassionate and sincere. For Chase, to place her as runner-up held his own limitations to a fault.

"Well, Ms. Bourque, this may just prove to be an evening to remember," His eyes searched to her very existence, fighting and pleading with his own sentiments while trying not to mislead her by what he had yet confessed.

"That's why we're here," her tone above a whisper. In all her sensations, she could feel her composure imploding. Advances and appetite, her desires were one in the same. Feeling, knowing and wanting to be lost in the moment would be forgotten in time.

To Chase, she was like a magnet where love stood as devotion, clinging to every reality that longed to feel her lips. Uncontrolled and with unbridled emotion he leaned in to kiss her, lost in his translucent escapes and any thought he had of Heather. It was forbidden and he knew it but he just couldn't help himself, any resistance that compelled him before lost all logic with the need to taste her. In life's stolen choices the unexpected and surprising collide as one. Upon hearing their names being shouted, the two suddenly stopped and turned in unison.

"Hey, I knew I'd recognize you two…even after all this time." A large, African American gentleman stepped up to both of them. "Is everybody else already inside?" Anticipation and surprise, fortitude and gratitude mixed with Chase's confusion.

"Excuse me?" Chase's hand released from Carly's, clearly seeing that this guy had made some mistake.

Or did he? What rose to the surface had come alive on Carly's face, the curvatures of emotion and what she planned for him all along. The insight and the sincerity that one could never take for granted, uplifted in a spirit that Chase could see grow instantly.

"What's going on?" Chase's head swayed between the two of them.

"What?" The guy held out both of his arms as if shocked that Chase hadn't recognized him. "Don't tell me you forgot about *me*, Chase?" His eyes kept widening, pulsating with every vibrant display of remembrance that came apparent to him now. "I know I'm as bald as a bowling ball and I gained about fifty-pounds, but ya gotta remember me, man. Charles Michael...*Chaz*? I grew up with you in junior and senior high school. Come on Chase, don't tell me you forgot about the good old days? It hasn't been that long, man, shit." Much to his surprise, Chase recalled everything and he recognized that this had exceeded coincidence.

"Why, I'll be damned... *Chaz!*" Chase lifted a smile, the beats of his heart drumming with excitement the moment he realized who the man was. "It's been forever since I've seen you."

"Yeah, man, that's right." Their hands met in a shake as they pulled each other into a hug. "At my sister's graduation, remember? Back in..." he pondered, though the moment he does, Chase remembered as well.

"Vaguely," Chase broke his concentration, knowing all too well that Carly had taken notice. Though, he just played it off, hoping it wouldn't dawn on her exactly when that was. "That was a long time ago, man. What a coincidence. What the hell you doing here?" But then realized, "What'd you mean, *'was everyone else inside'?*"

"Well, I don't know who else showed up but I confirmed my invite."

"Invite? What the hell you talking about?"

"I don't think Chaz realized it was supposed to be a *surprise*, Chase." Carly shed some light on the situation, glancing back to Chaz, wide-eyed and assertive. "I invited our mutual friends to join us tonight. At least the ones I found on Facebook. I wanted to surprise you with all our old friends from high school."

"*Oops*, sorry, Carly." Chaz shrugged, reaching out to hug her as well. "Just like me, jumping the gun on everything."

"You did what…when?" Chase's amazement superseded any expectations.

"Last night," she says innocently. "In my room, before I went to sleep." Her casual glance and meaningful stare bring together what she knew he held important. "So many people accepted my invitation; the restaurant gave us a banquet room."

"Wow, Carly, You're unbelievable…I don't know what to say."

In that one brief moment, Chase could feel it all coming together now. Her faith and trust that had put others above her awakened this serenity that had found him like never before. She was so pure, it was awakening to someone like Chase and it deprived his capabilities. Everything he had lost throughout time exposed the very core of his nature. Who he had become and what had enslaved him, found a guiding light in this forsaken tunnel he had carved. To persuade it and burrow out, conflicted with every sound conclusion and proved that it was never too late to dream. And where dreams formed into reality, nightmares still existed. So if Chase was confused about his feelings for his fiancé before, clarity now lay with this woman. A woman Heather could never be.

CHAPTER THIRTEEN

With their wedding date set, what started the weekend in cheerful anticipation now turned to disarray. She had not talked to him since morning, and by the time Heather went to bed that night, she had tried calling Chase three more times only to be routed directly to his voice mail. He hadn't checked in at the Hyatt where he said he'd be staying, and the fact that he was back in California, alone for the entire weekend, added to her anxieties. What the *hell* was going on? Heather lived on her instinct and every measurable intuition within her validated her concern. Trepidation brought awareness, deception brought alarm, enduring every inevitable compromise that ran through her disordered thoughts.

It was as if her friends couldn't wait to tell her and destroy her joyous triumph with contempt and jealous regret. Accusing Chase of what she thought to be the impossible. After all, what man would be crazy enough to not want to spend his life with her? But there was no denying it. The moment they alerted her to Chase's Facebook status and now these clips of him at the game, what Heather recognized immediately sent a cold, foreboding chill up her spine. Then she saw who Chase was with. She looked like the very same girl that was in the picture in his office. The one in the prom dress standing next to Chase. Heather had been jealous of her since seeing it. To make matters worse, now there was a decree she signed, hand delivered at Chase's estate, though the address on the envelope had been labeled with her apartment.

Did he actually have people watching her? Could she have been so foolish to think Chase's loyalty lay with her? Whichever the case, the facts on the prenuptial decree were clearly written. Without conception of a child, their marriage could be annulled.

The panic that ensued brought every restless thought within her to react. What could she do? What guilt could she devise to bring Chase to his senses? Though, in the life of the wealthy she was but a commodity, struggling to find her place in a past she'd known nothing about. If attributes were what he wanted and if ultimatums influenced his discretion, then what Heather had decided far outweighed her scruples. Whoever this Carly Bourque was, Heather could see that she was Chase's only friend on Facebook and the importance of that alone guided every misfortune she could conceive. Wherever Chase was and whatever he was doing, Heather was determined to find out all she could about this woman.

***

Chase could hear Carly jiggling the handle as her bathroom door swung open. Her smile met his embarrassment as her wide, humorous eyes greeted him.

"That's the second time I've had to save you now," she said with the butter knife in her hand. "I might just have to leave you in there next time, make you a permanent resident here in California."

"Sorry," Chase blushed. "Habit. I keep forgetting not to lock it." He stood there in his cotton, plaid pajamas, the ones Caleb picked out for him. "I suppose while I'm here I could try to fix that lock for you."

"Don't you dare. I like coming to your rescue."

"Yeah," Chase nodded with a smile just as inviting as hers. "I'm kind of getting used to it myself. You've been doing that since I got here," he said. His tone was humorous and sincere, they were comfortable with each other. Carly stared at him and in that brief, silent moment he witnessed her open generosity.

"That's what friends are for," her tone was just above a whisper as her soft, inspiring smile floated heavenly across her face.

"Friends?" Chase questioned, as if tempting his assumptions. However, if his assumptions reflected his thoughts, was it really temptation at all?

"Dear... old friends, Chase," Clearly reading what he meant. "If I didn't feel safe with you— for Caleb's sake, you wouldn't be staying here with us." She paused for a moment as her comforting eyes conveyed every ounce of trust she had in him. A reassuring dependence that could see how things were and a faith in her own accepting spirit of what the future may still return, securing it forever, and lifting their memories and passion to a second chance at love.

"Thank you, Carly." Chase took it all in, absorbing this fresh taste of honesty that she's shared since he's been here. "That means a lot to me...especially after all these years. And if I didn't feel the same about you and Caleb, I don't think I'd be here either."

It was honest, sincere and inviting and what it exposed before them, as it had all along, was how time can never fade what was in one's destiny. And Chase could feel that now more than ever. However strong, elated, and filled with self-contempt he felt, he knew that before he could ever have a future with Carly, he would have to reconcile the truth about his life and what was waiting for him back in Phoenix.

Odd. His only thoughts of Heather happened when they conflicted with his feelings for Carly. For a man who was engaged to another he was guarded. Carly didn't deserve to be misled or used as a pawn in his business or his life, and one way or another he would have to make it up to her and be true to her as well as himself.

If silence brought awareness, then the expression on Carly's face came as encouragement through her eyes. A warm, soothing smile showed with happy spontaneity that glowed on her face. What he brought and what he represented comforted her. To be free of all the cautions and put aside all the risks left her to explore what promise life had always held.

Her head tilted in a gesture for him to follow her as her smooth, petite strides directed them back into her front room. It was just the two of them, and as Chase followed behind, what trailed in his conscience was what the night still offered. It held him liable and awake, drawn to this compelling aberration of what distant memories bring. In all his thoughts and imaginable dreams, this fantasy that kept playing repeated every lasting memory of what it felt like just to be with her. To hold her and kiss her hounded his very soul having known it was forbidden.

He wondered how long he could keep up this charade, a façade that portrayed nothing of his life. But, then there was Carly and he didn't want to do anything to hurt her. He had fought off every emotion within and every relentless urge to taste her sweet succulence. All of this tempted him like never before. If he could make it through this night and weekend without further to diluting their friendship and trust, then Chase could answer to his own self-being and weigh all the options before him.

Just being with her now, seeing who she had become and what she brought to this earth tarnished his every accomplishment knowing he couldn't share it with her. But, oh how he wanted to fill her in on every detail of his life, nothing preserved and everything accounted for. All these years of thinking about her had definitely taken its toll.

It caught his eyes immediately as he sat next to her on the sofa, a bottle of wine, two chilled glasses, and their high school yearbook resting in front of them on the coffee table, gathering all the recollections of what their past imparted into the present. Time and gratitude, achievements and failure granted this passage to look back and not be judged or judge others.

Chase couldn't help but to stare at her again. Her soft, elegant splendor drew as much of her inner beauty as her outside had possessed. Even now, covered in her robe with glimpses of her red, silk pajamas that showed through from beneath, what Chase had envisioned shared every new light of endless possibilities. He couldn't help but query every thought that ran lucid in his head. If only he had the courage to look her up years before and if he knew the truth of his circumstance's at home, then he could pursue every deniable possibility that questioned his existence, deterring him from his happiness in a love-life that had gone completely off-track.

"What's all this?" A slow, encompassing grin pulled across his face.

"The wine or the yearbook?" Her playful eyes looked up as her highlighted brown hair hung loosely over her breasts covering her cleavage. Chase couldn't help but catch his prowling curiosity while trying to steal a glimpse.

Now, and all throughout the night, he imagined what she looked like underneath; soft, yet firm, with her pink body seducing his very soul. Heaven and paradise all mixed in the same security, building this foundation to discover what his imagination had left out.

"Everything, I guess." His tone now refocused, careful, yet assertive. He kept his eyes on her face. "This weekend's been one surprise after another…seeing the old crew from high school, where they're all at now, just makes me realize…well," he said with an undeniable sense of insecurity. "We've come a long way, haven't we, Carly?"

"I guess." She shrugged, tilting her head without true comprehension. "It's called life, Chase. Remember?" Her gallant eyes held to the stillness he had always claimed. "Life isn't about waiting for the storm to pass, it's about learning how to dance in the rain."

Hearing it come from her mouth echoed like never before. Like a reassuring prayer that delivered a true faith, he had every blind reason to listen to it for himself. To hear and understand what it finally meant. What it was to look ahead and take a risk, forgive oneself and make amends, even if it meant accepting ones own failures.

"Is that how you look at it, Carly? We all do what we have to just to get through this life? Get through the day or the week or even our past experiences, as well as our regrets?"

"What are you trying to say, Chase?" Her eyes and ears attentive. They hadn't talked about anything from that night and what it had meant to them over the years, but now in this one compromising, yet definitive moment Chase could feel it all coming to bear. Every affirmation that misled her from before and every blame and degrading lie that had burned him since, begged to let her know just how he felt.

"I looked at some of those people we went to school with, I mean, guys I'd seen nearly every day of my life—at least back in those days— and I wonder, *my God*, what the hell happened in your life? I mean, don't get me wrong, everybody's got their own circumstances and tough choices in their life. But I imagine luck has a lot to do with it…"

"I still don't understand what you're trying to say, Chase." Whatever he's saying or whatever it meant to him now, Carly could tell that it would mean just as much to her.

"My God, I've missed you, Carly." Sincerity and honesty clouded his eyes. "I almost forgot about that smile of yours. And how you could light up a whole room just from this caring aura that surrounds you. When I think about what I let get away, what we might have had…" He shook his head, holding on to the confinements of what she didn't yet know, what she thought she'd done and what he let compromise her ever since. If there was ever a time for Chase to be truthful about his past then that time was upon him.

"Tell me you've had a good life," His tone even more persistent. "Tell me it's been everything you've wanted it to be so far." He almost begged her to will it, free his own integrity and let it breath in new life. "I'd hate to ever see one ounce of pain in those heavenly, soft, brown eyes of yours. Any worries I could have protected you from…any sadness I could have stopped strips every fiber within me knowing that I wasn't there for you."

The distress on his face and the conflict in his tone caught her completely off guard, as if he looked for forgiveness in something she couldn't possibly fathom. In all her assumptions, theories and conjectures, what she could feel was that the pain was deep. Whether it was sorrow or amendments, or peace to secure fate, what Carly could read in his eyes and hear in his voice told a distant story that claimed her very soul.

"I don't know what to say, Chase." Every point and reasoning saw her own regret, blinded for so long now that she thought nothing would ever save her. "I guess…that could go both ways." Her blush took her to a place she hadn't been in for so long. This deep, tranquil embodiment that she hadn't felt since she was with him, consumed her every thoughts. Like never before, she wanted to hear him tell her what she had meant to him, even after all these years apart.

It's right then that Chase noticed, as Carly tilted her head back and exposed her chest. The sparkling, silver chain that she'd been wearing throughout the night now came so vividly clear to his eyes and all his recollection. He hadn't noticed it at dinner when she took her coat off in the restaurant, the pendent had slung down and hidden inside her blouse. Yet, now it was free, shining like new, the same amethyst stone necklace he had given her for prom.

"I thought that was the same necklace." Chase opened this door between them that had been closed for too long. "You've been wearing it all night, haven't you?" His eyes glanced back and forth between her and the chain. "I can't believe you still have it after all these years." His amazed yet gentle tone recognized the significance.

"Why wouldn't I?" Her soft, angelic voice called on every prayer within her and what this necklace had meant to her. It was more than just a gift, holding memories, thoughts and dreams, their joys and heartaches passing throughout time, yet woven in this comfort because it had come from him.

"I don't know." His head gestured to the jewelry's importance. Holding on to it after all this time and even wearing it now, brought ease to his worries as if they were never a thought at all. "I guess because it's been so long. But...then again, *I* still recognized it, didn't I?"

A long distant, pause followed, securing a trust and faith. There could be no mistaking what they had seemingly avoided. As his eyes held on the necklace and everything it restored, his arm slowly and ever so cautiously reached out, taking the chain in his hand as Carly's soft, accepting eyes followed along. As his fingers slid down the links, he felt every tremble and ripple within her, longing to feel his touch. A seduction of senses, awareness and fate clung to this moment of reason as Chase leaned in closer, with words above a whisper and a heart lost in time.

"I'm so sorry about what happened that night," he said finally. "I never meant to—"

"That's okay." Knowing it was as much her fault as it was his. "We were just kids back then. I was scared. I didn't think I could live up to what you..." She caught her thoughts, exceeding in a moment of regret. "Well, I completely overreacted." Her eyes looked away as if recapturing the moment. In all her thoughts and dreams, to have it to do all over again and greet what it could've and should've meant, would be to lift time and space, change fate with destiny and be always in his arms. "Besides, if anyone was sorry about that night, I am, Chase." Her head suddenly lowered to her own confessions, as if softening the blows of what she had done. "If it wasn't for me, I'm sure your life would've turned out differently. You would've probably been an all-star in the Major League's by now."

"That's not true, Carly." He emphatically stopped her. *Not this time,* he thought. If there was anything to come out of this weekend, anything at all to lift her out of this shame, then Chase would confide in his own remorse and come clean about what she thought, what he'd let her believe after all this time. "The fact of the matter is," he conceded. "I just wasn't good enough. I should have never let you think otherwise." His steady stream of honesty accompanied all the sorrow in his eyes. "There were never any offers for scholarships."

"But everybody said—"

"It was all rumors." Chase finally released the necklace, and in doing so, let go of everything that was holding him back. "The more people talked about it, the more it became easier for *myself* to believe. My injury was just an excuse, a way to face everybody's disappointment as well as my own failure."

Carly couldn't help but to reach out and touch his face, as if coveting his cheek washed away all the guilt he had been carrying for so long. What she'd thought wasn't important now. The only thing that counted was what this brought to them, understanding and feeling the pleasure that their company brought one another. Then, and only then, could fate describe a future, wash away doubt and replace it with joy.

"You asked about Caleb's father." The somber truth came to bear, as if sharing it with him released every awkward moment that they could ever face.

"Did you love him?" Chase whispered, not wanting to hear it, but in jealousy as in grief, what road to the surface was that need to know.

Her head subtly shook and ever so slightly eased this tension that came from heartaches, replacing them with fortitude and the gift of her son.

"Did he hurt you, Carly? Did he respect or love you like you deserve?" Chase could read something in her eyes, however vacillating, however evasive, the urge to free her anguish seduced him like never before.

"It wasn't like that, Chase." The grief in her voice came as her own hollowing, sad reminder. "You don't understand." Her eyes glanced away as if bearing a shame and indignity of refuge she's lived with since it happened.

Chase's hand now touched her chin, gently and ever so cautiously pulling her eyes up to his. Tender and warm, sharing a smooth understanding that whatever the circumstance, whatever the pain, he was there for her. Regardless of the past and what he'd missed, he was here now. In the constant need he felt to protect her, what he conveyed through his soft, gentle touch, gave her peace to finally tell him everything.

"I'm sorry," her words pull again. "It's hard…what happened."

"So, *you were* close?" He hung on the anticipation and somberness in her eyes.

"No." Her eyelids closed in one long, solid blink. "We were never close."

Hearing her say that brought an instant relief to his chest. A heavy load lifted from his conscience knowing she hadn't loved another. But how could Chase ever think of the unthinkable when it came to someone like Carly? What she gave in a heart that would never hurt anyone, should receive the same splendor in a life filled with happiness.

"Caleb's father and I only had one date." She had finally allowed herself to say it and in doing so, freed her strength enough to confide in him. Would he be able to accept it and live with it? And could he place the good over bad, just as Carly had done since Caleb's birth?

"Oh." *A one-night stand,* he thought. What she lived through and the strength it took to rise above it would all find its place inside Chase's hollowed heart.

"I know what you must be thinking." Her soft, courageous tone pulls on every thought her disgrace had once prescribed. Every single remembrance of what happened on that night conflicted within her soul on how Caleb was conceived.

"I'm not thinking anything, Carly." He tried to comfort the distress he saw in her eyes. "Whatever it was…whatever happened, you don't need to tell me."

She couldn't help but to feel it again. In all her recollections of Chase, this curiosity that compelled her imagination and dreams secured her in this trust and the awareness of the faith she had in him. Even after all this time, she knew what he had meant to her and confessing this to him now, so exposed and left to be judged, provided her conscious a chance to concede the inevitable.

"I'll leave out the details." Her eyes held what her breath released, free to replace shame and heartache with all that Caleb brought. Liberating and exceeding what it came to mean to her since the moment it happened, and looking into Chase's eyes, she knew he'd understand. "I think the only way I've been able to accept it is that I have Caleb and that's what's important."

"His father never tried to fight for custody?" Chase still couldn't comprehend the unthinkable.

"No." Carly shook to the absurd thought. "He's a union construction laborer in the city who's always out of work. The only time he did want visitation was when I wanted him to help with Caleb financially. Then he threatened for joint custody, which was the last thing Caleb needed in his life." Her eyes flutter to the ridiculous, absurd thought. "I never consented that night, Chase." Her words carried a tolerance, fighting to hold back these tears that clouded her eyes.

Then it suddenly hit him. The pain on her face and the healing she had succumbed brought forth every hounding measure that fixated in his thoughts.

"You don't mean…"

"I let him into my apartment after our date," Her head nodded her compliance. "I was young and naive. He forced himself on me and I didn't know what to do afterward. I was scared and all alone…and he knew that. You know I grew up in a foster home and I was never close to my foster parents. I had no one to turn to. When I found out about Caleb and told Ross…well, things just got worse with him ever since."

It left a hollow echo inside him the moment he realized what she was saying, a bleeding, burning, shattering echo that beat with every bit of his own agony wanting to mend the unaccountable. Feeling her pain, absorbing her grief, as if he blamed himself for not being there, not protecting her or loving her all those years they were apart.

"I'm so sorry, Carly." A breath of air escaped from his lungs. "I didn't know—"

"How could you?" The innocence in her tone reflected her purist thoughts. "Besides, there's nothing to be sorry about, not any more, it happened a long time ago. If there's any good to come out of it...like I said, I have Caleb and he's the most important person in the world to me, Chase. I don't know what I'd ever do without him."

Hearing her say that caused his frown to slowly dissipate, as if releasing this heartache for how he felt for Caleb. As Chase looked at it that way and thought of him, what collected in his thoughts, caved to his animosity looking to vindicate his vengeance. Caleb was important and just reading it in her eyes and comprehending it in her tone he discovered his own apprehensions and exactly what this all had meant to him.

How much longer can he keep this from her after she's shown all her trust and faith in him? How much can he keep searching for a reason not to take her, hold her, comfort her and taste her sweet caress? Every thought within him wanted to react without a consequence and every compromising interpretation denied those that held him back. In all the possibilities he could see sitting in front of him, what Chase had leaned in closer for, sealed his own preceding fate. As if taking her now secured their destiny by making amends with his past as well as his future.

"You don't think any less of me, do you, Chase?" Carly's soft, breath, delayed his burning desires, holding in her eyes the things she needed to hear. Waiting, hoping and feeling that whatever stayed in his thoughts, he would accept and hold no judgments against her.

"How could I?" His head gave a subtle shake as his hand gently, and ever so comfortingly reached out and rested against her soft, pale cheek. Her bravery and honesty exposed his admittance to the very same accords that held them apart.

Her cheeks lifted a smile to his tender caress, touching her hand to his forearm as goose bumps and quivers become the texture of her skin. The moment she looked into his eyes and read this overwhelming reassurance, was the very moment she could feel her own contentment and admiration, clinging to the same sensation that recaptured everything she'd missed out on. Only now it was here and she could feel it like never before. A woman like Carly, who was so secluded and protected from all the elements she feared—love and respect, passion and desire—weighed her greatest heartache knowing she could never feel it with anyone else but him.

"I was there, you know?" Thoughts and recollection twist in his head, enduring his regret that had once forbid him to say it. "What Chaz was saying...I was there when you graduated and I should have come to see you. Should have fought for you and never let you go. Then, I would've always been there to protect you." His eyes now shifted away, feeling his own resentment. "Instead, I was cowering away in Phoenix all this time. I should never have let what happen that night come between us." His hollowing heartaches now refocused back to her innocence. "It was my fault—what happened to you and what you've had to live with, and it pains me like nothing I ever felt before." His long silence caught every glimpse of what her memories held, for flashes like dreams always finds a way to define, secure the inevitable and restore visions of hope.

"Don't blame yourself, Chase. It's not your fault." Her hand began a slow, steady stroke against his arm as if trying to relieve his tension. He looked to her for forgiveness. "I knew you were there. I knew long before Chaz ever confirmed it."

"And you didn't say anything? How…how did you know I was there?"

"I never forgot that day," her keen memory recalled. "Funny how some things stay with you while others just fade away, lost in time without any recollection or thought at all. But, I remember *that* day, Chase. I remember how I felt when I saw you after the ceremony." She paused as the stillness in her eyes relived it again, keeping it inside all this time, never wanting to burden him by putting him on the spot. If Chase wanted to tell her, then she knew that he would, and if anything would come out of this, then at least Carly thought she would finally understand why he left without seeing her. "I can still feel my heart racing." She flinched, as every nerve in her body became restless endearment. "Just like right now," She pulled his hand off her cheek and placed it on her chest, the beats of her heart pounding with excitement. The touch of his hand and the warmth of his breath seduced every part of her body that yearned to feel him. This sweet, empowering man that she'd known since he was a boy captivated all her senses and freed her distant soul. "Can you feel it, Chase? Can you feel what I felt and still do?" She held his eyes and pressed his thoughts, compelling and restoring what Chase could no longer resist.

"Yes,"

"Then why, Chase? Why did you leave so fast? I tried to find you, but you were already gone. Why didn't you come see me?" She plead to his confessions as well as her own.

"Oh, how I wish I had." He looked straight into her eyes, knowing that now he would do whatever it took to be with her, and regardless of Phoenix and what existed with Heather, what Chase felt inside he would never mistake again. He loved her now, just as he always did, even after all this wasted, empty time apart, Chase felt that no other woman could stay in his thoughts like Carly had stayed with him.

"Then why didn't you?"

Chase couldn't answer her, couldn't admit what he had hid from for so long, that the effects that rippled through the both of them, held a consequence he could never have surmised. To feel it now and absorb its meaning helped him realize what he still felt for her. Hollow and forbidden, secluded in an emptiness the moment he'd seen her in the arms of another. Their lips pressing firm together in a passion that had seemed so obvious from where he'd been standing that to mistake it as anything else denied his heart to finally move on. But assumptions, like theories, have a way of superseding logic and if Chase would've known then what he was about to learn now, things would've turned out much different in his life.

"Was it because of Glen Sherman?" Carly finally said it for him. "Because you saw him kissing me?"

Chase nodded, keeping a look of sorrow that clouded his eyes, unable to say it and admit what he had seen, but then, *Glen Sherman?*

"Glen?" He shuttered, "Was that who you were with?" His memories of betrayal highlighted in his eyes, bursting with the thoughts

that compelled him to discover his own bleeding memory becoming even worse than he thought. "Wasn't that the guy everybody used to make fun of behind his back? That geek who thought he was God's gift to women?" Chase's tone changed entirely as a disgusted, uninspiring grin formed across his face. He realized what he was thinking and what he had done.

"Yes." Carly smiled at his absurd thought as her eyes widened to the notion of what Chase had completely misinterpreted. "You didn't actually think..."

"I did. I just saw you kissing—I mean—I didn't realize that was who you were with. Why were you kissing *him?*" The distaste soured in his throat.

"I wasn't," she chuckled. Slight, yet firm, her only way to defend what seemed so ridiculous. "That was all that idiot Glen. He came up from behind me, grabbed me and just started kissing me before I even knew what happened. Oh, Chase." She shook her head, releasing the top of his hand as she touched his tender, pulsating and masculine chest. "If only that jerk wouldn't have done that. Who knows how things could have ended up."

"*I know, Carly.*" As his chin rose he looked into her eyes that beckoned his desires. How could he have been so reckless and abstruse to unravel what he should have known all along? He realized that fate had denied him happiness. "I can't believe it. How could I have been so *stupid?*"

Though, what it had brought to Carly was an entirely different scenario. He was there because he still cared, to make amends and show her that he still loved her. It was obvious to her now that the reason he left was because of what he thought he'd seen, and the sight had truly hurt him.

"That doesn't matter now, Chase." Carly gently and ever so tenderly rubbed his chest as her eyes held a sovereignty that blanketed her heart. His smile brought her to her senses, holding, praying and hoping that he would never leave her again.

"What does matter, Carly?" Chase felt it as he breathed, needing to hear it just as much as his lungs needed air.

"That you *were* there. That you're here now and you never forgot about me…I never forgot about you. It's been like a dream. Ever since you friend-requested me on Facebook you're all I've been able to think about. You tell me how good it is to see *me*." Her breath turns into whimpers. "When actually, it's me, Chase. I'm the one who's been overwhelmed by it all."

Then he'd heard it. Everything that tainted this prize before him, mixed with gratitude and tender regret. What she believed had brought them together, Chase could only surmise the truth would tear them apart. How could he ever explain it to her and free his weary conscience? To come clean to her now and expose the unforgivable would truly destroy what they both now feel and that was something Chase would never allow. No, now more than ever, he knew he could never tell her about Heather and the circumstances of their engagement or the friend request he'd never sent. He would bury it forever and expel the insurmountable, breaking his own barren code just to have her so free and open, so pure with trust that he would never disappoint her again.

"There are some things you don't know about me." Chase

whispered to her innocence, confiding in himself to at least tell her about his success. The company he'd built into this empire that she could never have fathomed on her own, he built on the foundation that she had always guided. Obsession and devotion became his greatest strength and love and regret provided all his weakness.

"Will it matter in the morning? Will it ruin this moment that I don't ever want to end?" Her body craved his touch as his passion and endearment caressed her soul. Every bit that was a part of her and every bit of strength that she had ever known came by the grace of just his memory alone. There would be no more delay.

No words were needed for what was destined in their hearts, they were free to make amends, captivate and fulfill what had been evaded.

As Chase leaned in, all reason escaped him. His thoughts and memories collided. He could no longer resist. He wrapped his arms around her shoulders as their eyes met with acceptance, their lips touching firm with passion and their tongues reuniting in memories. A long, thriving, passionate kiss swelled into their conscience, and what was once forbidden had found them like never before. Chase just couldn't help it and what he felt in that moment released all of his worries. The only thing that mattered to him now was Carly, and to taste her purity, her sound peace and pleasure, lifted him to a place he had never been before.

Within that instant, their passion became unbridled, tastes mixing with lust as breaths turns into moans. If this was a dream, then let them never wake. If this was fantasy then let reality secure it. To be in each other's arms feeling the warmth of their splendor, brought all the necessities that their love would ever need.

Their tongues released as their lips separated and with every moment that awaited them, what burned into their sanity craved with desire, demanding to feel satisfied as Chase rose up, holding out his hand with lust in his eyes. He pulled her up off the sofa as he cradled her into his arms, her petite body hugging tight on to his wide, hard, demanding chest as his hands worked their way up to her shoulders, pulling off her robe. Anticipation and awareness spilled into their senses. His sheer strength alone, picked her up by the waist, straddled her onto his body with his erection full and throbbing. Every arousal peeked and yearned with sexual hunger and as he carried her down the hallway, excitement and ecstasy pounded in his heart.

Her bedroom door swung open as Chase used his elbow to turn on the light switch, gently and lovingly he laid her on a mattress that had never before supported or felt love. Not until now, as their lips met once again.

Passion, lust and desire intertwined, becoming apparent as they pulled at each other's clothes. Their bodies yearned to be touched and fulfilled an awakening in every want that found them.

Her breasts so tender, enticing and pure, that when his mouth circumference her pink, firm nipples, the soft, cushioned splendor that found his lips never wanted to release them again. The necklace he had given her drooped down her throat and sparkled like new. What he felt in this moment promised to last him forever.

He never wanted to release from her pure, tender sweetness but he knew he just had to, if only to discover, taste and savor her sensational, heavenly beauty. It was everything that controlled him as he felt her warm, heated flesh pressing up against the heat of his own. Friction and desire burned into lust as his lips glided across every inch of her luscious, goose bump rippled skin. So alluring and infatuating, he could no longer resist the rewards that awaited him.

His tongue worked its way down as his hands explored her smooth, shapely backside. Her buttocks enticing, it seduced his very soul. So round and firm that the humps of her cheeks aroused and ignited every sensation within him. If anticipation devoured lust, then every throbbing endearment his elation felt burned with the excitement that would forever fill his memories. She was everything he had ever wanted. Every desire, every flame that burned from this oxygen, this fire she released came from just her touch and her purity alone. If this was the beginning, then let him never find an end, and if this was fate, then let its magnificence secure his destiny. Forever intertwined, as if they've never been apart.

Moans had become her breath. Pants had become her air. Lungs that found this ecstasy twisted with Carly's fate. This yearning that completed her, plead with every rise in her pelvis for Chase to take her now, to feel his tongue and caressing lips taste the honey of her sweet succulence.

It was everything Carly wanted from the moment she first saw him again, every fantasy she had ever envisioned about him living up to her dreams. She found peace in his comfort and to look at it as fate had left her to discover it was what she had begged for all her life. She wanted Chase more than ever now and that thought alone left her with ambitions she would never confuse again.

His hands pulled down her panties as tender, pulsating touches caressed her smooth, soft skin.

She could feel his tongue now enter her body as her hips rose up to its splendor. Shrieks of excitement tantalized into her senses with visions of ecstasy invading her every thought. Would she live up to his expectations and fulfill what he'd fantasized all his life? Whatever the yearning and sensation that thrived inside their hearts, Carly had found the strength, longing and security to entrust it all to him.

He felt so good, so arousing and warm, that every sense of her wetness came strictly from anticipation. These expectancies that invaded her every thought excited and swelled to feel his throbbing, hard masculinity. Every hard, pulsating, tender muscle she felt seduced her also left her quivering in the excitement of him entering her, as if she couldn't wait any longer. Couldn't control this urge that wanted to wrap around his splendor. To resist it any more would be to resist her very soul.

His body so hard, so thriving with life, that to mistake its virile completeness would be to mistake pure perfection. From the rise of his shoulders to his firm, bulging six-pack he had built a fortress of new discoveries to what a man's body was supposed to look like. To feel it now and be in its presence escaped all time just to be lost with him forever.

She could feel his erection easing into her as his curving, rippling torso rested firmly on top of her. Her legs widened for his hips, which pushed gently against her thighs. Everything she imagined, as her body tensed up from his sheer size alone.

He worked his way fully inside of her and every inch that seduced her had also teased to bring her climax. It'd been so long; so painfully long since Carly had felt such pleasure, that no man could ever match what now completed her. She was his fully and with every stroke from his erection she felt what released her more was a dream that was now a reality. No more searching or fantasizing about him. He was inside of her now and she inside of him.

With every moan Carly released everything else escaped him. The only thing that mattered was what he could feel with each tight thrust. With a body of a goddess, her purity and magnificence built every sound measure that this was what love was supposed to be. He had never felt it so pure, not like this. To be here in its presence, to be a part of its beauty, left him to surrender to all he took for granted.

He wanted to last all night, never stopping in this ecstasy that had made him feel immortal. Her breasts so smooth, her body so tight, so gleaming and sound, he wanted to be inside of her forever. Though, he could feel forever coming now.

Her entire body wrapped around him as sweat filled his pours. No matter where he was, Carly wasn't done. With every push he sunk inside of her, Carly pushed back just as hard with her legs twisting to turn him over, feeling every inch of his erection sooth deep into her body.

Chase fought back his climax as anticipation and satisfaction mixed with every urge inside him trying not to release just yet. He could feel every tensing, pulsating nerve as Carly rode him fully, twisting with his sanity to hold on as long as he could. He could no longer mistake what happiness was supposed to feel like, for if this was ecstasy then let splendor always find them.

What seemed like seconds, lasted minutes and with every push Chase made, her pelvis arched higher. Carly could feel his hands pressed firmly against her hips; helping to lift her up to feel his full, thick, hardened length. With one long, high arching thrust, Chase released with all he could, feeling Carly take him in, tensing up as she reached her full and pulsating climax.

Depleted and worn she collapsed on top of him and as Chase's breath raced to catch his lungs, he wrapped his arms around her as their lips meet once again. The two in each other's arms, never to mistake what this truly meant to them.

"Oh my god," said Carly, exhausted. "Was this what I've been missing out on all these years?" Her smile lifted in a pure, sweet, inspiring heaven and it all came from being with Chase. What he brought and what they recaptured held a tranquility that enabled fate.

"Funny," he gasped, still out of breath. "I was thinking the same thing," His smile lifted to hers.

His secure, trusting smile made her feel so complete. Carly wondered why she had ever refrained from feeling him, but now that she had, she couldn't believe what he'd felt like. And if ever there was a truth that would expose what she felt, then she needed to protect it.

"I never stopped loving you, Chase." Her words came softly, honest and sound, exposing every memory that really wasn't a memory at all. He had always been here; placed in her heart and to believe it would end would be to believe there wasn't a God, a heaven or an earth.

"I realized the same thing the moment I saw you again…I never stopped loving you either, Carly." Chase finally admitted what he let destroy him. If there were ever any thought that he wouldn't conceive or consummate this undying love he always had for her, then what came to him now released him from his fears. She was everything he ever wanted in a woman and it was because of her that he found out his existence belonged here, in her arms.

A loud knock suddenly pounded on the front door as Caleb's distressed voice cried out. Carly's naked body leaped off the bed. Chase followed suit, each of them alarmed, rushing to get dressed. Chase quickly grabbed their pajamas off the floor not knowing which was whose. He handed Carly her top, then he reached over recklessly grabbing his underwear, which was loosely hanging off her nightstand.

Without realizing, he pulled the cotton briefs looped around the handle, yanking out the drawer as its contents spilled across the floor. Each of them rushed to put on their clothes and before Carly could realize what Chase was doing, she looked over to see, Chase holding her most embarrassing moment, the tool of her pleasure that she always used in place of him.

"Oh no!" she shrieked as her face blushed a bright, burning red. "Give me that." Yanking the Vibrator out of his hands. "It's not what you think." But when reading his eyes, it was obvious. "OK, it is." Playing it off with panic, she buried her head into her hands wishing it never happened.

Chase laughed. "It's OK, it's OK!" As she opened up her door and pushed him out into the hall.

"Just get out of here, get dressed. Caleb can't find us like this!" Her panic replaced her embarrassment.

As the door closed in Chase's face, the look in her eyes and the panic they expressed delayed his own thoughts about what made Caleb return home. It didn't matter what he found, in fact it confirmed that there was never another man. He wanted to be here forever, never wanting to let her go and the fact that she had a son, a special and wonderful son, had changed his conscience like never before.

He found every sense of his being, able to accept Caleb as his own, deny the unfathomable and what he'd always conceived. With his will and his passion they would never be unprotected again. As Chase beat Carly to the front door he saw the distress and bleeding pain on Caleb's face and Chase took it as his own. His arms reached out, not even asking 'what's the matter', just hugging Caleb as tight as he could, wishing *he* had been his father.

CHAPTER FOURTEEN

Carly's best quality was that of a loving mother, comforting and protecting, forgiving and warm. She had so many qualities Chase was now discovering.

But Chase knew all of his life that bully's look for weakness and no matter how protective or defensive Carly was when it came to Caleb, what she completely overlooked was that she needed to let Caleb face some things on his own. He needed to make decisions that would help protect him from aggression. Chase knew that Carly running to protect him would only make it worse.

Sure, Caleb was slow and was way too trusting when it came to certain types, but Chase could only assume that it was because Carly was always there making the choices for him. Chase was just too inexperienced in Caleb's nature. He didn't understand how a child like Caleb saw things or what he went through. He never wanted to put Caleb in any danger again, like the mistake he made at the ballgame. He felt discontented, yet assertive, and regardless of the cruel contingencies, Chase had thought it over more than once and was sure he knew exactly how to handle it.

Carly and Caleb put their trust in him now, and with all the facts that he avoided telling her, it burned in his conscience every time he thought about it, but there was just no way out of it. He already crossed that bridge and with no exit in sight. He had to do his best to forever keep it from her. As far as his wealth and confiding in her about that, Chase had put that on hold to concentrate on helping Caleb. Besides, at the time he wasn't even sure he had a contract in California. To reconcile that any further left him to discover that he had so much more to share.

Carly handled it all wonderfully and as distraught as Caleb was, Chase found it astonishing how easily Carly could calm him down. With just the security of her touch and the warmth and understanding in her tone, what she'd accomplished on her own all these years, Chase wasn't sure anyone else could overcome. Certainly no one like Heather and in his moments of comparing the two throughout the weekend, nothing Heather ever did had the potential to match Carly's heart.

Yet, that all seemed irrelevant now. Chase knew that Carly's main concerns lied with Caleb. It was easy for Chase to understand why Caleb had traded his signed baseball for the candy bar with the kid next door. He was scared and panicked, but when the other boy's mother wouldn't allow the trade, Caleb's anxieties spun way out of control. She had no other choice but to bring him back home and explain to Carly what happened, and apologize for making Caleb so upset.

"Now who is this kid *again*?" Chased asked Carly, as they sat in her kitchen on Monday morning drinking coffee.

All day yesterday he hadn't kept his eyes off her, the passion they shared reflected back to him in a warm fixation that coated his heart. The three of them had eaten popcorn and pizza while they watched pre-season football with Caleb on the couch. It was a feeling he'd been missing and Chase never wanted to let it go.

"His name's Marshall." Carly answered, her concerns clear.

Both of them showered and dressed, taking the opportunity to discuss her son's new trouble at school while Caleb was getting ready in his bedroom.

"And he's Shelly Blake's boyfriend?"

"He's a jerk Chase. He's the one that should've gotten suspended." Carly's frustrations shook with her head, "And Shelly's parents are complete ass-holes. You can't believe what I had to go through with those bigoted idiots."

Her remarks took Chase by surprise, widening his eyes to the first time he heard her swear. But, considering the circumstance, it was certainly understandable. She was angry at those people for hurting her son, and Chase had already devised a plan to give Marshall a deserved payback.

It turns out Marshall had apparently been seeking his own vendetta against Caleb. Without Carly's knowledge, Marshall was the student that watched over Caleb's after school study class. He teased and picked on Caleb and threatened to beat him up if he didn't bring him a candy bar every day. What Chase had inspired set a new tone completely, he wasn't the type to run from indecision. Chase set the standard and if there was any way to beat a bully, it was to beat him at his own game. Embarrass and humiliate him and let him know everything has a consequence.

"I can only imagine Carly, I'm so sorry." Chase takes a moment, as he looked into her eyes with sincerity in his voice. "We never really discussed this, but what *is* Caleb's condition." He hesitated briefly, trying to find the best way to understand. "I'm mean, I know he doesn't have Down Syndrome and he's certainly not Autistic…"

"The umbilical cord got caught around his neck when he was born Chase." Carly understands his curiosity came as sincere. "It briefly deprived his brain of oxygen leaving him with cognitive difficulties. They call it Mild Hypoxia."

Chase nodded his head, understanding clearly why Caleb's a little slow. He knew it had to be simple, and he also conceived the care that would be essential for Caleb would probably be needed for life. Though, if there was one thing for certain to Chase, they couldn't always be there for Caleb and now was the time for Caleb to face people like Marshall.

"But, I really think this is something he's gonna have to handle for himself," Chase continued, lifting a confident, meaningful smile to what he assured Carly next. "It'll only get worse if you bring the principal into it. Trust me on this, I know how bullies are. Once Caleb stands up to Marshall he'll never bother him gain."

"How can you be so sure Chase?" Carly wanted to cry. "What if he beats Caleb up?"

"He won't." Chase lifted a confident smile trying to reassure her. "All Caleb's going to do is give that kid his candy bar. Trust me, after that thing takes effect the only thing that Marshall will want to do is run to the bathroom. This will work and it'll teach Marshall a lesson. If that doesn't work, then I'll go in with you to see the principal and we will all have a talk with his parents. Don't worry, I promise I'll handle it all. You just go to work. I have plenty of time before my plane leaves. I'll call a taxi and take Caleb to his first class. Who knows, maybe we'll run into Marshall and I'll put a stop to it right then."

His tone came strong, caring and protective and as Carly had thought about it, she hoped Chase was right. She knew it did have the potential to get worse if she brought the principal into it again. Chase told her he would handle everything and as he kissed Carly goodbye, he and Caleb stood on the porch watching her leave for work. What stood to his attention was how much he was going to miss her

CHAPTER FIFTEEN

Chase couldn't stop thinking about it his entire trip home, all the care Carly had shown him through the weekend, her accomplishments from the heart, surprising him with a high school reunion, all the fun they had at the baseball game and then at the pier, reflected his memory of the girl he once knew who had now become a woman.

A smile met his eyes when he reached for his wallet, another surprise of many, as he sat in his seat on the airplane. Chase looked inside, still not believing that all his money and credit cards were there, what he pulled out from behind his license stood now to be his most prized possession. Holding the picture he'd taken of Carly receiving her diploma at her graduation. The recollection it brought and the irony it instilled held the power of forgiveness forever in his thoughts. If rewards are what he was looking for, then Chase had found it all, even if it meant denying Heather a future.

He knew he didn't love her, not truly. What he shared with Heather stood as a shallow comparison to what he felt for Carly. Now more than ever being back in the Bay Area with the one woman he had truly loved his entire life, he knew he could build a future with Carly.

As Chase put the picture of Carly away, what came to his thoughts no longer stood as assumption. She'd been so kind, so compassionate and understanding; he wanted to pay her back by coming up with a wonderful idea on how to do that. For now, while he had time, still waiting for his plane to taxi in on the runway at Phoenix's Sky Harbor International Airport, he touched his Facebook application on his phone, instantly noticing all the friend requests he'd received since Carly's surprise for him on Saturday night.

There was Charlie Brooks, the guy who had all the looks and girls. Only now, he was on his third divorce, bitching about all his child support. There was Robert, the mechanic and racing nut, still playing with his toys and drag racing professionally. And Dave Clark and Joey Townsend, the biggest burns-outs in school, so it seemed appropriate that they now run a medicinal marijuana dispensary in Madera. Seems some things never change. There was Jesse and Johnny and most of the baseball squad. Every name on his friend request lifted Chase to a memory that still warned him of his own. Where he was living, what he did for work and why he had never been married, all found the conversation just as intriguing.

Of course, Chase evaded the obvious and it still conflicted him knowing he had to do so, but in time as in faith, Chase could only surmise that things would come out differently. Nothing seemed to matter anymore, at least not when it pertained to Phoenix. And to face his biggest dilemma was to face his own insecurities, knowing what awaited him wasn't going to be easy. Though, no matter what, he had to make things right and trust in himself to finally get tested, to find out if he was sterile and meet the truth if he wasn't and taking Heather for whomever she truly was and gaining an understanding that this weekend had changed him forever.

Then Chase saw it as he clicked on his last request and the reality set in his eyes left him completely numb. Ironic eccentricities twisted to subdue him, pulling him in a force too overbearing to comprehend. It was Heather and she'd found him on Facebook. Even when talking to her this morning about the airport pick up she never gave him a hint that she knew about his status. He was sure she'd received the prenuptial decree and still she had said nothing. Whatever was going on with her was entirely out of her nature, but still none of this was fair to her. As much as Chase felt for Carly, he knew he'd put both of them in a situation that neither had asked for. *How could he stay with Heather knowing he had cheated on her with Carly? How could he be with Carly knowing he had made her the home wrecker in all of this?* Whichever the case, the scenario was all the same, Chase was the one who had reached the unspeakable and to ever free himself, he would have to free the both of them.

***

You know exactly what I'm talking about, Kelly!" Heather snarled into her cell phone as if scolding an adolescent. "You and Sydney put him up to this, didn't you? There's no sense in denying it. You two've been jealous of me ever since I started seeing Chase."

"Oh, Heather, that's ridiculous." Kelly's objective tone tried to rationalize her emotion, yet she knew that in some small way, however distracted her accusations were, Heather was right. "It's not that we're jealous of you, dear, it's that...well," her tone coaxes, "you're a bitch."

"Pardon *me?*" Heather gasped. Her anxieties and disgust evident.

"Sydney and I have given you every opportunity to be a part of this family. Yet, in that conniving little bird brain of yours, you see it as a competition."

"Funny you mention competition, Kelly. Was that what this was all about? Setting up Chase with old flames?" Her tone grew harsher, conspiring in a mind too incensed to see reason.

With every bit of information that Heather unleashed Kelly thought to only taunt her, to plant in Heather's mind what was already past reason.

"Really, Heather?" The premonition exposed her thoughts. "Have your own insecurities already reached that level? We haven't even heard from Chase since he left. How do *we* know who he's with?"

"Oh please," Heather snarled. "Carly Bourque, the girl he was with at the game…" she paused. "The same girl he took to the prom?" She casted an accusation that only made her seem more desperate.

Kelly knew all too well whom Chase was with, but she would never share that with Heather. Whether he was faithful to her or just catching up on old times, any speculations that were being cast, she wanted to make sure they had strictly come from Heather.

"So what are you saying here, dear?" A grin on her face, enjoying every minute of Heather's panicked anguish.

"I don't know what I'm saying," Heather quickly snapped, realizing she was fighting a battle with no real weapons in her hands. "I just wanted *you* two to know that *I* know what *you* two are up to," her tone hard and angry.

"Well, I'll keep that in mind, dear." Kelly kept her composure, knowing it only dug into her deeper. "Sid's at the airport to pick Chase up now, I'll let him know when he returns home tonight."

"Oh yeah, right," Heather smirked. "How dumb do you think I am?"

"Umm," Kelly pondered. "Is there a chart to go by, maybe something on the lower end of the graph?"

"Funny. Real cute, Kelly. It's no wonder I avoid you and that husband of yours whenever possible."

"Get to the point, Heather." Kelly had become more than frustrated and leaned towards Heather, annoyed.

"What would Sydney be picking up Chase for?"

"Uh…" She cocked her shoulders, sarcastic and taunting all in the same breath, *"because, Chase asked him to."*

"Yeah, right." Heather's eyes rolled with obstinacy. "Was that *before,* or *after,* he talked to me this morning?" Heather's challenging tone took another turn.

"What are you talking about?" She had caught Kelly's complete attention.

"Where do you think I'm at now?" Her words driving with expectancies as she exited to Sky Harbor Airport. "I'm getting ready to pick Chase up. Why on earth would Sydney be here to get him?"

"Oh shit," Kelly hissed, good question indeed, as if feeling the inevitable circumstance of Sydney's interference coming to implode.

"What's wrong, Kelly? You finally realize that Chase can't wait to see me?" she gloated as the only thing she could believe would secure her in all of this.

"If that's what you need to think, to help you get through all of this, then knock yourself out honey. You just keep on believing that. But right now, I have to go."

Within that instant the line had gone dead. Kelly could feel it as she breathed. Each second she delayed, predicted the inevitable. She had warned Sydney about Chase's reaction to how he'd set him up. Yes, Kelly knew everything now, the demanding conscience of a loyal wife making Sydney come clean. Of course, the final outcome was all in Chase's hands and whether Kelly liked it or not, in the back of her mind, she had definitely liked Sydney's plan. But knowing these two brothers like Kelly knew them; nothing was forgivable without serious repercussions and just what Kelly had feared; her instincts took over as she dialed Sidney immediately if just to give him fair warning and caution him that something wasn't right.

***

"Where the hell you at?" Sydney's frustrations rose as he drove down the terminal looking for Chase.

He had everything and still no answers, though Sydney was just relieved that Chase had finally answered his phone and was talking to him again. Of course that was all preceded by Sid picking him up now and what stood in his conscience was what he still had to tell him. To shock and prepare his brother for the truth, come clean to everything he had done. It was all for Chase's own good and the good of the company. No matter what Chase thought, Sydney knew that Chase would've done the same thing to him, using anything at his disposal to secure their contract. To be misleading about the rest, well, that had all been Chase's doing in the end. As soon as Sid found out what happened over the weekend, he would show Chase the proof about

Heather and make his brother face his own ghosts, to see Heather for who she was with the hope it would finally force him to get tested and find out if he was indeed fertile.

"I can see *you*," Chase guided him in. "Just keep on coming, I'm right on the other side of this bus up ahead. You can't miss me."

For most of the flight home, Chase thought about what he was going to do to Sydney. Yelling or threatening him wouldn't be enough as far as Chase was concerned. No, Sydney had definitely crossed over the line to just give him a pass. Regardless of how things had turned out over the weekend, what Chase could never forgive him for was using Carly and Caleb to deceive Montoya. What else could it be? He had to know that Caleb was slow and sitting on the border of what's considered normal. Why else would Sydney choose for them to meet him there? A meeting between them both after all these years apart, stood to only reason that they would show their true emotions, all for the pretense of Montoya and the improvisation that Sydney had counted on from Chase.

Oh yes, Chase knew his brother all too well and to think any other way would be to deny the vindication he was ready to complete. Just to let Sydney know how pissed he was and that he should never have fucked with him in the first place, set him to conceive this awful idea the moment he saw the cement barricade blocked from Sydney's view.

Sid had gone way out of his way to deceive him in all of this and if it was just to put him on the spot and test his own reason, then Chase could admit his own sense of shame and what he'd done over the weekend. But for now, there was no way Sydney was going to walk away from this clean.

Sid loved his Mercedes and bragged about it ever since Kelly let him get it. It was his only comfort away from their family vehicles, and if there was anything Sydney cared about more than his family, it was that pretentious car of his. So, Chase thought, *why not?*

"I can't see shit," Sydney lashes out again. "That damn bus was in the way. Oh hell—"

"What?"

"Kelly's calling me."

"Goddamn it!" Chase blasted, "Never mind that. Will you just come get me?"

"Alright already!" his frustrations shouted back. "Is it safe to go around that bus? Can I get to you from the other side?"

"If you hurry," Chase's harsh tone was a ploy to keep Sid frustrated.

"Are you *sure?*" Sydney leaned over to the passenger seat, trying to get a better view.

"Yes! Now! Hit It!" he screamed in alarm and panic.

Without thinking, Sydney floored the accelerator, taking his brother's word. His tires peeled smoke as if he was trying to beat another car that was never even there. He swerved around the bus, picking up speed, looking over his shoulder as the impact stopped him short. A hard, crushing impact that caved in the entire front end of his car, causing his airbags to go off and leaving his grill stuck in the engine with coolant leaking all over. Steam sprayed out from everywhere. All of it happened within that instant, before Sydney had even known what the *hell* was going on.

A crowd quickly gathered, as even Chase was shocked by the

damage. He quickly looked around thinking, *Oh shit, what have I done?* His legs carried him as fast they could around to Sydney's driver side window. It was obvious he was dazed and confused his only reaction was to swat away the deflating air bag as he looked over his steering wheel to the enormous cement barricade that had now become part of his car.

"What the hell just happened?" he gasped, looking around as more people came running over. He was obviously all right and about to lose it, when he suddenly saw Chase's face appear in his window. "Didn't you see that fucking thing sitting there, Chase?" His panic quickly turned to heartache. "What the *hell* man! My car!" His hand wavered over to the wreckage. He was almost in tears as he looked back to Chase and shouted, "My car, man...*do you see my car?*" His distress became even more sorrowful.

But then there was *the* look. That satisfying, gratifying look splattered across Chase's face and reflected in his eyes, which left no doubt that Chase had done it on purpose.

"What?" Sid cocked his head. "Was that funny to you?"

"Yeah." Chase nodded in delight as his grin pulled even tighter. "How's it feel to hurt and destroy what you love? Huh? Sid, tell me that. I don't give a damn about your car! Do you realize what you did, what you made me do?" His anger was piercing. The moment he realized his brother was all right, Chase's only concern laid in Sydney's deception. The fact that the only thing hurting on him now was his crushed, materialistic ego made Chase think it was a far better alternative to how he'd really wanted to hurt him.

"Oh, come on, man." Sydney realized he'd been had. "You

would've done the same. You can't tell me it didn't feel good to see her?" he said, trying to find logic in his own inimitable way. "But the important thing is—did you get the contract?"

Chase just couldn't believe it. *Had he been this way himself? Was he looking in a mirror that reflected all of his past aggressions?* Whatever his standing reason, Sydney had no right. Regardless of how Chase felt now, what reconciled in his heart was just as bad as Sydney, he could've stopped this entire charade. But deep within him, his regrets stood as shallow as his treason. To deny it now and forbid what was to come would only prelude the inevitable. He had to cast out his own demons, find a way out of this mess and he had thanked God that Montoya had come to reason. At least now he would have his chance to move on, find a different life and it all started here. He must correct things with Heather. Knowing she was waiting for him at the terminal, he gave Sydney a farewell.

"Yeah, Sid," Chase's eyes peel his anger. "I got the contract," His smug, tight jaw grinds his distaste. "It's this one, right here," Holding up his middle finger and then he walked away.

"Chase! Come on, man—Chase!" Sydney pleaded. All to no avail as he saw his brother's backside slowly fade and disappear into the chaos.

If anger burned for vendetta, then what Chase felt inside torched his very soul. He had no one to blame but himself. He should never have gone through with this in the first place. He should've come clean from the very beginning and just played it off as his brother's interference, telling Carly who he really was, never hiding his wealth or his engagement. And now everything was in such a mess. Such a drastic, complete mess, that Chase wasn't even sure he had the tools to fix it.

He heard a honk and looked over as a disparaging, distraught look consumed his entire face. The small, shallow beats of his heart dropped into his chest, prohibiting the endearments of what he'd felt over the weekend. The only thought that he retained was what he was going to tell Heather as he watched her car pull up to the curb like a hearse taking him to his own funeral.

She honked again as Chase stepped over. The only thing he had were the clothes he was wearing that Carly had bought for him, not even taking it into consideration what Heather would think about that. But as soon as he opened the door and sat in the passenger seat what came to his awakening made him realize his own faults. He'd been just like her, never thinking of it until now. But, hearing her say the very first thing out of her mouth left him to feeling what he should've felt all along.

"Oh my God," Heather leaned over to kiss him. "What are you *wearing?*"

"What?" Chase pulled back, his lips never touching hers. The only thing that hit him was the panic of his guilt twisting with her words. Every aberration that had confused him before found this clarity in his heart, as his ears finally comprehended it.

"Well, you don't have to be so alarmed." Heather noticed his panic, knowing where it came from and wanting the truth to come from him.

"What's wrong with what I'm wearing?" He refocused, trying to tame his guilt and rely on his instincts, knowing he had to tell her. Only now wasn't the time.

"A bit drab, *isn't it?*" Heather's tone was arrogant.

"What?" His hands flared out. "I told you I lost my wallet. It's not like I'm going to a formal affair."

"Yeah, but honestly love," she smirked. "What you have on isn't even appropriate for lounging around the house. I mean..." she chuckles. "Where did you get those shoes?"

"Wal-Mart."

"Wal-Mart!" she gasped. "It's worse than I thought. You might actually need to get a tetanus shot."

"Oh, Heather, stop. It isn't that bad. They're actually very comfortable."

"Comfortable enough to at least give your fiancé a kiss? I mean you've been gone all weekend. Don't you even care you left me to fend for myself?"

"Don't you think you're over exaggerating?" His eyes gave a subtle roll. "You'd better just go, the transit cops are waving for you to exit."

"Hmm," heather pouted, putting the car in drive as she hit the accelerator.

"Slow down!" Chase shouted, "You're going to get in a wreck!"

"Oh, really?" She gave a smug tilt of her head. "You didn't seem to care when it was Sydney smashing into that barricade."

"Yeah," Chase nodded rational and sound. "Maybe because I don't, he had it coming. Us on the other hand, I do care about," He looked over calmly. "Now please Heather, slow down."

She eased up on the pedal as her thoughts consumed her suspicions. She had so much to talk about she didn't know where to start. In a mind of stolen choices, hers were pre-decided. *Has she lost him? If she did, could she ever get him back?* All of her prevailing insights stood everything to gain just to know those two warranting questions, and when looking into his eyes, she knew she had his cure. The provocative sexual entrapments that had always enticed him before. A seduction of his senses that he'd never refused, and by the grace of her own conniving arrogance she felt her beauty was all she ever had needed to entrap him.

"Where are you going?" Chase noticed her route. "You have to get in the southbound lane."

"*Southbound?*" she leered. "I thought I was taking us home."

"Home?" He caught himself questioning what he had never questioned before. "You mean my house?"

"What?" Heather couldn't believe what she just heard. "I just assumed it was going to be our house. Funny how all of a sudden it's changed."

"I didn't mean that the way it sounded." He cautiously looked over, careful not to make contact. "I'm just not thinking straight right now. Sid really pissed me off this time."

"Are you at least going tell me what happened between you two?" She paused for a moment if only just to hear it come from him.

"That's not important right now." Chase held up his palms, trying to play it off. "What is important is me getting to the office."

"Work?" she flared up, "Now? But you just got back. You have to change out of those ridiculous clothes you're wearing. I thought we could—"

"I don't have time, Heather. There're some stipulations that've been amended to the contract and a deadline on top of that." Urgency and stress find his reprieve.

"So you did get it? Whatever that job was in California?"

"Yeah, Heather." Chase glanced over. "The Veterans Hospital in San Francisco…yeah, we got it." He realized right then that she never even cared what he did, how he made his money or the importance that his expertise brought to his company. No, Heather only cared that he made money. To construe it any differently, left him with his own compromise from what he had witnessed in California. Carly had to make sacrifices throughout her entire life, living on a fixed income yet she found the will to share what she couldn't afford—with him. As much as Chase hated to admit it, Sydney was right. Heather would never give him the time of day if it weren't for his wealth and all the toys that came with it.

"And quit dogging my clothes," he suddenly found himself adding. "The person who bought these for me couldn't even afford to. So, show some respect, Heather. I'm lucky to be wearing them after the way my weekend started out."

"What does that mean?" Heather started to pout. "Who bought them for you?"

"A friend." He looked over with no more caution in his eyes or shame in his tone.

"That girl you were with?" Her eyes flash anger. "Carly Bourque, the same girl you took to the prom?"

There, she'd said it, bringing it all into the open. Unleashing what she knew and confirming her suspicions. To see it on his face and to read between the lines allowed her to expose her inner-self and confront him here and now.

"How do you know her name?" Chase turned to her surprised.

"I saw her on Facebook." Heather's eyes hardened noticing his shock and questioning it again. "That's right, I found you on there and she's your only friend on Facebook. Why's that?" Her accusations flare.

"I have lots of friends on Facebook," Chase quickly defended. "I saw your friend request and relationship status." He creased a grin, knowing that he'd ignored them. If Heather wanted to hear the story then Chase was going to tell her.

"You do? You did? Then why didn't you tell me about all of this? I've been after you for a long time to get on Facebook."

"I didn't *get* on Facebook, Heather," Chase confessed. "Don't you get it? This was all Sydney's bullshit."

"Sydney?" She shook her head, though she knew he'd been behind it.

"Yeah." Chase's frustrations grew. "And he did it all just to get this damn contract. Why do you think I'm so pissed at him?"

"But, I saw you on T.V. at the game. With her and that boy…"

"Yeah, So?"

"Why? Was that who you were with all weekend?" Her face clouded over. Up until now Chase had forgotten what he felt for her. To say he didn't care would be to deny his own will, torn between his love for Carly, and Heather, a woman who had just been his lover.

"I lost my wallet," Chase tried to explain. "I didn't even know how I was gonna get back on the plane…"

As Chase began to explain the events that unfolded through the weekend, what he left out was the night he'd shared with Carly, forever hidden inside his heart until he could see her again. From the fate of his truck to the Mexican guy that had fixed it, Chase told her everything and it all rested on the fact that Sydney had set him up. All so they could get Montoya to release the amending contract and finally award it to them.

"So, it was all because of that poor, orphaned girl and her son...Montoya's son?" Heather came to understand. "Oh, love, what a nightmare it must have been for you, stuck with that *retard* all weekend."

Chase quickly turned, flexing his brows the moment he heard her say it. His instant reaction to what she'd just said caught him completely off guard.

"Do you realize how awful that just sounded, Heather? My God, what the hell's the matter with you? Show some goddamn compassion!"

"Honestly, Chase," Heather succumbed to her tears. "You've never spoken to me like that before. What happened over the weekend? It's like I don't even know you anymore. That's no way to speak to the woman that's going to bear your child. You leave me alone all weekend with nothing but your short, little phone calls. Never answering my texts and you don't tell me anything that's goin' on. I get this damn pre-nup hand delivered to me with no warning at all. And now this outburst...I'm only repeating how I heard you refer to *those* kinds of people your entire life."

It was all out before him as Heather pulled into his office parking lot. Every grieving memory and every thought that remained, came tarnished from a lie that Chase swore he would never commit. To be truthful would mean to disregard their plans, regardless of repercussions. Chase knew in his heart that he would never be happy, or never restore what he found in California, if he didn't end this now. He had to honor Carly the only way he knew how instead of making her into the evil seductress she would seem in all this. If anyone was at fault in the end Chase knew he had only himself to blame and someway, somehow, he would have to confess.

"You must think I'm a complete fucking idiot." Chase looked harsh as her car came to a stop in front of his office doors.

"What?" Heather looked shocked, widening her eyes. "What's wrong with you Chase? Why are you talking to me like that?"

"How come you've never showed me your pregnancy results Heather?"

"What?" Her heart began to panic as she felt her throat drop into her chest.

"Did you go off birth control without telling me?" Chase held a steady conviction, exposing her for who she was. If there was any truth to come out of this than Chase would start with his own.

"My God!" She cried out. "No Chase, what an awful thing to say. I would never…"

"Oh, spare me your bullshit Heather." Chase had had enough. "I got news for you sweetheart, I've known a long time I can't have kids." Finally admitting it to himself and any disregard he had of Heather. "But *I will* tell you one thing," He held up his finger, putting himself in a position that he thought he'd never want to do. "I'm gonna find out once and for all. And for your sake…," he stopped. The anger on his face piercing with resentment. "I just think I need some space from you for a while."

"What are you saying Chase?" Her tears fell uncontrollably, unwilling to believe that they were over.

"I'm taking you off the guest list to my estate until can figure this all out. Don't bother coming over anymore. You won't be allowed past security."

"But, I already picked out my wedding ring from that jewelry store you had credit with. See?" her tears poured, as she showed him her finger.

"Well," Chase returned a spiteful smirk. "I'm gonna cancel my credit with them and they'll probably report it stolen. If I were you, I'd take it back." He said with no remorse at all.

His words echoed to her as she sat there sobbing, watching Chase slam the door behind him as he just simply walked away and headed into his office. All Heather could do was stare and feel every ounce of her control she had over him fade away as she watched him lock the entrance making sure she wouldn't follow him inside.

It didn't matter to Chase what others thought anymore, this was his life and he wasn't going to let anyone deny him that. If Heather were indeed pregnant with his child then he would honor that. But now more than ever, Chase understood that honor and devotion didn't mean he was bound to get married. Even if he was never meant to be with Carly, what happened over the weekend made him want to try and live up to what he started, finish it here in Phoenix and be brave enough to carry on.

CHAPTER SIXTEEN

The staff had gone home for the day and Chase was all alone in his office. All the revisions to the contract were under way with every specification set in place, everything that was needed to bring his status back to hero. Yet, what remained still held him to make amends.

He hadn't talked to Sydney since he left him at the airport, knowing it was only a matter of time before he would definitely make his appearance. In everything that happened, what led up to this point had held him accountable for everything he'd done. For a man who was looking to rectify his life, what Chase was feeling left him completely distraught.

There's just no escaping these unmerciful warnings and hard, tearing regrets that will forever question ones character. Everything within him wanted to just leave and go back to San Francisco, but what made him stay, he looked forward to facing head on. The tears on Heather's face and her desperate pleas that begged him, *"Why?"* brought everything from his past spiraling into his future. *Could he even begin to feel or imagine the pain that Heather must be under?* Of all the warnings he'd heard coming from everyone, their regards had been out of concern for his trusting of Heather. Yet, here he was, living up to the very same imperfections he'd always thought would come from her. If Chase had ever looked for a sign or peace in his heart, he heard it calling his name as he stepped out into the front office. It had come to give him life and clarify meaning. If there was ever a moment for Chase to step up and face his indecisions, then the storm is upon him and it was time for him to dance in the rain.

"Kelly!" he called out, recognizing her voice immediately. "That you?"

Seeing her now brought everything into perspective. The look on her face and the self-reliance in her eyes shouted out the inevitable as she walked over to where Chase was standing.

"I owe you something, Chase." Her tone was a bit harsh, though it held a calm, yet assertive look.

"Look, Kelly—" Chase had reached his own conclusions. In all the years of knowing his sister in-law, what Chase knew most was that she wasn't afraid of anyone. *"Ouch!"* he gasped, feeling her cold hand slap hard against his face. "What the *hell* was that?"

"Who the *hell* do you think you are, buddy?" Her finger pointed into his chest as if probing every word with each hard stick of her finger.

"Kelly, I know—"

"Oh, no you don't, Chase!" Her tone flared up. "I don't get you guys, you know that." The shake of her head turned to disgust as shock and terror led her convictions. "You think what you did doesn't have repercussions? Well, he may be your brother, but he's *my* husband, not to mention the father of my children. You could've killed him with that stunt of yours. I've been at the damn hospital with him ever since it happened. Did you know that? Huh?" She pointed to him once again, causing Chase to flinch. He tried to dodge her anger but Kelly just kept yelling. And with every push she shoved him with and every finger that struck, Chase took it all in, knowing he deserved it and knowing in his heart that she was the only one on this planet that could ever get away with it.

"I know, Kelly, I know. I'm sorry. Just please stop hitting me. I wasn't thinking. But you have no idea what he did."

"I know, Chase." She took a long deep breath. "And you better believe Sydney got a piece of my mind as well. I'm mad at the both of you. But you two have got to stop this, make this right for everyone concerned, damn you."

She walked over to him as her hand touched his cheek where the red from her slap still burned. "I love you, Chase," her tone soothed. "You know that, honey. I just want you to be happy. Whatever happened in Frisco between you and your old flame, if it makes you happy then screw everyone else. The only one you have to answer to is yourself."

Everything she'd said, Chase had already felt. The dire consequences of his shame had brought humiliation. What he'd done and how he'd handled it brought grief to him and he didn't know how he would fix it, or how we would live with what he'd done to Heather. But most of all, how he would explain to Carly that he might soon be a father.

"It's over, Kelly." His tone came unrepentant. "Heather and me—it's over."

But Kelly already knew everything. Sydney had confessed it all. The tapes Sydney had on Heather and the truth about her pregnancy had exposed Heather's only motive to be with Chase. And to help him escape what could've been had restored Kelly's resolve to tell Chase everything.

"I had a feeling," she answered in a soft, inspiring tone. "Heather called me and pretty much let it all fly. I don't know anything about Carly Bourque, but I do know something must've happened between you, because I don't think I've ever seen you like this." Her hand rubbed his shoulder as her smile filled his senses. "If what you're looking for is some kind of understanding in all this, some reason or forgiveness in whatever you feel you need—in, I don't know, to move on—then you don't have to forgive anyone, and that includes *yourself*."

She focused on his conviction and the future that remained. "Now," She cautiously approached just how to tell him. "There's some things?" She gestured to the front. "I wouldn't let him come in here until after I spoke with you. But I'll tell you right now Chase, this thing with Heather, he did it for your own good."

"What do you mean?" His faced grimaced, immediately catching what she said. "This thing with Heather?"

"Sid had Heather followed, Chase. He used that same private detective you guys are always hiring." She felt reluctant to express disapproval and just needed to make Chase understand.

"You gotta be kidding me Kelly!" Chase flared up again. "When's he gonna stay the hell out of my affairs?"

"I know Chase, but he did it for your own good. The PI gave him some pictures of Heather smoking when she said she was pregnant, along with a taped conversation she had with a friend. You're going to want to hear what's on it. I think you're going to be quite relieved when this is all over."

As Kelly spoke, she could hear Chase's phone ringing in his pocket. A pause turned to hesitance as they both assumed it was Heather on the other end. He reached for his phone then held it up to his eyes. Seeing Carly's name and number immediately put a smile on his face.

"Well," Kelly sighed. "Apparently, it's not who I think it is." She waited for Chase to say something and when he didn't, she concluded it was indeed the only woman he'd wanted to hear from. "Is that her?" She waited, breathing in the excitement. She could see it as he looked at his phone. "Is it Carly?" Her curiosity and insight lifted a smile.

Chase nodded, warm and inviting, hesitant to answer as his eyes revealed his thoughts.

"Well, that's my cue." She graciously excused herself. "I'll go get Sydney. Just remember what I said OK, Chase?" She waited for him to acknowledge her before she turned and walked away.

In all her thoughts and sound conclusions, it's what she saw on Chase's face that restored her own peace. Kelly understood how he'd been taken by it all and with each step that took her away she realized she'd been taken by it as well, knowing in her heart she couldn't help but to listen in. To hear Chase for the first time in her life knowing that true love has touched him.

"Hi." Chase answered, watching Kelly walk away. His cautions swayed his thoughts, hoping Sid would at least take his time so he could talk to Carly in private.

"Hello there yourself," came Carly's pleasant sounding voice, a voice of acceptance and passion, harboring the endearments that found her since the two of them reunited. "I was wondering how everything went for you…and," she paused slightly. "To tell you the truth, I just wanted to hear your voice again."

"Well, it's definitely nice to know you're thinking about me." Chase disciplined his thoughts to what he really wanted to tell her.

"And you?" Her tone was cautious. "What've you been thinking?" She leaves it up to him, wanting to hear him say it, if only to relive it again. Wanting to prove to herself that it hadn't been a dream.

"I'm still trying to wake up." Chase slowly led her in.

"Wake up?"

"Yeah," His humor lifted, fading in the remembrance to her true feelings. "I still haven't found anyone to pinch me, 'cause if what happened over the weekend was a dream, then I don't ever wanna wake up."

Silence became endearment and desire ignited its flame, feeling, praying and hoping that what her heart had now found would never go away.

"Well, if I was there," She played along, "I'd pinch ya."

"No, that's okay," His relief coincided with his chuckle. "Just hearing you now, I know what happened between us over the weekend really did happen. Didn't it, Carly?"

"Were you disappointed? You don't sound disappointed."

"I'm not…and for that matter, it doesn't sound like you are either."

"How could I be?" Her tone moved to a pitch that let his imagination consume him.

All throughout the weekend Chase studied her every gesture. How she walked, how she breathed, laughed and felt, all filled his senses to every expression that enveloped her face. He got to know her so well, that he could feel every part of her emotions, and hearing her on the other end he relived it all again.

Her teasing little smile, the gestures of her nods and waves of her hands, the way her hair fell just across her shoulders lifted him to a place he could feel himself being. Oh, to breathe it in and exist in its fulfillment brought truth into the open with a need to expose all the secrets.

"You know, Carly…" Courage provided faith. "There are some things about me that I need to clear up—I mean," he stumbled. "Well, take Caleb—"

"Oh," her excitement interrupted. "That reminds me. Caleb has something to tell you."

"That's right." It had totally escaped him. Once again finding him in a detour. "He was a bit nervous this morning. How did that whole thing go?" He could hear Carly's breath as she panted through the phone, picturing her smile and all it meant to him.

"Perhaps I should let him tell you for himself," Carly's happy tone said it all. "He's been so excited, Chase," she whispered in the phone. "He's been dying to tell you what happened ever since he got home." She paused in the moment, collecting her emotions. "You were right, Chase. Thank you for understanding and helping out in all this. He really looks up to you, you know?" Her words sweet, honest and endearing, carrying what he felt the second she'd said it.

"Not as much as I look up to him, Carly." Honesty had found him and he knew as he said it that it was truly how he felt.

Carly smiled, feeling her heart soothe into her chest. It had been so long since she had felt that way. Every time she spoke to him, anticipation and expectancies had gone hand in hand. He hadn't disappointed her since they'd reunited and everything she felt about him brought her the faith to secure it, dividing her heart from the contingencies that had always protected her before. If this was how fate had worked or how destiny had judged perception, then there could be no mistaking what she craved to always have.

"I'll go get him."

He could hear the slight tremble, the endearment in her voice and the hidden complexities he felt were his own. He never expected it, not like this. Every endowment, every discovery of what he missed out on, brought him to his own heart wrenching decisions, never wanting to tell her about Heather. To free her from the pain and save himself in the process led him to the question: *was it to save Carly from heartache or was it to save his own ass and forever becoming a bleeding, desperate soul?'*

"I know, mom. I know."

Chase could hear Caleb's voice, a bit muffled but clear, as Carly handed him the phone. If influence provided security then just hearing Caleb call Carly 'mom' instead of mommy lifted a smile to his cheeks. The conversations about his childhood helped Caleb begin to understand himself. To feel like a man, to face challenges and decide for himself gave him pride that Chase instilled just from being around.

"Chase!" Caleb's excitement flared the moment he took the phone. Chase pictured his cocky and proud expression. "Boy, buddy, can I tell you what happened? I want to tell you what happened to Marshall when he ate that—what do you call that stuff *again?*"

Chase started laughing, hearing his glee and the earnest respect he felt in standing up for himself. But what he noticed most in all of Caleb's excitement was that for the first time Chase could recall, Caleb wasn't stuttering. He sounded confident and proud as if he was some kind of Super Hero and it all came from Chase and the chocolate laxative he replaced for the candy bar.

"It was just something that makes you go to the bathroom," Chase laughed, hearing Caleb's gratifying voice, knowing obviously it had worked.

"That's what he did, buddy," Caleb's excitement rambled. "He went poop in his pants," he suddenly hesitated. "Mom said I could say that. He pooped his pants right in front of everyone. We were all laughing at him and boy, buddy, you know what happened then?"

"What's that?" Chase kept his composure though he wanted desperately to laugh.

"Marshall got *mad*," Caleb's voice swayed toward his tendencies. "Then he said the F word. Oooh, that was bad. You don't say the F word, buddy." His excitement kept growing. He shouted rambling muses at everything he felt, "Oh, and I also get to come home now. Mom said I don't have to be there with Marshall and I can take the early bus home. That's good, huh, buddy?"

"It sure is." Chase's inspired smile never left. "I'm real proud of you, my boy and I know your mom is too."

"Boy!" Caleb recognized the one thing he'd envisioned. "I'm your boy? Does that mean you're going to be my new dad?" Random shouts of glee filled his expectations.

"*Caleb!*" Chase could hear Carly quickly take over. "Say goodbye to Chase now sweetie, okay?"

"*Oh, mom,*" Caleb's disappointment sounded. "How come? I want to say more to him and tell him I love him." His innocence held Chase's influence.

"I love you too, my boy." Chase savored his endearments, if only to secure that they will see each other again.

"Sorry about that, Chase." Carly came back to the phone. "He can get carried away sometimes," she said, a bit embarrassed yet relieved knowing Chase would understand.

"It's not really a bad thing, is it Carly?" Chase captured the moment and with it came the need to hear it come from her lips.

"Um—" Hesitance and reason mix with the unknown. "I'm not sure how to answer that. What do you want me to say?"

"It's not up to me. It's what your heart's telling you that count's. After the weekend, I think you know exactly how I feel." However, when silence met anticipation, Chase revised his thoughts, not wanting her to feel any pressure to vocalize what he'd just admitted himself. "Sorry, Carly, I don't mean to put you on the spot. I just can't wait to get back and see you."

"So, you're coming back?" She broke her silence.

The moment she said it, Chase could hear the instant joy in her tone, which brought him answers and the spontaneity of her happiness lifted his joy to new sensations. It had only been the weekend, yet so much had progressed that he had to find his chance to tell her.

"Was there ever any doubt?" His tone was more determined. "I don't give a damn about that job. My only reason for returning was to see you and Caleb again. Don't ever forget that, Carly. I know last weekend—what happened—means just as much to you as it does to me. You can't deny me that, not now."

She could feel her heart beat faster and every word freed her soul. She had been unable to admit it up until now. "I'll never deny you again, Chase and the way you are with Caleb, how he feels…I've never seen him take to anyone like he has with you. I know it's only been a few days, but it's like—I don't know. You hear what he calls me now? I've never seen him like this before, but this confidence he has, all comes from you. Whether you can find a job here or not, I'll help all I can but don't ever mistake how I feel about you. I just don't want to get hurt again and I can't put Caleb through that knowing how he feels about you. If this isn't going to work out between us then tell me now, Chase. Let me have what we had over the weekend once more and I promise you it will last me forever."

It had all become so nourishing, so honest and free, that to deny what fate had finally restored would be to deny time and space and forbid all that was heavenly. No, Carly didn't deserve to be put through such despair. The only thing she deserved was to share his wealth with him and to live life to the fullest. He had to expose that much to her.

"I've been wanting to tell you something for a while now…and if I don't say it now," he paused, reconciling his moment. "I…well—"

"What?" Her cautions pulled at him, as she felt the beats of her heart slowly diminish. Her throat swelled. Her conscious and every deniable thought told her to get ready for what she didn't want to hear.

"It's my job. I mean…" He stumbled, feeling his insecurities coming to steal his heart. Everything that led up to this and everything that remained promised to haunt his thoughts. "It's not *really* my job."

Relief instantly found her as troubles avoid despair. It was all going so perfectly, that when Carly first heard his reluctance, what gathered in her thoughts she thought would come to destroy her. Though, how could she have ever surmised that what she was thinking touched so close to home?

"Your job? You actually scared me there for a moment. I had pictures of you telling me you were married, have a family or something. My God," she sighed again. "Believe me, you don't want know *what* was going on inside my head just then."

This pain that grieved him suffocated him like never before. A verity so close he could feel his heart shattering through his chest. Carly deserved the truth, but he couldn't expose his shame. He felt lost in his own convictions of what was wrong and right and this guilt and disgrace bled from his own misery, like nothing he had ever felt before.

"Yeah, I suppose I don't." His conscience overshadowed his fear. "It's just that...well, maybe we can talk about this later? There're some things I need to take care of right now."

"Oh." She noticed his sudden change in mood. "Ok, I just wanted to call and give Caleb a chance to tell you what happened. We'll have time to talk later. Won't we?" Her insecurities surfaced, feeling that whatever had deterred him, had come from her. She should never have confessed what made her panic because if desperation seemed certain, then she had only herself to blame.

"Of course we will. I'll explain everything when I see you again. It's just that right now," He looked up, seeing Sydney come through the front door. "I really have to go."

"Okay, that's fine," She said, sensing his hesitance. "Call me when you have a chance." As if one last prayer would solidify what she'd always felt for him.

"I will, Carly. Good-bye."

"Good-bye, Chase." Her breath echoed into the phone like faded thoughts and memories, wondering if she would ever see him again. Whatever had changed in that moment, there was no doubt Carly had felt it. When it was time, she would listen to whatever he needed to tell her, taking in what she could and comprehending what she couldn't, even if it resulted in losing him.

CHAPTER SEVENTEEN

The northern coastal breeze stretched across the Bay and eased into the city. Landscapes and skyscrapers met peeks and inner valleys, with people filling sidewalks in an array of social ethnicities. A mixture that had brought back so many memories, it was as if Chase had never left. Even feeling what he felt now, trapped in his own prison, his aspirations seemed to have faded into remorse.

He'd avoided it so often that it became second nature. The confession he'd refused that awaited his every standard, but try as he had, no words could ever explain it. All for his own self bleeding needs when so many had been counting on him.

The instant Sydney handed him the tape of Heather and the pictures of her smoking and drinking, what Chase refused to bargain for was more humiliation. It just didn't matter anymore, and he didn't even care to listen. Regardless of what Kelly demanded, he wasn't sure he could ever trust Sydney again, certainly not with something like this. The way Sid felt about Heather was obvious, he would do anything to stop them from getting married. He had set him up the entire time, confessed no remorse and held no shame, residing on the facts alone that he'd did it all for Chase.

But Chase was certainly no fool and had called Sid on everything. From the moment Sid kept Montoya's amendments from him, to the friend request he had sent to Carly, Chase put it all together and the extremes in which Sydney used had only built upon more contempt.

It was obvious Sid had Carly investigated and found out about Caleb. Chase was sure he used the same PI he had spy on Heather and Sydney had used it all to format his plan. However, when Chase had confessed to Sid about how he felt for Carly and what had happened between them, it only pushed the issue and Chase ended up consulting Sid about what should be done now. After all, Sydney was still his brother.

Of course Sydney's reasoning was simple; just don't tell Carly about Heather. In Sid's eyes there was no reason to ever confess it to her but that would mean Chase would have to bury it forever. An easy concept to someone without a conscience, though in the complexities that remained, it would always be there. To Sydney, it was all a welcoming relief that Heather was no longer in the picture. Despite all of her transparencies, if Chase didn't want to face the truth or couldn't admit to himself that he'd been played, then the only fool Chase had to deal with was the one he saw in the mirror.

If anything at all, Chase had to know for himself. It didn't matter what Sid thought, Chase had to know, if just to move on. There had to be no contingencies or anything to ever tie him to Heather again. Because if what Sid told him was true and the tape was indeed authentic, then the only way to free this guilt would be to get tested once and for all, which was exactly what Chase had done.

God, the humiliation and contempt he had to put aside just to free his guilty conscience had all been so embarrassing for him. It was as if the only way he could be with Carly was to amend what he'd done to

Heather, turning the tables on her to what she supposedly had done to him. The awkward, distressing blame he'd put on himself drowned in this predicament and it had all been self-inflicted.

He heard his name being called as he headed through the doorway to the examining rooms of the fertility clinic, the beats of his heart subtly fraying from his existence, pulling on the outcome that so much had been resting on. His nerves of steel suddenly collapsed, replaced with the heartaches of the truth that waited. The walls, the ceiling, even the door closed behind him and echoed his fate, sounding the forbidden even though he had to hear it. True, it had only been a few days since Chase was here last and the humiliating circumstances of that visit alone made him hate this place. What he had to do in the back room of the clinic, the provocative DVD's and sex magazines all supposedly to get him in the mood, left him with no doubt that he'd sunk to his lowest level.

Worse perhaps was the embarrassing moment when the nurse had examined him. After all, he was a man and she was quite attractive, but the pencil she had placed in her ear Chase could never have assumed would become a weapon.

"Well Mr. Bishop." Said the same nurse that had stayed with him in his room. "Are we over our little episode we had the other day?" she asked as she took his pulse.

"I don't think I'll ever get over that." Chase answered, still angry and embarrassed that all he could do was stare at that pencil. "But at least I'm not wearing a hospital gown this time. I won't be such an easy target." He said with humor, trying to play off his humility.

"Don't worry Mr. Bishop." She smiled. "Men have no control

over that, it's a natural reaction. Yours isn't the first erection my pencil had to swat down, and I can assure you," she glanced up. "It won't be the last."

The moment she reminded him, he could feel it all over again, clinching his knees together from the pain he had felt. It played like a movie in slow motion. Feeling his erection rise when she touched his inner thigh and her immediate reaction when he watched her grab that bright, yellow pencil. Like a warning flag, she swung it like a home run slugger with a hammer as she struck the head of his penis causing it to collapse like a wet noodle.

"Well," Chase grimaced. "You don't have to worry about me. I don't think my boy will ever salute you again." His charm, once again, tried to diminish the entire awkward matter.

He watched her leave, giving him a smile and it came apparent to Chase that she actually enjoyed it. However, he couldn't think about that now, he had to concentrate on why he was here. As he waited, what crowded into his every thought and what blanketed his soul, was that he would finally know the truth and he could accept what God and his fate had left him with. He knew that too many lives now depended on the outcome.

Chase didn't have too much time to think. Though, what raced through his head made him fear the worst. He had blamed himself for having to come to this point, and for the first time in his life Chase didn't care about his manhood, the arbitrary standard that kept him from being a father. What he thought would make him feel complete had now made him panic. For what he'd feared his entire life was the fact that he could never sire a child. Now what he'd hoped for was just to soothe his tarnished regret. To never have to tell Carly about any of this or to be sterile and accept it as fate, would mean to exile Heather to a faraway land, just like in a fairy tale, though it couldn't be more real.

He tried to remain calm as he heard a knock on the door. A man who built his reputation on intimidation and confidence, now came to claim him with desperation. Every scenario crossed before his eyes and every shameful act stood as his own aggression. Eyes that harbored fate, held sheer determination, brought him the strength and the will to listen to the doctor.

Their eyes met immediately as he entered the room. He was an older gentleman, perhaps reaching fifty, white and confident with his suit showing under his lab coat. He was cleanly dressed and shaven with not a hair out of place, holding an assurance in his face that conformed strictly from his demeanor. Everything needed to feel secure and trusting, and Chase could only assume it came from his years of being a fertility doctor. The couples that came here were just as desperate as he was, but their ironic differences twisted to the duplicities that made it so wrong for what he wanted to hear.

"Mr. Bishop." He held out his free hand as he stepped over to Chase. The only thing Chase saw was the file he held.

"Doctor Dudik." More irony came as Chase said his name, rising to greet him and whatever awaited him now. "Are those the results?" Chase's eyes gestured towards the folder.

"Just your chart, Mr. Bishop." The doctor could feel his stress, like so many others before him, torn from desperate afflictions. "Your fertility results should be in the system. Excuse me," he said as he stepped around Chase. His casual, prominent strides now came to a rest as he took a seat in front of his computer screen, clicking on the mouse and pulling at Chase's nerves, coming to the conclusion and any aftermath that remained. "Here it is now."

"And?" Chase's anxieties pulled at him.

"Perhaps you should take a seat." The doctor's hand gestured towards the chair beside him. "You say you had an accident when you were a teenager?"

"Yeah." Chase hated repeating it.

"You were cut directly on the scrotum itself?"

"More like punctured," Chase nodded.

"Well, you *are* fertile, but not in the aspects I'm sure you're thinking." His eyes looked over, bringing no conclusions at all. Nothing to relieve the circumstance that has him here to begin with.

"What?" Chase squinted, giving him not a hint of reconciliation at all. "I'm not quite following you here, doc. Can my boys swim or can't they?"

"It's not that they can't swim," the doctor met Chase's intellect. "It's more like the pool has been drained. You're definitely able to sire a child, but the chance of that occurring without some help seems highly unlikely."

"What do you mean by help?"

"I believe the reason for your low sperm count is in direct correlation to your accident." Though, when seeing Chase's confusion, he once again spoke in layman's terms. "I think you have scar tissue damage that's blocking the flow. Luckily, I can repair the damage with light surgery. It's not one hundred percent guaranteed to correct the problem, but if it's what I think, the odds are in your favor. Of course, the only way to know for certain is to probe a scope inside the scrotum sack itself and take a look."

What's the use? Chase had thought, confined to this prison once again. There was just no end if he couldn't even have a beginning and there's nothing to continue if it stopped him from even starting. It took every bit of his strength to be here, left with what he heard, to conceive just what it meant, held him to believe it would always be there to haunt him. For a man who stuck with the odds it defied him once again knowing that anything was possible. With the fate of Sydney's friend request and everything it restored, he could see it no other way. Life was full of compromise, hidden and obscure and to seek and rise above it left even the strongest vulnerable to failure.

As he stood up and thanked the doctor for his time, Chase realized he had no answers. He had no other choice but to listen to the tape and hear it come directly from Heather. As painful as it would be, the only way to believe that she had been this monster and he'd been so stupid was to finally hear it for himself. There was nothing to confirm one-hundred percent that he couldn't sire a child. If he was looking to clear his guilt and live with what he'd done, then he'd failed once again and it would forever be there to question. Of course, if 'forever' had a place to confine him in this predicament, then 'forever' in his mind, should only last for nine months.

Could he hold out that long and confirm that Heather was indeed lying? Or, would he deny his shame and always keep it from Carly? Whatever the decision, the test was now before him and everything in him said Heather was indeed a bitch.

He had an entire crew of locksmiths from his company's residential division change all the locks on the doors at his estate in Phoenix. With Heather's constant phone calls that he refused to take, he felt it was only a matter of time before she stalked him to reconcile and right now she was the last person he wanted to talk to. For a man who needed to dance in the rain, the storm that was passing through had left him stumbling to the waltz.

He was glad he took Heather off the approved guest list, she would never get past the guarded security gates at Costa de Oro, so he felt relieved in knowing that his home would be secure while he was away. It was hard, because at one time he did actually care for Heather. But, if what she'd done to him was true, absolutely and unequivocally true, then Heather deserved what she got and that had meant cutting her off completely. At least for a while, until he knew for certain that she was, or never was, carrying his child. Besides, with the new stipulations in the contract it appeared, at least over the next two years, that he'd be spending most of his time in San Francisco. Montoya demanded that he be the on the job supervisor, throughout the project and even assumed extras in trade for a Master Builders multi-million dollar cost over-run.

Chase didn't mind, at least he got the contract with no legal battle. The new stipulations were sure to cut into their profits quite a bit. Yet, in the end, they were set to take in over forty-five million dollars. The fact of that alone and the publicity that was due to come out left him with no doubt that he had to tell Carly about his wealth.

***

Chase had been gone for only a week before he returned to San Francisco. He was glad to be back, because Heather wouldn't quit hounding him. He avoided her phone calls and most of her texts, and he still met her reluctance about taking back the ring. He warned her in one text he would report it stolen and if she didn't want to be arrested she had better take it back.

In his absence, he took the initiative to make sure the photo studio had mailed out Carly's present before he'd left. The one single endearment to secure what they'd shared and their weekend to remember that expanded all their possibilities. The smile it was sure to bring to her and the joy that would find her when she opened the package, would confirm once and for all that Chase has always loved her.

He no longer kept in touch with Carly on Facebook. It became their common practice to text and talk on the phone. Since he'd been back he hadn't been able to spend much time with her, the main fact considering what he was going to do and waiting for his fertility results to come clean if he had to. He loved Carly and wanted to spend the rest of his life with her, making all the preparations to ask her the one question that he hoped her answer would secure for eternity.

He now found Facebook intriguing and also addicting, catching up with old friends he hadn't seen in over a decade. With new requests coming in all the time, Chase had started to send some himself, he felt completely comfortable with the system and was glad he never accepted Heather or their relationship status on his profile. In the back of his mind though, the hidden conceptions remained that Heather could always message Carly if she wanted to.

It was something he had to accept and there would be consequences if she did. He still had the incriminating tape back at the Hyatt where he'd been staying and planned to finally listen to it when he returned that night. Though, if hearing it was what stood to unequivocally release him, then Chase was determined to finally see it through, live with his conscience and deny Heather's deceit. It would mean another night without Carly and he was still susceptible to the guilt that remained. He had told her the company placed him at a Holiday Inn in San Rafael, at least until he could find a suitable apartment.

Sure, Carly wanted to see him and Caleb asked about him all the time, but Chase always made the excuse about his long hours, never confiding in her that he actually owned the company. Everything had been riding on today and the fertility test confirmed what he hoped would give him the courage he needed to ask the ultimate question and to purchase the ring to seal their fate, but instead it left him more confused than ever.

He thought about her as he started up his new Escalade, one of many toys he'd kept from her. He had been here in San Francisco to remodel their new office with most of the work already underway. After all, Chase had an appearance that was in direct correlation to how his company was perceived and as far as his business competence, he would never lose sight of that.

Chase's sudden change in demeanor came as an unexpected surprise to Sydney. He was stunned at how empathetic Chase had become toward his fellow man, at least when it wasn't Sydney he was looking at. But what surprised him most was the new foreman Chase had hired and the truck he'd given him. This was way off Chase's usual pace for people who had earned those positions, but when Sydney objected, Chase didn't want to hear it and just called it a 'leap of faith'. Even though Chase was still mad at Sid for what he did the brothers had always found a way to forgive. Chase took the incentive to pay the deductible and the ticket on probably one of his most outlandish paybacks yet. If just to smooth things over, knowing the two were now even.

Carly had been busy herself lately and even though she never let on about Chase's new situation, Chase could sense insecurity in her tone whenever she hinted at seeing him. Though, to her credit, she never held it against him, never demanded or seemed accusatory one way or the other. Whatever was troubling him, Carly had been prepared. She would wait, if only for the chance to be with him always.

Chase was still worried about her having to work where she did, another reason of many to finally tell her about whom and what he really has. After everything was over and finally out in the open, he had hoped he could get her to come to work for him. They needed an administrator in the office. The pay was good and the position carried full benefits. Though, he'd hoped to keep it in the family, make her a part of all of this and plan for a future for the three of them.

She'd been telling him about her job and how she'd been suddenly moved up the ladder to a new position, holding it all on account of Chase and the fear he must've brought Andrew. She was currently in charge of weeding through applicants with Andrew to prep for interviews for a recent job opening. Of course Chase had seen it as strictly an opportunity. The very fact that she had to work for a man that used his position to manipulate woman made Andrew susceptible to his own weakness, so Chase had devised a plan.

His office wasn't in the best of neighborhoods and from working there recently he got to know the community. The route from his hotel took him through some unsavory streets where he could see the prostitutes of all kinds, men, women, transgender as well as the drag queens of Polk Street. One in particular that always tried to wave him down.

What Chase had done on that morning set an entire new standard for what the Drag Queen Miss Margaret had been asked to do in the past. Chase thought he actually looked attractive with long legs and a pretty face and if one didn't know any better, you'd swear he was a beautiful woman. An easy portrayal to someone like Andrew and Chase had no doubt he would definitely try to seduce her. Of course, the only thing he'd told Carly was to send her right to Andrew. It was up to Carly to determine what she saw and did after that.

She had agreed of course, knowing nothing about Chase's vindication for her. She found it a bit odd that he was being so evasive, but Carly took his word and promised to send her through. If jealously stood in her way to exactly who this woman was, then it all justified the moment Carly sat down to interview Miss Margaret.

***

Is that an Adam's apple? Carly noticed right away. Miss Margaret's obvious wig, fake eye lashes and nails assembled this tall, slender girl's body whose attire didn't really fit her. She wore all the wrong clothes and exposed all the wrong cleavage. For someone who wanted to work in an office, she was more set to appear at a burlesque show performance. It left Carly with no doubt about what Chase had been up to and it was also obvious this was the type of girl Andrew would go after. Whether it was to relieve the pressure on her or set Andrew up for harassment, what had begun to unravel before her appeared to be much more sinister.

"So, Miss…" Carly waited to hear her name.

"Oh, honey, you can call me, Miss Margaret." Her tone became rather alluring. "That's what I go by, during working hours that is."

"Ok," Carly hesitated, trying to comprehend what she just heard. "How long have you known Mr. Bishop?" Carly had been dying to ask.

"*Who?*" Miss Margaret replies in a voice far from elegant, trapped in a body that just didn't fit.

"*Chase Bishop,*" Carly leered. "Your reference."

"Ohhh, *Chase.*" She gestured with her hands, folding both of her palms down exposing her somewhat manly knuckles. Her dark skin was no help with the make-up she used, but still she held an attraction that Carly now tried to define.

"You know honey, I wouldn't put too much effort in all of this. *I know what to do.*" She held her hand across her chest, not even playing along, just strictly here on business. "Now," her voice suddenly changed to a deep, hard growl. If there was a frog in her throat, then it had to be a bullfrog, because there was no way that sound would come out of a girl. "Just tell me who he is, I'll take care of the rest." He barked once again. No more disguising or pretentious extravagance. If

Carly had wanted revenge, then now was her chance to get it.

"Yeah," Carly nodded a subtle acceptance. Her eyes opened wider as she began to lift a smile, a curved lustrous smile that bent to this awakening that just exploded in her head. Intrigue and astonishment mixed with bold apprehensions, conceived the inevitable as she showed Miss Margaret to Andrews's office.

Miss Margaret followed along, seductive and swaying, which resulted in Carly noticing that every set of eyes in the office had now looked over their cubicles. Steady stares and provocative comments, sneered and whispered as they headed to the back. With each step Carly took her smile grew wider. *How did Chase come up with this? What was she doing going along with it?* All had met her caution as they stepped up to Pam's desk located just outside of Andrew's office.

"I have Andrew's next interview, Pam." Carly held her timid and elusive thoughts as she tried to shield Miss Margaret from her view.

"Oh." Pam looked up, never even noticing Miss Margaret behind her. "I don't have anyone scheduled right now." She looks back to her monitor and opens up his appointments. "No, no one."

"Well," Carly cautioned, if only to persuade Pam. "I don't think she'll be able to reschedule. Is there any way you can squeeze her in now?"

"Who?" Pam now noticed the evasiveness in her tone.

"Margaret," Carly answered as she slowly moved out of the way.

"That's, *Miss* Margaret." She peeked her head out as she said it, as if emphasizing the word as well as herself to exactly what and who she really was.

"Oh." Pam could sense something right away. "I didn't see you back there." She then suddenly refocused to this woman standing so provocatively before her. "Can I see your credentials?"

"My…" she stumbled, taking it completely wrong. "Well, nobody's ever called it that before, but my boy's still *hangin'* around." She winked, and then gestures down below to where her hand rested on her crotch.

"Oh," Pam hesitated for a moment. *"OH!"* It suddenly hit her. "What is this, Carly?" Not believing, her eyes questioning her thoughts.

"It's an interview." Carly sways her eyes, leaving them both innocent to whatever happened next.

"An interview?" She stared at Carly, meeting the vengeance that came to stare back. She and Carly had been at odds ever since Andrew had her alone in his office and now with her new promotion Pam had assumed Carly was playing along. Why else did she suddenly turn on her and act like she was avoiding her if she hadn't been corrupted by Andrew? Sure, Pam had been fighting him off and he'd become even more persistent, but this…here and now? Was this actually what she was thinking, could this be Carly's revenge? Every nerve within her decided Andrew's fate. If vengeance had a partner than Pam was all in.

"It's just an interview, Pam." Carly curved her brows, coaxing with every gesture as she waited for Pam's approval.

"An interview, *right,*" She nodded as a devious, corrupted smile pulled across her face, bending to all her thoughts. As her finger reached down to press the intercom for Andrew's office, the expectations that awaited left a hallowed chill in her bones. "Your next appointment's here Andrew." She looked back up to Carly.

They both kept their smiles as seconds foretold his fate,

harnessing their own discoveries to what this would mean to so many women that worked here. The payback, the sheer, undeniable revenge to take place, instilled who had the power and in this one single, blissful moment what came as opportunity would bring Andrew's demise.

"You said my day was clear," he barked back through the speaker. "Appointment for what?"

"The position you listed," Pam said while she tried to keep from laughing. "It's your next interview. A Miss Margaret."

"Miss?" he answered immediately, catching his full interest. "As in *single*, Miss Margaret?" And when Andrew heard silence, he questioned again, "*Well?*"

"Shall I send her in, Andrew?" Pam looked back to Carly as a gratifying fulfillment met both of their eyes.

"No, wait!" She heard some shuffling in the background and before she could say anything else, his office door swung open.

"Andrew," He startled Carly, though she tried to keep it professional. "This is Miss Margaret." Stepping out of the way, she saw his eyes immediately light up as Miss Margaret came into his view.

"Margaret." His lips pulled alluringly. "So nice to get to know you. Thanks for coming in." He ignored everyone else around him.

"That's *Miss* Margaret sweetie," her tone was tempting and alluring. "And I can see by the looks of *you*, I've come to the right place."

"Indeed, you have," His tone was even more inviting, swelling to all his pretensions as he took her arm into his. If Andrew was looking for excitement, then the moment he laid eyes on Miss Margaret the excitement showed in his pants. His erection reflected his appetite as he led her into his office, his head peeping out through the closing door, making sure no one would come to disrupt them. "No calls. Pam. I don't want to be disturbed, *at all*. Oh, and thanks, Carly. You can go now." His final words before closing the door behind him ignited laughter the moment he had disappeared.

It was just so crazy, so wonderfully crazy that Carly had to hug Pam right then and there. They both started laughing and carrying on so loud that anyone within range had begun to take notice. They just couldn't help it. It was way too funny. The anticipation alone made them race to his door, gluing their ears to the panels while trying to listen in and with each second that passed more and more colleagues took notice. One turned into three, three to six and before the each of them had realized, practically everyone was outside Andrew's door.

"What's goin' on? Who's he with? Was that really a woman?" All echoed the questions that their laughter drowned out. If it's Andrew's time to finally get caught and to expose himself for what and who he truly was, then let no doubt come to influence what was taking place in his office. Lust of the forbidden, saliva exchanging fate, protrude to a label that now shall always precede him. If there was ever a fitting end to the humility that had found him, then what's happening behind his closed door opened the pages to his epilog that awaits.

***

Oh, *Miss Margaret,"* breaths of seduction escaped his lips. Howls of ecstasy anticipate her body and as the moisture from her tongue still seethed into his pallet, Andrew leaned in to have another taste. "You're going to go far here…I have plans for you." His lips pressed again as her thick, swollen tongue reached down his throat.

"I have plans myself," she stressed her seduction as their tongues untwisted. "You big, strong, hunk of man, you." Her enticing breath came in rapid gasps as Andrew felt her hand reach down to his crotch. Her robust, wide fingers gripped firmly around his penis. Stroking and rubbing as pleasure took over Andrew's senses, pouring through his eyes and melting on his face.

He had no idea what he was about to enter, because what he presumed as natural actually held an entirely different concept. He never realized that what they were about to share was anatomical. The only thing Andrew could perceive was the sheer passion that had found him. She was so easy and willing that there was no doubt he could definitely have her right here and now.

He grabbed her free hand and placed it on his belt line and as Miss Margaret took over, he leaned back against his desk. His arms braced him as he heard his zipper go down and felt his pants drop to his knees. This filled all his expectations as Miss Margaret dropped to hers.

Pleasure and lust burst into pure splendor. Excitement and ecstasy came with each stroke of her hands. Like a true professional, Miss Margaret knew what to do and before Andrew knew it, he could feel her mouth around the head of his penis sliding a condom down his full erection with her lips.

Her throat had found him now and with every deep lasting swallow, what exposed Andrew in the moment had now come to find him. As his hands grabbed her head, guiding with each stroke, Miss

Margaret suddenly stopped.

"Oh please, sweetie," her voice a bit low and harsh. Andrew considered the moment, but just excused it. "I know what I'm doing by now," her voice soothed back. "I mean if anyone should know what a man likes, *I should*." And Miss Margaret went back to work.

He just couldn't take it, he wanted so much more. She looked so sweet and erotic he had to taste her sugar down below. No longer could he resist what his tongue begged for and as Miss Margaret stood, he placed her bottom where he had been leaning.

"It's my turn, baby." He began to pull down her skirt as her long, muscled legs pushed and lifted up her buttocks helping him to ease it off her hips.

"Safe sex, sweetie," Miss Margaret suddenly stopped him. "There's a condom in my purse."

"I'm already wearing one." Andrew's blind lust drove him even deeper.

"Not for you, sweetie, for me," Miss Margaret said as he fully exposed her bare bottom. Her skirt and underwear flew over his shoulder, but he hadn't comprehended what she had said. In the mind of the closed and the weak and shameful, what came to stare him back, there could be no mistaking.

Was that a penis? His eyes focused more. *IT'S A PENIS!* Awoken by his disgust, he stood shocked with fear. "Oh, *my God!*" Cries had come from his lips as shame consumed his eyes, pouring through every awakening that had come to find him now. "Who the hell—we—they—what?"

"I don't mind if someone joins us, Sweetie," her soothing tone came softly at first, then faded into a growl. "However, that's going to cost extra."

Just the word alone echoed in treason. As his panic took over, he quickly buckled up his pants, scouring around to gargle with anything he could find, wiping off his tongue and the inside of his mouth, as if using his sleeve like sand paper in the hopes of grinding off his disgust and any trace of Miss Margaret. Revenge, a cold incentive began to sink in. *Those bitches* taunted his thoughts and corrupted all of his blame. Though, if there was any horror in exposing what they've done to him, then Andrew was staring at it now. Knowing that what just happened, he made the commitment that these events would have to be taken to his grave.

"Get the hell outta here!" he exploded from all that was grotesque. "You sick th—thing!" He stuttered, unable to find the words. "Oh my God...*oh my God oh my God, oh my God!*" Panic and horror met chaos and concern.

"Well, this was a wash out. You had me all excited." Miss Margaret stood up as everything else hung down.

"Uhg!" Andrew almost vomited. "Just get out! Uhg!" His shoulders rose up, consuming his entire neck. "Get the fuck outta here, now!" He threw her clothes. "And don't tell *anyone* about this. Oh my God!"

"God has nothing to do with this, sweetie." She put on her skirt then added, "And if you're thinkin' of layin' one hand on *me*," She leaned in, leering over Andrew with a threatening look in her eyes and a foreboding tone as his voice came hard, deep and offensive, conveying just who was exactly is in control. "I'll kick the shit outta you."

The last thing she shouted as she collected her thoughts was, "Well, that was interesting." Her voice retreated back to its soft, tender feature. "Don't bother, sweetie, I'll let myself out." As she headed towards the door she tossed her fake hair across her shoulder as if mocking Andrew. Every ear listening, every laughter waiting, all came out in the open as she opened the door.

An entire group of people were pressed up against the door and when it swung open the sheer force alone sent them all crashing into his office.

"It appears we had an audience, sweetie." Miss Margaret looked back to Andrew as her high heels stepped over Pam and Carly, dodging the rest. It was up to Andrew to explain it now.

"Oh, very funny you two." Andrew stood there disgusted as they all rose trying to refrain from their laughter, though in moments like these, it only takes one comment to incite a hilarious riot.

"What's wrong Andrew, didn't expect frank and beans for lunch?" A random remark flies.

"Yeah, literally Frank, huh, Andrew?" Another follows.

They all started laughing uncontrollably and merciless. If there was ever a time for Andrew to find a new career, it would have to be as a magician because he quickly disappeared.

Oh, Chase, Carly had thought, *this was the best one yet.* If Carly was looking for this day to end, it would be just so she could tell Chase what this gesture had meant to her, what *he* meant to her, giving herself to him fully and to find out what was really holding him back. If not for her, then for the sake of her son because she knew how much

Chase had come to mean to them. The encouragement and strength, and the confidence that Caleb had suddenly gained lifted to the prayer that Chase had answered.

It all came from Chase with his wit and his care, seeing Caleb as normal and treating him as an equal. If there was ever a time for Carly to believe that her and Chase were meant to be together, just knowing the independence that Caleb had now found restored her self-assurance as if he'd always been capable.

CHAPTER EIGHTEEN

For months it had been all over the news broadcasts and in television commercials on every channel. The U.S. government was undergoing a new census, which meant there would be a door-to-door approach to confirm who lived where.

Carly thought she considered every caution knowing Caleb would be home alone, going over every possible scenario that crossed her weary head. She felt secure knowing that at least her next-door neighbor Rogine was there to check on him until she could get home.

Her neighborhood started to come alive at this time of the day, with school busses filled with kids and mail carriers in route. Service vehicle's and stay at home housewives flourished in a surrounding where practically everything went unnoticed and today was no exception.

His tiny, awkward legs carried him down the sidewalk. A short distance for many, though to a man of his proportion, conforming in unity to that of an elementary child, and the lengths in which he traveled, at times, made it the equivalent of crossing the Sahara Desert. His tousled, red hair and matching, full grown beard met a wrinkled face leaving no doubt that he was a fully mature man. However, to an adolescent mind animation distorts reality.

After all, who would ever suspect a circumstance like this? In all the crazy thoughts ever conceived in Carly's head, the Census Bureau was the last thing to ever cross her worries. Certainly no one like this ever came to her door, and even though she and Caleb went over every possibility that would ever come to question, what knocked now meant more training would be needed.

Caleb knew he wasn't supposed to answer the door to anyone except for the only one he could trust, which was Rogine from next door. Usually she was home and didn't mind checking on him, but of course on days such as this nothing was certain. He knew what to do if someone tried to break in, but this? There was nothing in place to explain what he saw and Caleb's instant joy and delight came the moment he looked through the peep hole.

Caleb immediately swung the front door open. "You are in my cartoon!" He looked back to see the television screen and as his excitement mounted he turned to the small man. "They said you are a leprechaun! But, how did you get out here? How come you dressed like *that?*" intrigue and fantasy sounded from his voice as he immediately concluded what he saw.

"Is one of your parent's home, kid?" His deep, frog-like voice overshadowed a body that didn't match, as small beads of sweat rolled off his forehead. He'd been walking for hours and it was obvious he was tired. Nobody was answering their doors and he needed to take a break. His pants were getting soaked from the spray of lawn sprinklers and worse off perhaps was his small, inadequate bladder that was ready to explode. He needed to relieve himself and with every empty knock, he was just glad that *this* door had finally opened.

"Why, did my mom send you?" Caleb's innocence flared as he was once again completely overwhelmed by what he was looking at.

"No, kid," the little man shook his head. "Uncle Sam did. I'm with the Census Bureau, your mom or dad home?" He noticed Caleb's disposition and tried to look past him but Caleb stayed in his view.

"I have an Uncle Sam?" Caleb's surprise led him to more confusion. "My mom never told me I have a uncle. Is that why you are here? Because my Uncle Sam wants to see me?"

"What?" His eyes squinted down as a hard frustrated crease formed across his brow. He thought to himself, *'great'* having been under these circumstances before. It was obvious who he was talking to, noticing Caleb's mental state right away. "No, kid," he said, shaking his head again. "That's just a saying. Let me talk to your dad, if your mom's not home."

"My, dad?" Caleb looked to him trying to figure this out, his slow mind coming to only one conclusion. "His name is Ross. He is mean and makes buildings. Oh, I know!" His excitement suddenly exploded. "Is that why you are here? To tell me Chase was going to be my new dad?"

"Look, kid...." He bowed his head, actually wanting to cry. "I don't know anything about that. I just need to know who lives here." His knees began to buckle, not sure how much longer he could hold it.

"Me and my mom do. She lets me come home before she does. That's good, huh?" Caleb kept staring down, believing what he sees and trying to comprehend just what it really meant.

"It sure is, kid." His humbling uncertainties confused him more. "I'll just have to come back." He began a slight dance, trying with everything he had to hold back the pressure. "But, for now, ya gotta help me out, kid, 'cause if I don't use your porcelain throne, I'm gonna have an accident right here on your porch."

"My porcelain throne!" Caleb's eyes opened wider. "I have a porcelain throne?" His excitement carried him to a fantasy that now seemed more real than ever. "Is that why you are here? Because *we're* under the rainbow?" His excitement took over completely as his arm lifted up, pointing like a bird dog to a small, colored spectrum fading in and out of the sprinklers.

"Oh *man*." He realized immediately. This wasn't the first time and he knew it certainly wouldn't be the last. "Yeah right kid. I'm here for the pot of gold."

"I knew you were the leprechaun in my cartoon!" Caleb jumps with joy. "You just had to dress like that so no one would know who you are, huh?"

"Sure, kid, sure." His frown met disbelief.

"Do I get to help you find the pot of gold?" Fantasy and coincidence mixed with Caleb's delight.

"Whatever makes you happy, kid." Grunts replaced his tone as this tiny, restless gentleman danced even stronger. The inside of his thighs began to tense up as he tried with all his might not to relieve himself in his pants. "You can believe whatever and call me anything you want. Just, right now, I'm beggin' you kid, you gotta let me use your bathroom."

"Sure," Caleb said and immediately let him in. His smile opened as wide as his strides, and led the humiliated man to an even worse fate than he'd thought.

***

The afternoon had been pressing, and with what had happened earlier, Carly found herself spending the rest of her day explaining to upper management exactly what had happened. As far as she was concerned, she was just simply setting up an interview anything else that followed was strictly Andrew's doing. She'd been so busy with her and Pam calculating their story that she was a little late with her usual call-in to check up on Caleb. For a mother who'd always curved her incentives on the security of her son it helped ease her worries knowing that Caleb had been doing fine while he was alone.

It became so routine that she stopped second guessing her own insecurities. The confidence Chase had restored in the both of them only proved the point that Caleb had been ready for this. But what Carly was hearing now made no sense at all.

"What do you mean, you're feeding Skittles to the leprechaun?" Confusion met her brows, pulling her thoughts toward what Caleb was saying.

"Yeah, mom, that was because they are the same color as the rainbow." His excitement kept flaring, living in the fantasies that kids played on.

"Oh," Carly shared. "Skittles, huh? Rainbows and leprechauns, I get it."

"Yes Mom, and we're under the rainbow and the pot of gold was under the porcelain throne. That's why I'm feeding skittles to the leprechaun under the door." His excitement still blazed.

"You're doing what?" She gave a chuckle, not sure what he was saying now. The only thing that she could assume was that he was playing a game. Though, with a child like Caleb, nothing was certain and the more Carly thought about it, the more her inner voice told her something wasn't right.

"I'm feeding skittles to the leprechaun, mom. Red, green, yellow, orange, blue, just like the rainbow."

"OK, Caleb that's good." Carly questioned her own judgment. "So, you're just playing, right? There's no one else there with you?"

"Ah huh, mom, just me and the leprechaun."

Slightly muffled, Carly heard a noise in the background. As her nerves began to panic, her next course of action would be to decide if it was real.

"Do you have the T.V. on, Caleb?"

"I do, mom. I was watching cartoons when the leprechaun followed the rainbow."

"I see," she said, feeling more relieved. "Has Rogine come to check on you?"

"No, mom, just the leprechaun."

"*Caleb!*" Her frustrations rose again. "Will you stop with the leprechaun? This is important. I wanna know you're okay."

"I'm okay, mom. Now can I go feed the leprechaun more Skittles?"

"Yeah, Caleb," Her thoughts were clouded. "I'll have Rogine come over and see how you're doing, okay?"

"Okay, mom, bye."

He said nothing more as Carly listened to the dial tone. She was always worried about Caleb, trying to curb her emotions when it came to him. Yet, no matter how well he was doing, the plain fact remained that he was easily susceptible to confuse reality. Sure, he was only home alone just under an hour, but the time he spent alone was all Carly could think about. Where was he getting this, leprechauns and rainbows, a pot of gold and porcelain thrones? What could possibly be going on over there? There's no plausible way she could leave work now, not with everything that had happened today.

Each time she tried calling Rogine it went directly to her voicemail and after the third try the only thing she could think of doing was to call Chase and see if he would go check on Caleb, hoping in the end that her only humility would come from being a worried mother. She'd confused such situations before and to be absolutely certain of what Caleb meant, you had to be there just to decipher it for yourself.

***

Chase was on his way back to his office by the time Carly called. He was confident of his new foreman, Hector to handle things until he showed up. He had already notified the local laborer's union to send out some available workers earlier in the week. The unions were much different in San Francisco and Chase had to abide by their strict rules. In Phoenix his labor contracts permitted him to hire any union member he wanted but here in California, if you want to hire new employees that weren't supervisors you had to call that union rep and they would send out workers who were usually next in line on the available hire list.

Chase didn't like not having the power to interview, but the work was already underway and he could never have known that Caleb's father Ross belonged to the same union. He hadn't even met the new workers he hired and all of their paper work was sent directly to their Phoenix office. He had Hector handling the work for him, and he was more than confident in his ability. From the moment Carly dropped him off to get his damaged truck after the Cheer for Hope Center's opening, the confidence Hector restored in Chase left him with no doubt that he could trust Hector from here on out.

He was kind of a handyman and the first thing Chase noticed when he returned was that Hector took his advice and filled the pothole he'd tripped over. He had his truck fixed when he said he would and even painted it to match. But most of all, what met Chase's trusting perception was when Hector found his wallet lying underneath his truck. The only thing Chase could figure was that it must've fallen out from the inside pocket of his jacket when he fell. But when he'd opened it and noticed nothing was missing, Chase offered Hector a job as his lead foreman, instating him in the union and giving him a truck like all of the other supervisor's get.

Chase was surprisingly close to Milpitas when Carly called. His expectations about Miss Margaret had been strictly overridden from her worries about Caleb. Chase didn't mind, in fact he liked playing the hero and wanted to see Caleb again. If anything would come out of this day, what he now planned for tonight would provide all his incentives to be truthful from here on out. He knew it was time to quit living in this lie and tell her about his company and his wealth, knowing that Carly, has and always will, accept him for who he truly was. Everything else precluded that, and if this were his chance to come clean Chase would take it and explain to her just exactly what she meant to him.

Chase could only assume, like before, that Carly was worried over nothing when she asked him to check on Caleb. But, still in a surrounding he was unfamiliar with; he was always a man of precaution taking the incentive to come in unannounced. Carly had a key hidden on the porch and as Chase opened the door, what met his eyes in that moment left a lot to be explained.

"*Caleb,*" He said as he stepped inside, his head tilting as he saw Caleb sitting with his legs crossed in front of the bathroom door. "What are you doing, buddy?" Closing the door behind him and noticing Caleb taking Skittles and shoving them under the crack.

"Hi, Chase!" He immediately jumped up and went running over.

"What are you doing, buddy?" They meet with a big hug. "How come you're sitting there like that?"

"I'm feeding the leprechaun Skittles."

"You're what?" Chase chuckles. "But, then…"

"I'm a regular person, damn it!" An unknown voice—a man's voice——came from the obviously locked bathroom.

"Hello?" He walked over as Caleb followed along. "Who's in there?"

"Leroy Stoutmire."

"*Who?*" Chase asked, trying to figure out why he was even there.

"I'm with the Census Bureau. I just wanted to use the bathroom."

Oh shit, Chase thought, clearly understanding now. "Sorry man this lock's broken."

"*Ya' think?*" His sarcasm called out the obvious.

"You see, Chase," Caleb's excitement exposed his confusion. "He is Leroy the Leprechaun, and we are looking for the pot of gold under the porcelain throne!"

"Oh, for Pete's sake kid," Leroy's frustrations were more than apparent, "Enough already! Between you, that leprechaun crap and those goddamn Skittles…I just wanna get outta here, man. Whatttaya say, huh? Can ya help me out?"

"You should not say that word, Leroy the Leprechaun," Caleb burst out, "The other leprechauns will get mad."

"Goddam it, kid, I'm *warnin'* you!"

"Ooooh." Caleb hid behind Chase.

"Hey, easy there, Mister!" Chase immediately defended. "I have half a mind to call the cops. You should've used better judgment when you met Caleb." Knowing perfectly well the man knew what he meant.

"Hey, it was either that or piss on your porch. Will ya just get me outta here, *please?*" he pled.

As Chase pried the lock open, everything became clear. This small, awkward looking gentleman with red hair and a beard, captivated the adolescence that anyone like Caleb could misconceive.

Chase couldn't help but laugh as this small gentleman stormed out and down the hall, listening to Caleb cry, "What about the gold, Leroy the Leprechaun?" with every step that took him outside.

Chase couldn't believe it as he hugged Caleb right then and there. If innocence had a foundation, then Chase had found his. In all his thoughts of what he had just witnessed, what he felt in his heart was just how wonderful Caleb was. He'd never heard or seen anything quite like this, if this was a sign that he'd always wanted to be here then it all started with Carly as he pulled out his phone.

***

"You've gotta be kidding me?" Carly burst out with laughter. *Oh my God.* You must've been laughing your head off. I have no idea what I would've done."

With Caleb inside watching cartoons, Chase smiled as he stood outside on Carly's porch, thinking about what he'd say and how he'd confess; the only thing that crossed his mind was to actually show her and explain the confusion that started it all in the first place.

"I need to see you," his amorous tone confided.

"That would be wonderful." An instant relief now soothed into her soul. She wanted to see him so badly lately that it was all she could think of. "Just tell me when and where."

"Right now."

"Now? That might be kinda hard, I mean, considering the Miss Margaret stunt today. I have to see if I still have a job," she said with no remorse and only humor in her tone. "You're terrible," She laughed. "That story's gonna be a legend in this place from now on."

"I certainly didn't mean to get you into any trouble, Carly." Chase was glad she took it so well; however, under the circumstances he wasn't sure how she'd react. "No matter what happens with your job, I can assure you you're going to have plenty of options from here on out."

"Well...thanks." she responded, not exactly sure what he meant.

"In fact, that's one of the reasons I want to see you. I need to show you something when you get off work. Do you think you can meet me and Caleb at my new office in Montoya's district?"

"Caleb?" she questioned, gathering her curiosity. Obviously with a man like Chase, nothing could surprise her now.

"Yeah," Chase explained. "He's a part of this too." His tone carried the relevance of what he needed to confess, hidden in his own guilt for not coming clean in the first place. Money could never change someone like Carly. But Chase hoped that if anything came out of this day it would be for her to see him for who he truly was and know that he's the same man she'd fallen in love with.

"A part of what, Chase?" Carly's thoughts bent to his vagueness, enduring the inevitable and what she'd hoped would be a future.

"I think it'd be easier just to show you at this point. What do you say? Can I take Caleb with me and you can meet us there when you get off work?" His voice perked up, encouraging her to commit to what he already had. "I would never let anything happen to him." His sincerity reflected his earnest devotion, inspiring from his heart what he could feel more than ever.

"I know I've only been in his life for a short time, but he means the world to me. I love him as much as I love you." He let go of his thoughts and embraced their future, entrusting that she felt the same way.

"You love me?" she smiled, as beats of her heart raced with the endearments of what she could feel coming.

"I've never stopped loving you." His thoughts conceded to what he could no longer suppress. "And if I don't explain…," he stumbled, trying to free what had trapped him since the beginning. "I just need to show you. It will be easier for the both of us if I just show you."

"Ok," She responded to the mystery and urgency in his voice.

Whatever his reasons, obviously they were important, and as the small beats of her heart still raced with her conscious, what prolonged the inevitable, searched her every thought. "Just give me the address, I have GPS." Amorous thoughts now soothed into her soul.

In all her delight and amusing realizations, what came to her now was more than she'd ever hoped for. *Could it be what she thought? What she imagined he would ask her?* Chase was so wonderful, so honest and caring and she had never known a man quite like him. Strong and domineering, yet gentle and understanding; he held a sincerity that was so contagious she could feel it whenever she saw or spoke with him. She waited so long, so painfully long, that if he had wanted her to meet him on the moon she would somehow find a way to get there. Regardless of what anyone in this office thought, what stood to be most important was for her to just go and see him as if everything depended on it and nothing could wait.

CHAPTER NINETEEN

The work was well underway by the time Chase and Caleb made it back to his office. He explained everything to Caleb the easiest way he could. The suit Chase was wearing, the truck they rode in all became a reference for Caleb that indeed made Chase important. And with every earnest reflection Caleb returned, just being with Chase alone made Caleb feel secure. The bond they shared and the devotion they embraced held the highest significance to a mind trapped in fantasy and believing once and for all that Chase was going to be his dad, held them both to a circumstance that fate had designed.

Chase had fully loaded semi's coming in and out all day from their main office in Phoenix. Even though Chase had Hector supervising the workers that were unloading all the heavy machinery and equipment in their warehouses, he phoned to meet him up front when he and Caleb came pulling in. Of course, what caught Chase's eyes right away was the taxicab sitting in the parking lot. Chase had also found it a bit odd that Hector was standing out front.

Shit, Chase thought, seeing Heather step out of the cab. *This can't be happening, not here, not now,* knowing Carly was due to be here as well. As he saw Hector walking over he asked him to take Caleb with him before going back to work over by the semi's so he could have a chance to talk to Heather alone.

"What are you doing here, Heather?" he said, eyes resentful and in a voice full of distain. He now felt in his heart how everything had changed.

Heather looked at Chase with discomfort, refusing to believe she had lost him, especially to someone like Carly with her underprivileged way of living, cursed with a mentally challenged son. This idea held Heather in contempt to what she couldn't believe was happening.

"Is that anyway to greet me?" Heather's taunting, smirking pout came with all the fabrications that only she could have manipulated. "If you won't see me in Phoenix, then you'll have to see me now. After all, I'm still carrying your child," she sneered, leaving herself open to every lie she had sustained. "Less than two weeks ago I was planning our wedding. Regardless of...whatever this—this whim was." She gestured to Caleb who was walking away. "I'm willing to forgive you. See," she announced as she held up some papers, her desire begging him closer. And with each step she took only confirmed her demise.

"What's that?" Chase questioned, keeping his same tone.

"I signed our prenuptial agreement." Holding it out for him to take. "I'm willing to forget all about this foolish nonsense and move to San Francisco with you." Her chin smugly rose.

"Spare me the bullshit, Heather!" Chase flared back, finally letting it go and condemning what she'd done. "I know the truth."

"*The truth?*" Heather spited, shaking her resentments to what her eyes brought into view. Curving up a grin as if it was her last desperate hope to have him.

Of course, where sympathy rides on distress everything goes wrong and who Chase saw pulling into his parking lot, held all the misery that he would have to explain. Everything he hid was now plainly in view with all his deceit coming to drown him.

"Is that the tramp?" Heather mocked, looking back to Chase and seeing his fear. "Is she coming to get her little retarded boy or is she here for you too?" She taunted him as if she had a claim to whatever she thought Carly had coming.

"Shut up, Heather." Chase's resentments burned, knowing Heather was about to ruin the most important thing in his life.

There was no precedence for him now or nothing to explain just how he felt. He was so afraid of losing her and knowing Carly could never forgive him for such a thing, knowing he had slept with her while he was engaged to another woman who was supposedly carrying his child had been eating him up. The thought of that alone twisted his fate and in a love that had just rekindled, he wondered if it could ever be strong enough to forgive what he'd done.

"Hi," said Carly, greeting him with a warm, endearing smile as Chase opened up her door. *"You look sharp,"* Gazing at his suit, searching her own expectancies and the urgency of his wanting to see her. "What's going on?"

Chase didn't say anything as he helped her out of her car, hugging her in a hard, desperate embrace.

"Oh, my," she said, taking her by surprise and as the moment passed, he wasnt letting go. "What's going on, Chase?" Carly could suddenly feel that whatever was happening, it wasn't good.

"You just remember, Carly," Chase slowly whispered, breathing in desperation he could no longer bear. "I love you more than anything in the world." His urgency pressed because no matter what happened now he never wanted her to forget it. "You and Caleb..." he paused as he looked at her and hoped that what he showed her with his eyes would forever seal his feelings. "You two are the most important people in my life now and I don't want ever lose you again."

His desperate pleas and solemn emotions echoed to her. Everything she felt told her something was indeed wrong, and as her feelings exposed her conscience, she noticed Caleb was missing.

"What's wrong, Chase?" Her panic succumbed to her worries. "Where's Caleb? Is he alright?" Carly's panic rose with her voice.

"He's fine," Chase tried to soothe and quiet her, though considering what was coming it seemed to be impossible.

"Is that *his* name?" Heather suddenly smirked, stepping toward them as she heard what they were talking about. The moment she did, she noticed Carly turn with resentment. "The little retarded boy," Heather mocked, posing with her contempt in a voice that told Carly she was inferior.

"*Excuse me?*" Carly snapped, completely over taken with anger. "Who the hell are you?" She stared fiercely. "And you better just watch out how you refer to my son!"

"Shut the hell up, Heather!" Chase quickly intervened. "Not here...not now," His eyes tightened in as his jaw started to flex. "Just go—now!" His voice more determined, spiteful and angered.

"Who is she, Chase?" Carly turned to him, suddenly changing her expression to a deep amorous look.

"Oh, as if you don't know," Heather stepped around to the both of them, taunting and ridiculing with every step that she took. "I'm his fiancé." She held up the ring Chase let her pick out while he was in San

Francisco. "And you, I presume, are the little gold digger Chase has been having his fling with?"

"*What?*" Carly could feel her throat drop into her chest. Panicked beats of her heart pounded at what had left her so exposed. She turned to Chase immediately with eyes of swollen humility. "What's she talking about, Chase? Who is this woman?"

"*As if,*" Heather's malevolent voice cast aggressions that preyed on Carly's soul. "You're just after my fiancé's money, while I'm the one carrying his child."

Then she had said it, laying everything out in the open. The pain and humiliation in Carly's eyes consumed with remorse as she heard the truth come out.

"You're what?" Carly turned, shock and dismay collided and depleted her. In all her desperate hopes there could be no forgiveness for what Carly was feeling now. Chase had used her, and if this was his revenge for what she did to him years ago. Her awakening had been swift.

"That's a Goddamn lie Heather and you know it!" Chase burst out, trying with all he could to reconcile what he'd done. "I already told you they're gonna report that ring as stolen, I certainly never picked it out for you!" He suddenly turned to Carly. "Don't listen to her Carly, it's not what you think."

"Then what is it, Chase?" Tears clouded her eyes as shouts turned into blame. "You had to come back and get the one girl you never had, right?" Her embarrassment and humiliation fed on anger and disgust.

"That's not true, Carly. You know I'm not like that. I love you. Don't listen to her. She's lying."

"Oh, Chase," came Heather's ferocious tone. "You can't possibly be serious about this parentless foster girl? Even after I signed this." Heather flashed Carly their prenuptial agreement.

"What did you just say?" Carly's disgust flared even more. "Have you two been making fun of me, Chase?" As Carly read the names that would be joined in marriage and the date on the decree, Chase bowed his head knowing nothing could explain this. Outrage and remorse mixed with pure anger as Carly looked to him with resentment in her eyes. A hard slap followed as Chase took in the pain feeling every tear that flowed down her face.

"Where's my son?" Carly demands. "We're getting the hell out of here."

"You can't, Carly. Not like this. Please, just let me explain." His tears swallowed heartache and everything she meant to him.

"The retarded boy?" Heather couldn't help but to intrude. "He's over there at the warehouses, and the sooner you get him and leave, the sooner Chase and I can get on with our lives."

"Don't worry lady, you can have him." Carly stepped past Chase. "If you can stomach him that is." Her eyes gave him one more revolting stare as she suddenly turned to Heather. "And don't disrespect my son again," she warned with cold, burning eyes of hate.

"Really, you *slut*," Heather spit out. "As if you had a chance. It's all in the genes you see."

"What?" Carly got ready to deliver what she warned.

"I come from a higher stock." Heather flaunted her tenaciousness. "While you obviously come from the genes of a bad chef."

"Meaning?" Carly stood there ready to deliver her fate.

"Let's just say the first pancake in your kitchen never does turn out quite right." She laughed, mocking her resentments all at the sake of Carly's son.

Anger and hatred found Carly right there, realizing that if she stayed and listened to one more insulting word she would end up striking Heather and going to jail was the last thing she needed to worry about. She knew had to get Caleb.

"Get the hell out of my way!" Carly shouted as she pushed past the both of them.

Chase tried to stop her, but Carly pushed him away. He immediately turned to Heather, warning her to leave or he would call the cops. Hector had been watching from where he was standing and the moment Carly shouted he ran over to see what was going on. Chaos and confusion left Caleb to fend for himself, a boy who had found new confidence.

Caleb wandered off to the last semi around the back, he never even noticed that his mother was there. Everybody had gone to see what was happening except for one worker that was throwing the packing blankets back into the trailer.

Caleb saw him immediately as he stepped up to where the man was standing, catching him off guard as he threw the last of the blankets in.

"Caleb?" Ross squinted, not believing his eyes. "What the hell are you doin' here?"

Though, Caleb just stood there, his expressions provided the words that said it all.

"I asked you somethin' boy." Ross' voice turned harsh. Whether it's the fact that Caleb was slow, or the way he was conceived, what Ross hated most was knowing Caleb was his son.

"I do not like you." Caleb finally spoke while keeping his distance. "You are mean to me and my mom. I have a new dad now. His name is Chase and this is his place and he is going to make you go away!" The peaks in his voice never lost their pride; straight forward and capturing all of his resentment without a stutter in his tone at all.

"What?" Ross stepped closer, though Caleb held his ground. "You mean Chase Bishop, the owner of Master Builders?" Ross suddenly realized that he was talking about his boss. "You mean your mom's fuckin' him now?" Spite flaunted his anger and everything he resented.

"That's bad!" Caleb runs at him, swinging with both fists. For the first time in his life he was defending himself like Chase had taught him. "I am going to tell Chase and he is going to make you go away!" His yells kept repeating in an uncontrollable rage as Ross tried to subdue him in a hug, struggling with all his might just to keep him under control.

Caleb only got worse, kicking and screaming even harder with years of suppression giving him the strength to hit Ross in the face. With each punch Ross felt collide against his cheek, his animosity and hatred consumed him in a panic. His eyes soured with contempt and his thoughts burned intolerance. Without even thinking, Ross peeled Caleb off of him and threw him as hard as he could. Caleb landed in the back of the semi's trailer. The force was so strong he hit his head on the steel frame, opening a cut. Ross noticed the blood right away.

Caleb laid there motionless and as Ross saw what he'd done. Stolen apprehensions mixed with fear and alarm so he searched for a refuge and anyway to hide his dirty deed. If there was a devil disguised to walk among us, then the demon was inside Ross. He didn't check the boy for a pulse or show any concern. His only thought was to make it all go away. There had been nothing to feel in an empty soul and nothing to save what should've never been born.

He quickly threw some more blankets on top of Caleb as he closed the trailer doors. Without any hesitation at all, he walked around to the side of the truck giving his okay to one of the drivers, as the truck clicked into gear for its journey back to Phoenix.

***

The last semi was leaving as Carly made her way around back. Tears mixed with panic as hopelessness crowded despair. In all her sorrows, the pure streaking terror that consumed her every breath lied in the fact that no one, including herself, knew where Caleb was. Her lungs kept shouting as if pleading a prayer, *God find my boy and let him be safe*, but no matter where she looked, Caleb wasn't there. She felt a hole grow inside her heart with every empty swallow.

Chase had everyone join in the search while Hector stayed with Heather waiting for the police to arrive. Chase's heart feared that something was gravely wrong, taking all the blame and swallowing his own grief as his cries for Caleb kept coming.

It all came to light when Carly made her way to the warehouse in the back. She saw Ross by the machinery going about his work as if nothing was wrong. Standing by the equipment away from all the commotion, the hate that took over her far outweighed the coincidence of him even being there at all.

"You bastard!" Carly screamed out as she instantly ran towards Ross. "Where is he? You son of a bitch!"

"You crazy bitch, get off me!" Ross tried to defend himself as Chase came rushing over.

"Easy Carly, easy," Chase pulled her off him.

"Let me go!" Carly turned on Chase. "That bastard's done something to Caleb! I know it!"

"How does she know who you are?" It quickly caught Chase's attention, reflecting fire in his eyes as he turned to Ross. "And why does she think you took Caleb?"

"What's he even doing here, Chase?" Carly's disgust rolled with her anguish.

"He's one of the workers I hired…the union sent him out. Why? Who the hell is he?"

"That's Ross, Chase," Carly's hate rolled off her tongue, "Caleb's father."

Remorse found pain as hollowness found fusion, and as the two mixed together sheer indignation took over Chase. Bending in a fury, he immediately took hold of Ross and demanded with all his vengeance for him to show them where Caleb was.

"You fucking coward!" Chase's rage now boiled. "Where is he?" Chase shook him furiously, overpowering him as if he was a rag doll. Except Ross just hung on denying any involvement.

"I have no idea." Ross fought back. "I didn't even know that fuckin' bitch was here with that retard!"

"You fuckin' bastard!" Chase immediately threw him to the

ground. As others come running over, Chase straddled him pounding in a wrath as he beat Ross senseless. Over and over his fists struck his skull until finally everyone tackled Chase and he rolled off of Ross. Everybody around them rushed to Ross' aide, keeping Chase away as Ross lay there bleeding.

"I better call an ambulance!" A worker looked up to Chase as he took out his cell phone. "You hurt'im pretty bad."

"Fuck him!" Chase said, still furious. "We need to find Caleb! That's the *only* thing that matters right now!"

Carly buckled to her knees fearing the worst. Her cries catered to her anguish as heartache depleted her soul. And if emptiness found blame, then she secluded it and made it her own. She'd strayed from the life that kept them so safe, putting her faith in a memory, and trust in a man that she didn't even know. In all her misery, shame and grief, what revealed her only hope was that Caleb was near, that he was alright and would be back in her arms soon. There's no other way this could turn out, regardless of how bleak it seemed. If hope had a prayer then let it find her now, if peace has an ending, then let it guide her to its fortune. Show her the way and deny its plausibility and search her heart to keep Caleb alive.

***

In the hours that passed, Chase found himself in the shallow refuge he made for himself, redefining his existence. He questioned why this had happened too many times, and every time he did, his heart found no answers. *How could he fix what was impossible to save and* how could he deny what he had undoubtedly ruined? To search for the answers would leave him in shame, and knowing he had no safe conclusion, only drowned him more in his heartache.

When the police arrived they wanted to place Chase under arrest. But, when they heard the entire story it was Ross who was truly suspect. Heather was no help and Chase had to have the authorities remove her from his property, filing a formal complaint against her for harassment and stalking.

He was desperate and alone in his hotel room at the Hyatt, finding no sleep in a night that invited desolation. Every time he tried calling Carly it went straight to her voice mail. Obviously she was avoiding him, and the fact of that alone only held him in his misery. *How can he ask her to forgive what he would never allow? How can he find rest until he knew Caleb was safe in her arms?* Every thought within him held him responsible for Caleb, and he would never rest until they found him safe once again.

***

It had aired all over the news, though the bulletin had come out too late. By the time the authorities became involved and alerted the media over two hours had passed and still there'd been no sign of Caleb.

Carly had been with the police, scouring for recent photos of Caleb and blaming Ross for his disappearance. Chase had beaten Ross so badly the authorities still hadn't had a chance to question him, only taking him to the hospital where he'd been admitted. Carly had been so hysterical that the authorities wouldn't release her until the EMT's had a chance to look her over as well. Of course, the last thing she wanted was for them to release her to Chase. She blamed him just as much, if not more, for what had happened to Caleb, but she blamed herself for ever trusting Chase and letting her son get so close.

Everything she thought of Chase turned out to be a lie, a man reconciling forgiveness just to play this cruel game in the end. *How could she have ever fallen for such a deception? How could she ever find peace knowing her son was still missing?* She searched her soul to believe that everything would turn out all right, denying her worst fears with every tear she shed.

Sleep had been useless in a night so intense, but with coffee as her crutch it was her worries that kept her from slumber. The rocking of her grief and the hardships she endured kept these restless beats from drowning her in a torture that never stopped. She kept her cell in her hand as she sat on her couch, waiting for any news. But, the only number that kept calling was the one she refused to answer. Chase. But she couldn't even stomach his voice, and he was the last person on this earth she ever wanted to hear from again.

There was a package waiting for her that had been too big to fit in her mailbox. When she finally got home she noticed the mail carrier had placed it against her door. As she looked to it now, lying on the coffee table as if larger than life and sealed in a gold frame, all the memories of what Chase had done were erased. The surprise he'd mailed her before he left for San Francisco only traded in her thoughts of why he'd kept it for so long. It was the picture he'd taken of her receiving her diploma. It came with the gratification she was supposed to feel had she known he was actually there, but now Carly wasn't sure how to feel, so she turned the picture over along with every trace of him in her mind. The only one who mattered was Caleb. She would torture herself forever for allowing this to happen, and as she thought of him now, knowing how scared and how alone he must be, she prayed for him to forgive her and prayed to forgive herself for what she'd done.

***

It had been over fourteen hours since Caleb was reported missing, and as two truckers were taking turns driving back to Phoenix, their music selection that had lasted through the night had now finally found morning. Each one of them providing an entire different taste of artists in an assortment that lasted them through the trip and as the truck pulled into Master Builder's main equipment yard, the noise the other driver woke up to found immediate disapproval.

"Goddamn it, Ernie, turn that shit off!" Sonny scowled as he climbed up front, "If he ain't George Jones, then I don't wanna hear it."

"Relax, Sonny, we're pullin' into the yard now. You can handle a couple more minutes." His smile turned over.

"I don't think so." Sonny turned on the radio and poured himself a cup of coffee, "I wanna hear the mornin' news."

It was an improbable circumstance and so they looked to each other the moment they heard "Master Builders" coming over the speaker. Sonny turned up the volume as they heard the news about the missing child. Each one of them looked to the other wondering if it could actually be possible, and as the truck came to a stop they both jumped out and ran to the back. What met their eyes as the trailer doors swung open proved their intuitions were correct. For there, in front of them lay Caleb, wrapped in a shipping blanket, asleep on the floor. He had some dried blood on his forehead as well as his knuckles, but from what they could tell he seemed all right.

"He must've been pounding on these doors pretty bad," said Sonny, as he gestured over to some dried blood smeared on the inside of the trailer doors.

Ernie woke Caleb and took him in his arms, telling him it was going to be alright and that they would call Chase. They immediately noticed the smile gleam wide across the young boys cheeks. And as Sonny began to dial, they were both relieved that he was fine. Each looked to the other, wondering how Caleb ever got locked inside.

***

Carly had showered and dressed, somehow finding the strength to get ready for the day and had planned on going to the police station in the city. Feeling hopeless, she heard a knock, frantic and pounding, hearing Chase on the other side. Though, in all her hesitations she knew she had to answer for the sake of her son and any word he might have heard.

"If you don't have Caleb with you then get the hell out of here, Chase!" Her anxious shouts echoed through the door, fighting any urge to free the lock. "I never wanna see…"

"They found him, Carly!" The desperation in his voice came as relief.

"What?" Her door opened, "Where?" Her concerned cries asked. "Is he ok, Chase? Dear God, tell me he's safe." Elated tears consumed her face, just hearing Chase say it and seeing it in his eyes was all that mattered.

"I guess other than a little bump on his head, he's fine." Chase fought back every temptation just to hug her. "They found him in Phoenix."

"Phoenix?" She wipes her tears, *"How?"*

"You were right," His tone lowered as sincerity and regret found him like never before. "It was Ross. He threw Caleb in the back of one of our empty semi-trailers. My guys found him when they got back there this morning."

"And he's ok?" Worries and fears faded from her conscience.

"He's fine, Carly." Chase confirmed it once again, lifting up a smile that could never lie about this. "He's at my home in Phoenix with my brother, Sydney and his wife, Kelly."

"When are they bringing him back?" Instant panic met her again. "I have to see him. When's the next flight out of here?"

"Are you kidding me?" Chase tilted up his head. "I chartered a jet. Come on, it's leaving from San Jose just as soon as we get there."

It was everything he'd wanted in that moment, with Carly hugging him, as warm aspirations hit her face. Thinking became trust, vengeance became her guilt. The only thing that mattered in that instant was what he was telling her and before she knew it they were on a plane headed for Phoenix to reunite with her son.

***

"I'm so glad you're alright, honey." Carly talks to Caleb on Chase's cell while sitting across from him in a small, custom jet with downtown Phoenix in their view. "I'm so sorry, baby. I'll never let you down again. I promise."

"I'm ok, mom. *Really*, this was fun." His excitement pitched up. "I got to beat up Ross." For the first time in his life he didn't refer to him as his dad. "Then I got to be a truck driver and I have new friends, Mom. Jason and Jacob, and they have Wii, and I am in the desert mom, at Chase's house. Did you know that? It is like a big castle, Mom. Really."

Ramblings and excitement found Carly's ear as her joy and content looked over to Chase. Everything she felt found passage and strength, knowing at least Caleb was safe. From the moment she hung up the phone, Chase confessed everything. His engagement to Heather and how she lied about her pregnancy, to the sealing of his fate and finding out he was sterile. Even when he told her about Sydney and the friend request he'd never sent, Chase took all the blame knowing he should've told her the truth in the first place. His wealth, his life, his home, or his company, meant nothing to him now if he couldn't share it with Carly.

As their plane touched down, everything she'd ever meant to him and everything they could ever be had exposed the true man before her as Chase now held out a ring. Holding their future in the palm of his hand he could see in her eyes that she wanted to commit. Clear on her face and as bright as the sun, he could already feel her answer.

Everything life had promised just to share it with each other forever.

"When did you get that?" Carly's soothing eyes ask. Though, the smile that had lifted could not be mistaken and what Chase proposed to her now, she knew was always meant to be. No more doubt or required answers, just the look on his face provided everything she needed, accepting it not only as fate, but what should've always been.

"I bought it the same day I got back to Phoenix. I was going to ask you to marry me when I asked you to meet me at my office. I'm sorry, Carly. I was just trying to do the right thing with Heather. But, our weekend only proved to me that I was living a lie, so I broke it off with her the minute I got back. I love you Carly and you know how much I love Caleb. I want to be his father. His real father and I want him to carry my last name," he paused briefly as sincerity took control. "I know even after everything that's happened, you still feel the same. If you tell me you don't love me, that you could never be in love with me, then I'll have this plane take you and Caleb back home and I'll never bother you again."

Echoes found sound, hearts beat with pleasure as contentment and endearment mended two lost souls. Tears swallowed remorse and regret found happiness, and with every word that Carly felt, she restored them all within a whisper. No more comprehensions or needed conclusions. She felt it the very moment he told her Caleb was safe. No matter how hard she tried to fight it, her heart was sealed the moment Chase had asked her. No more words were needed as she leaned in, holding up her hand as Chase placed the ring on her finger forever sealing their love with a long passionate kiss.

She stayed in his arms for the rest of the trip, and even when the police convoy sped them away to Chase's estate, her pure jubilation and devotion stayed cradled in his arms. Secured and rewarded, capturing everything he'd ever meant to her, surpassed all her dreams as they drove past the guarded gates to Costa de Oro Estates.

She felt like Cinderella, and Chase was her prince, though as the reality unfolded, nothing could prepare her for something like this. Grand towering Spanish tiled peaks met a sandstone pavement below. Rock gardens and cactus with huge, wrought iron gates exposed a fortress of wealth and prestige. With each beat of her heart came the shock of what she saw as she looked up to Chase with amazement in her eyes.

"How rich are you?" Disbelief found her thoughts.

"I'm worth millions, Carly." Chase just smiled, sure she had never even realized until right now, nor would it ever matter to someone with a heart like hers. But as their caravan came to a stop and Caleb came running out, the hesitance Carly felt showed clearly through her eyes as Chase leaned in comforting and warm. What inspired to bring her peace found fortitude in his answer.

"What's wrong?" He asked, holding his breath as well as his heart.

"It just makes me wonder." Carly's tone faded in a hesitance.

"What?"

"What could I possibly ever give you that you don't already have?"

As her door opened Caleb barreled into her arms. Chase breathed in a whisper as the three held in an embrace.

"You already have." He looked down at Caleb with proud eyes and peace in his heart. If dreams were meant to be fulfilled, then time must be erased. Love and devotion cradle hand in hand. Fate, as in destiny, must play the same role and Chase knew this feeling with every awakening in his body. Dreams reunited and breaths turn into one, clinging in the essence that had come from, *The Friend Request*

EPILOGUE

Chase and Caleb sat beside Carly at St. Luke's hospital on the university campus in San Francisco. She was resting now and as Chase began to read Caleb a story from a book he had bought from the gift shop, what came to mind stood to be his proudest day of all, he was here with Caleb and he would always be his protector. He had a son to carry on his name now. In all of his worries what brought him contentment was Carly was his wife and she is a great mother. No matter what, he would always be there for her. He will comfort her through the bad times and cherish the good. No matter what, he realized, life had given him a second chance at love and he could never take that for granted again.

"Hi," came a voice, suddenly appearing through the doorway.

Chase looked up instantly as Kelly and Sid entered the room,

"Jason! Jacob!" Caleb blasted out, running over to greet the two of them as he accidently woke Carly.

"Hey you guys." Chase stood up. "I can't believe you flew all the way here!" His tone expressed his joy and his face gleamed a smile.

"You kidding me," Kelly answered. "We wouldn't miss this for the world. How you feeling Carly? Glad it's finally over?" Kelly stepped over to her bed.

"I'm doing just fine Kelly, thank you," Carly said, as she sat up against some pillows. "That you back there, Sid?" She looked his way.

"Of course Carly," Sid's excitement provided every bit of happiness his cheeks would allow. "No way I'd miss this. I'm so happy for you guys. When can we see?"

"You're acting like a little kid at Christmas Sid." Chase couldn't help but take notice and return the same glow.

Just as Chase said that, a nurse strolled their baby inside the room. He was wrapped inside a blanket, wide-eyed and awake as he laid quietly on small mattress in a roll-a-way crib.

"Oh my gosh." Kelly held her hand to her mouth, "Is that him?" Her delight was so vivid it was as if her smile would shine forever.

"That's my new brother!" Caleb quickly shouted the moment she asked. "And I got to help name him! I love him, and you do to, huh?"

"I sure do baby." She stepped over and gave him a hug.

Sid came around to look as well as the nurse took their small, innocent son and handed him over to Carly.

"Man, Chase." Sid reached out and grabbed Chase by both of his shoulders. "I can't believe it." He stopped briefly, turning Chase towards him as if posing him for a picture. "Look at you man, you're all grown up. A year ago your life was a complete mess, now…" he paused, gesturing out to his new family. "You're a family-man. You have a beautiful wife that loves you, you have your sons Caleb and Carl, and not to mention that palace in the heights you call a house. Man, bother I sure am proud of you." Sid gave Chase a hug, and when turning to the rest of them they all looked just as proud.

"To the best urologist around!" Carly's voice raised up, cuddling their baby, Carl in her arms. "To Doctor Dudik!"

"To Doctor Dudik!" They all said, giving a salute to the doctor and the successful surgery he performed on Chase.

It was all Chase ever wanted and he realized it the moment he reconnected with Carly. This life he'd made here in San Francisco had brought him everything he'd been missing, and to feel what the heavens had bestowed him, lifted him up to a place that his heart had never felt. To be in its magnificence and claim what he'd forsaken, granted him this fortune that would secure him now and forever.

Chase looked back to Sidney, giving a grateful nod of his head.

"Thanks Sid." Chase said, pleased. "Thanks for interfering between me and Heather back then. I don't think any of this would be happening now if you didn't. I owe it all to you bro."

"I love you too man." Sid nodded his head and flashed back a smile. "Oh," he suddenly remembered. "Speaking of Heather." He pulled Chase aside. "I thought you might get a kick out of this." He pulled out a newspaper clip he had in his shirt pocket.

"What's that?" asked Chase, puzzled.

"Read it." He handed it to Chase. "It's a clipping from the Arizona Republic News. I printed it to show you. I thought you might get a laugh out of it." He smirked a satisfying grin.

Chase began to read as his face curved up in a smile. A chuckle turned into a laugh as he tried to hide his humor. "They caught Heather in Las Vegas trying to sell that ring there!" He seemed just as pleased as Sidney. "They extradited her back to Phoenix for grand theft."

"Yeah," Sid chuckled. "How cool is that?"

"That ring retailed for twenty-five thousand dollars. I warned her it was considered stolen property, that the store reported it."

"It isn't your fault Chase. That's what that greedy bitch gets. See you in five years honey," Sid scoffed.

"You know that old saying of mine Sid?" Chase looked over with serenity in his eyes.

"How can I forget?"

"Well," his voice swayed up. "The storm is finally over Sid," he paused and then slowly gleamed a heavenly smile. "And for the first time in my life, I think I've finally learned how to dance in the rain."

If heavens can hold Angels and God can bestow grace, then what Chase was feeling now could never be mistaken. He had come a long way and life had granted him a second chance. He was a man with new hope, visions and dreams, and he owed it all to Carly and their sons Caleb and Carl, knowing they had changed him forever. To be in glory and accept it as fate, is to look destiny in the eye and forever protect it.

Made in the USA
San Bernardino, CA
03 April 2015